"Sissons' voice (on both, stage and  social fabric of modern British ; honesty, curiosity and thoughtful for talents like his. The stories of incomplete without them."

Raymond Antrobus, author of *The Perseverance*

"A powerful story of family and culture echoing the great Northern tradition. Proudly working class."

John King, author of *The Football Factory*

CAUTIOUS, A BOAT ADRIFT

CAUTIOUS, A BOAT ADRIFT

Tommy Sissons

Published by Repeater Books

An imprint of Watkins Media Ltd

Unit 11 Shepperton House

89-93 Shepperton Road

London

N1 3DF

United Kingdom

www.repeaterbooks.com

A Repeater Books paperback original 2023

1

Distributed in the United States by Random House, Inc., New York.

Copyright Tommy Sissons © 2023

Tommy Sissons asserts the moral right to be identified as the author of this work.

ISBN: 9781914420658

Ebook ISBN: 9781914420689

Printed and bound in the United Kingdom by TJ Books Limited

Factory chimneys spewed out a pollution largely unchecked, threatening the washing on the line and challenging the pride of housewives and mothers who scrubbed stone steps and edged them with scouring stone; who wore head scarves or turbans and "pinnies" and baked bread; who black-leaded open fire surrounds and kept an iron kettle on the hob; who recycled old clothing to make flock rugs; who juggled ration cards and helped each other; who clothed their children in homemade wind-jammers and hand-knitted balaclavas which could be rolled up and adapted to commando-style skull caps. Hunslet people were resilient and strong in spirit.

Les Sissons (2000)

Contents

MAY

May 2017 (I)

The second time Brenda died, Grandad Norman trudged around the house indefinitely, with no real place to rest. The day following his return from the hospital, he busied himself staring at the places she had been. Like a dog whose owner had left the house, he perched on the rug and stared, as if he could stare her back into existence. She would rematerialise, surely, on the armchair, on the end of a cigarette stub, in a shroud of smoke. When this proved futile, Norman nosed through the back garden, toppling gnomes, disturbing the odd earthworm with a curious finger as its towed its corner. Neighbours said he was searching for something, or that something was searching for him.

The ex-foundry men in the Conservative Club, soon to be carted off to the factory in the sky, sank warm pints, their leathered bellies swelling like globes. *It's 2017*, one said to another. *Globalism's dead* and the sun was out. A rare May heat for Leeds. The sort of heat you want to lock the doors on, so it can't escape. A terrier wheezed on its haunches. A prune-skinned dear sat on her doorstep, her feet in a bucket of water, asleep. Children were happier, their faces pinched, burnt. A fiesta of life, adjacent to the A61, was underway. I was speeding towards it, on towards Hunslet.

I had but twenty minutes more to be visibly happy, and my joy was rarely observable, so even when the car started its routine shudder I did not care. I grinned, half-crazed in amusement at the bastard thing. Then, drawn to a halt at the side of the motorway, I regarded the worn-out engine of my Vauxhall with a laugh. It was the perfect day to celebrate a death. After more than twenty years, the curse of the witch had been lifted. No longer would mothers bundle their toddlers inside at the sight of Brenda waddling down Jack Lane, Windsor Blue clenched in her teeth like a firecracker. Cups of milk could be lifted in celebration. Cats could roam freely without fear of being kicked. Birthday parties could resume without the police being summoned on a noise complaint. Even when the roadside mechanic arrived, and conjured up an extortionate price, I tipped him cheerfully, thanked him for his service, and would not come to regret it until later.

Hunslet. *"Hūn's creek", the Anglo-Saxons had called it, "Hūn" being a man, the "creek" being an inlet from the River Aire. "Aire" itself originates, most likely, from Common Brittonic "Isara", meaning "strong river".* I played with the words, let them sit against my teeth, let them flow out. Hunslet. *A man and his river.* Somewhere, the Anglo-Saxons, axes in their backs, reclined in peace.

As I cut off the A61 onto Hillidge Road, I killed the speed. Respectfully, my car fell to the pace of a hearse, and on reaching Grandad Norman's house, the time for smiling stopped completely. The quiet was noticeable. The terraced house was waiting, sniffing the concrete, the hot rubber of the Vauxhall's wheels, the aged pigeon droppings. It was newer than it had once been. Newer than the house that had stood there before it, but considerably older than the new builds that encircled the Oval. In Norman's opinion, much of Hunslet had lost its character, as had many parts of South Leeds since the slum clearance, since the regeneration. The curtains were drawn. The bin lid was propped open above a bulk of bags. Flowers, like the bodies of old ladies, were gathered on the doorstep. The sort of flowers that said, "Aye, we *are* polite for pretending we care. I would have dropped off a bottle of whiskey, but you *are* an alcoholic these days, Norman." Those sorts of flowers. Hunslet.

Locating the spare key where it always was, under the potbelly gnome on the windowsill, I slipped inside. The faint waft of burnt toast. The lingering smell of tobacco — not that of Norman, that of Brenda. It was as if she still existed in the untouched ashtray. A narrow and empty corridor, decked with framed family photos. Mam and I, in a chalet in Butlins, on the beach at Skegness, in our garden in Nottingham. Brenda's daughter, Sherry, tanned in her sickly pink wedding dress, mouth open in mid-belch. Pride of place, above the open door to the compact kitchen, was a framed photo of three doctored Leeds United shirts. HUNTER on the left, BREMNER on the right. WHITBY, our surname, was printed on the back of the shirt in the middle.

The living room was deserted. The television sat expectantly, a muted sports channel talking to no one. On the mantlepiece, boxing trophies from Norman's twenties, palm-sized golden gloves, figurines of fighters supple with youth, a black-and-white photo of two boys with bruises for eyes, were silent. In the kitchen, the window had been tampered with, as if someone had tried to break in. I gently deposited my bag on the sofa and, on noticing the comfortable black leather shoes by the door, went silently upstairs.

I found Grandad Norman in his bedroom sleeping, spread-eagled across the armchair. The print of Brenda's body was still visible in the sponge of the mattress, so deep that the springs were unable to breathe. Norman's face was turned up to the ceiling, where a nicotine stain grinned down, watching over him. He was skeletal for a large man. Having once been the annual Father Christmas at the White Rose shopping centre, now even his jovial fat had escaped him. The slight shadow of hair occupied his wattle. Spittle hung from his lip. With one slipper off and his meagre chest visible through the parting of his bath robe, he was as if a human sacrifice. I unlaced his fingers from the vodka bottle they were grasping and went to empty it.

When I returned to Norman's bedroom, I perched on the bed and watched him sleep. Mam was due to arrive that evening. I would wait until I could tell her face to face; tell her that he had relapsed after so long, tell her to brace herself before she saw him. It had always been assumed that he would go before Brenda, and that on that day we would tell her what we thought of her. Several times before, however, we had discussed the possibility that Norman may surpass her and that, in that case, much would be required of us. The work to be done was monumental. It was good work. It was work we were blessed to do. In dying first, Brenda had lost, and that, if nothing else, restored some kind of begrudging faith in God.

There was still something of the old cock of the walk about Norman, even in drunken sleep. His life before the death and, indeed, before Brenda, was still gathered around him. It was still present on him. The slight unconscious curl of his lip, as if rising to play his harmonica, his stomach still harbouring an untold joke. Tumbling down from the bedroom window, the rare Yorkshire sun filled his face, made it look supple in the areas it had become sunken. In the hand of the sun, he looked almost unfettered, yet terrified of the liberation that had leapt so suddenly upon him. He had always been young for an old man. His hair had been white since he was thirty. That didn't age him. It was his body that was nauseating, emptied as it was, a missing person poster discarded on an armchair.

Mam and I would stay for a little while yet. We would see

him through the period of mourning. I said a prayer for the first time in ten years as I listened to the life at the window. The summer was coming and thank God for that. Outside, a goal had been saved. A child's balloon had taken flight. An ice cream cone had been dropped on the curb. Happy hour was approaching in the pubs and the houses and the city. Even the moors were alive and thrashing. A man was there, in the howling winds, shouting at no one, heard by no one, all alone.

Double Rations

Old Massey was the Hunslet greengrocer. A dour man, perhaps in his mid-sixties, exceeding his life expectancy with little known arrogance for this fact. His first name cannot be remembered or recovered. He was not seen often outside of his shop. He is said to have sold an apple to Lord Mayor George Brett once. His life, it appears, was as unremarkable as the next man's and, in fact, there is no sufficient evidence to confirm he ever existed. For the sake of imagining him, however, it is fair to assume that he ate his tea late, after closing the shop, as this would be common enough for all shopkeepers. He may have known one or two killed in Normandy, this being also unremarkable. He will have loved someone once, perhaps. Let us imagine him with a mauve tie and a carefully kept white coat.

Old Massey's shop was under the protection of the Mercers, a local gang headed by three brothers, who had made a small fortune from the gambling habits of the miners and steelworkers recently returned from the war. The Mercers would take bets at football matches, boxing rings and dog fights. They had been protecting Old Massey's shop since rationing came into effect, since fruit and veg became targets for theft. This is not to say that anyone had ever stolen from Old Massey's greengrocers. There are no stories to suggest they did, excluding the customary apple occasionally snatched by a hungry child. It is fair to suggest that Old Massey was paranoid, and by the time the local men had gambled all their money away, he had even more reason to be so. By this time, business was slow and Old Massey was in debt to the Mercers.

Jim Whitby knew Old Massey as well as anyone else; that is to say, not well at all. Yet, as he was a loyal customer and as his son Norman had not been known to pinch, Jim had been entrusted with protecting the shopkeeper from his former protectors. In exchange, Jim would receive a double ration of potatoes and cabbage, something which he could not afford to turn down while he himself was out of work. Every day, Jim would keep watch from opposite the shop, sometimes pretending to read a dated newspaper, sometimes stooping to mend the soles of his boots for five minutes at a time, sometimes simply watching, unsure of what he would do if the Mercers did show up. To assume he could fend off three armed toughs on his own was daft, but he was willing to take a beating for the rations he had so far received. May the Lord make us truly thankful.

On the evening they did come, the shop had just closed. The pale and hollow faces of mothers were retreating into the dusk and the mangy cat that hissed at the drunks was clawing a mouse on the cobbles. The day we eat like cats — that'll be day, and angels will drape the lamp posts. *As Jim collected his spuds, a car crept up against the pavement and sat in contemplation. Old Massey and Jim, both being upstairs in Massey's living quarters, could see it from the window. The men in the car were preparing themselves, the streetlight illuminating the occasional cheek, the brim of a cap, the shred of a knuckle. The streetlight caught the cricket bats, and Old Massey quietly collected his week's takings and concealed them beneath a floorboard he had tampered with. Seeing the bats, he had seemingly lost faith in even Jim to protect him, and when the old lose faith in the young, there is nowhere left to turn. Having cheated death this far, the shopkeeper was prepared to relinquish himself, but not his earnings, never his earnings. Jim watched in interest and wondered momentarily where those scraps of money would eventually go, with Massey having no family of his own.*

"Reyt", Jim said, jumping to life, seizing the pan and kettle. "We need to boil water. Quick."

As Jim feverishly set about the cast-iron stove, the most rotund of the three Mercers drummed on the door of the shop. The tallest, gauntest

Mercer cast aside the roseate stub of his cigarette and leaned to peer through the window, to survey the categorised goods in their crates, doused in shade, giving nothing away. The water was rippling on the stove. The youngest of the Mercers, a pale, freckled bulwark, took four strides back and turned. The steam was beginning to sigh from the pan, to trickle from the kettle, when the shop door came down. A drill of boots. A cacophony of hollers could be heard from below. It seems likely the Mercers tore the place apart. Having ransacked the takings box and found it empty, the brothers set about toppling the crates, upending the tables, flinging the scales across the room. Carrots and onions rose in clouds, fell as sleet. Brown paper bags sliced through the air. Pears rolled clumsily across the floor, rushing to reach the road. A cabbage was launched through the window. The instrumentation of shattered glass saw the cat outside take flight, as each fragment came to rest as frost in the street. The pan was ready. The kettle was ready.

By the time the three Mercers took to the staircase, Jim was waiting above them. His feet were planted on each side of the banisters, each hand brandishing a vessel of boiling water. All four men were familiar with the situation. In the barren lands of France, a lone Nazi gunman stands before you, separated from his division, half-mad with the nausea of war. His Walther P38 is staring you down, and you, unprepared, have no weapon raised. Jim had been there. The Nazi had been shot from a distance before he could act. The Mercers had heard of a similar happening from a brigadier in their regiment, perhaps the very same event. Jim had been lucky, and the Mercers would have to count on similar luck. Yet on the confined staircase, no one was there to shoot Jim from a distance. The dim umber walls would yield to no bullets.

"Tek one more step", Jim warned. He surveyed the faces of the men below him. Bewilderment painted them. The youngest tightened his grip on his cricket bat, as if it would shield him from the coming wave. The gauntest, eyebrows twitching, glanced quickly at the door. The most rotund held Jim in a fixed glare, did not blink, did not move.

As nobody spoke, Jim continued. "I happen to be Jim Massey. I'm Massey's nephew and I'll tell thee now; I've come to stay with my uncle for a while. I know he owes thee money and thee shall get it. Until that day, thee best not darken our doorstep. It's not just me that's Massey's nephew. There's more of us. Why, I could summon a whole street of nephews. Don't think I couldn't. They've got bats too, and all the boiling water going. Take that as a warning, and get gone."

The Mercers did not move at first. The most rotund was yet to blink and, momentarily, Jim thought the man might lunge up the stairs towards him, with little care for the consequences. Then, carefully, the brothers retreated. Jim listened to them, making certain he could hear all three as the men crept through the carcass of the shop and out into the street. Returning to the window, where Old Massey waited with his head in his hands, he watched as the Mercers gradually climbed into their car. The rotund man, being the last to join, turned his face up to the window and caught him watching. The two were interlocked then, for a matter of seconds, as the Mercer absorbed everything he would need. The shape of Jim's nose. The way his mouth hung. The side of his skull that his hair fell on. When satisfied, the Mercer ducked into the car, and the three men drove away.

Jim stayed with Old Massey for an hour before he left to return to his wife and son. "Always take care of thissen, and never run t'bluddy police." As he walked home, he found himself glancing down each and every snicket. All that greeted him was the smoke that lived with the houses, the familiar neighbour. The ghosts of some ten thousand men could be down there and, due to the smoke, they would never be seen. Felt, perhaps. Some ten thousand soldiers. May the Lord make us truly thankful.

Jim cursed himself for having gotten involved. The cabbage and potatoes hardly seemed worth it. They were worth it though. There was no denying that. Without them, how would he properly feed his wife? How would he feed young Norman? His only child, as of late the lad *had shot up like a beanpole. The boy was the future. A loss of food would stunt the poor bugger's growth. It didn't bear thinking about. Still, Jim wondered why he had pretended to be Old Massey's nephew, and most important of all, he wondered how he could ever help Massey come up with the money he owed.*

May 2017 (II)

I was raised by Mam alone in Nottingham. We went to Skegness once a year. It was the nearest seaside getaway. It also marked the eastern edge of England and the beginning of something alien, the sea, and subsequently whatever hazy space lay beyond the watery boundaries of the archipelago. Mam was an art teacher at a secondary academy near Sneinton; a school I avoided going to for the very same reason. She would come home on weekdays with fingers made of ink and paint splattered across her top. Sitting on the beach in Skegness, she would draw the coastal shelf, the waves, the sky. When I was of primary school age, I would huddle in a towel, like a mollusc, beside her and she would point over the North Sea. *There's Den Helder; and that there's Texel. They're in North Holland, which is in the Netherlands. The Netherlands isn't England. It's a different country altogether.*

I would point with her, my hand sticky with ice cream, and pretend I saw the islands she was referring to. All I could see was the still face of water lifting the sky, consuming the sun and the light, until the sea was sombrely luminous. I don't think she saw the islands either. We'd imagine we saw them. I'd picture little people going in and out of cottages, floating serenely on boats, going for walks on dunes that sprouted purple flowers unapologetically. I don't know what Mam imagined. She held me and England held her, and we reclined into each other. England wouldn't let us go. It took us home when the holiday had ended and reminded us of the leaking roof and read the newspaper silently in the front room and spluttered over cigarettes in its armchair.

Mam's mother had not lived since Mam was born. Mam had taken her place. She was an extension of her, an extension of invisibility. In many ways, half of me was an extension of invisibility also. Mam was everyone's mam. You could borrow milk and sugar off Mam. You did not talk back to Mam. She was one of several mams who managed the local neighbourhood with authority. They would congregate at doorsteps to find out what needed fixing, to make sure no one went hungry. Even the little hoodlums who laughed in the face of police would embarrassedly accept a clip round the ear from the mams and be sent to return whatever they had stolen from the off-licence. Every Sunday, on finding their teenage children asleep, and fearing a late arrival to church, the mams would slap them with a wet flannel and the howls of disturbed sleep would lift the rooftops.

Mam, like her fellow mams, saved aggressively. She never bought herself clothes and made a habit of upcycling everything she owned. She snored loudly and sang Siouxsie and the Banshees in the kitchen. She was missing two teeth and two others were silver. She hated commercialised Christmas trees, the glitzy pink ones in St Pancras that were designed to sell perfumes. She wanted to find more time to read. She probably mollycoddled me as a child. I think she quietly knew I had taken drugs in my life but would raise hell with me if ever I told her. I think she would be secretly disappointed if I hadn't, for concern I had not spent my youth defiantly. She did not like to think of us as working-class but referred to herself as working-class when distancing herself from middle-class women she didn't like. She wanted to find more time to learn about politics. She didn't trust any of them.

Mam's voice was constricted. It had been squeezed into a strained attempt at standard English by austere speech therapists in the late 1980s. *Repeat after me: How now, brown cow.* To enter the world of education with a County Durham accent had been dangerous. Such teachers were the enemy within. Such teachers were likely to be friends and family of recently crushed miners. They were not fit to teach England's children. Mam's voice had been workshopped, dismantled, and reproduced. It was now an image of a voice. It sat on the end of her tongue like an acidic sweet. Her short *a*'s remained, but when the occasional Northernism found its way to her teeth she unconsciously swallowed it back.

She had taught me how to hide my Nottinghamshire accent when on the phone to employers. This hadn't been necessary until I became a journalist at the *Nottingham Herald*. Until that point, I had not worked a job in which a voice was required. I began my career in journalism writing the obituaries section and, two years later, have not progressed much since. My accent, if anything, aided me in producing the obituaries. Every mourner feels more comfortable talking to a reporter with a familiar, neighbourly twang. The austere drone of the South wouldn't do. Widows would call to tell me about their late husbands (it was almost always the men who died first), and I would *mmm* and *ahhh* and occasionally call them *duck*. I would purposefully broaden my accent to put them more at ease. If I was to be an obituary writer, I'd make sure I was the best obituary writer around; a celebrated trailblazer of the death column. People would be blown away by my obituaries. Then I would hang up and return to my work voice. Often, I would hope a widow would tell me about a death that was particularly suspicious — something that suggested a murder — that way I could try to accompany the more mature journalist who would be sent to report it. But no. No mysterious circumstances. Just heart attacks, hapless accidents and common diseases.

"At least this can be a new start", Mam said, as she slapped the bacon into the frying pan. It was the morning after she had arrived. Norman was asleep upstairs, in bed this time. He had barely recognised us when he had come to. He had mumbled deliriously and gone to the toilet. Then, after we had brought him water and paracetamol, he had gone straight to bed and not budged since.

"Aye", I said, "as soon as the funeral's over." I buttered two slices of bread and dumped them on a plate. "I was convinced she'd outlive him."

Mam nodded. "Your sixties is a young age to die."

"Well, that's thirty fags a day."

Mam flipped the bacon, kept her eyes on it. "Dying and being resuscitated, then dying again less than two weeks later. Something in the universe wanted rid."

"Don't bloody blame it", I said. Then, imitating a priest, "I am the resurrection and the life. And here till next Tuesday." The bacon was razed in the pan. Fat frothed like gums of land. *Raze the houses. Raze the unions. Raze the industrial bull.*

Mam scowled at me. "Don't let Grandad hear you say things like that."

Norman ate in bed. We talked to him. The smacking of his lips answered. "How are you feeling this morning, Dad?" *Smack, smack.* "Have you seen how many flowers? We'll have to get some vases. Sunflowers and tulips and—" *Smack, smack.* A scrap of pig was stuck between his teeth. He dislodged it with his thumb and stuck it under his tongue.

"Who brought 'um?" Norman asked. "Cus if it wuh that

Ron Barnes, I dun't want 'um. Always sniffin' round our Brenda, he was. Bloody get."

Ron Barnes had died two years earlier; at the start of spring when everything was beginning to breathe again. A lot of flowers came up when he went down. Not many of them stuck around for long. Norman ate cucumber sandwiches that day as a cloud of old women, and some young, dressed in black looked each other up and down at the reception. More paper plates were left over than expected.

We brought the neighbours' flowers to Norman, organising them around him as he read the accompanying cards. *The florist was in his counting house, counting all his shrapnel.* Petunias from Mary, tulips from Paul; both of whom Norman had once seen weekly but had not seen now for a while. Indigo and salmon pink and plum and vermillion. The sun once more washed the room and, sinking in amongst the teeming colours, the rotund heads of light, Norman looked almost like a painting of a small Tudor prince, solemn faced, going about an inconvenient duty, his bathrobe a grubby jerkin. This was his Hunslet, and he'd bloody well keep it in order. There is, after all, something childlike about mourning. You need to learn to walk again; you need to learn to speak again.

At request, Norman's record player was brought out to fill the gap that, for that moment, words could not. The Watersons were dropped beneath the pin, their shearling jackets, their caps stuck down. They rotated, intoning the death of the winter and the coming of the summer. The infinite continuation. Things that could not be changed. *And send us peace to England.* As always, Norman murmured along with them. He had done so when I was a child. He would drive us to the Dales, tapping his finger on the steering wheel,

Norma and Martin's voices rising from the cassette tape. We were going to Malham Tarn. A man and his grandson and the water.

"What was that song you used to sing, Dad?" Mam asked, as the record came to an end. "There was one about Hunslet wasn't there?"

"Oh aye", Norman murmured, brushing the discarded sympathy cards to the edge of his bed. "Wuh a Hunslet rugby song. Me father used to sing it me."

"How did it go again?" Mam started humming, trying to lighten the mood. Her recollection of the tune was largely inaccurate. She hit a high note and laughed encouragingly.

Norman listened, looking down at his lap, then, with a small tight smile, began singing in a rich, breaking voice. "Napoleon talks of war, boys, and boasts his mighty force." Sherry and Wayne would be arriving soon. They would be in Hunslet by the afternoon. They would arrive unceasingly and would not be stopped. A significant part of my and Mam's work would be keeping them at bay, holding them at a distance as you would a copperhead snake. "But vain his aim, despite his name, to ride the world's high horse." Brenda's daughter, pink gin in a pink park. Her husband, the London wide boy, wide as London pockets. *Big man, flash car. The flashier the car, the smaller the—*. The hand turned the wheel. The hand of the clock swept. "While waters wash the shore, boys, our own we shall retain." Norman's eyes were lit up. His chin was raised. He was bellowing across the room, his bloodless face beginning to gush. "We've swept the seas before, boys, and so we shall again." A pigeon took flight from the windowsill. It would return when the song had subsided, as sure as a song always does. "And so we shall, so we shall, so we shall again." As sure as the mountains sink into oblivion. As sure as the

roses poke their heads above the parapets of grass, the miners
above the parapets of slurry. As sure as I can only know of you
what you tell me. "We've swept the seas before, boys,

and

so

we

shall

again."

Phantom Hand

Norman's father had lost his right hand in the factory. This was what was told to Norman and this was what he believed. He went out in the morning with the hand and came back without it. Norman's mother screamed. Of course she did. He was always losing something or other.

They didn't eat as much after this. There weren't as many potatoes or cabbages all of a sudden, and often Norman's father would stay awake through the night, boiling water. Local lads started calling him Captain Hook, despite the fact there was no hook to point to. When Norman reached his teenage years, he started telling friends that his father had lost his hand at war. A Nazi had chopped it clean off with a meat cleaver, but, in response to this, Norman's father had taken both the Nazi's hands. There was now a handless man in Düsseldorf with a vendetta against the Whitbys, but with no ability to shoot them, should he manage to track them down. The local lads stopped calling Norman's father Captain Hook after this, shortening it to Captain instead. This was preferable. Still, when Norman became employed at the foundry, the story his father had told him hung over his shoulder, and Norman found himself excessively cautious about where he placed his hands.

"Norman, lad", Big Henry bellowed, clapping his hand on the youth's shoulder. "Call it a day. I know yus eager but yer can go now."

It was true that Norman had been overzealous at work, ever since his first day a week earlier. He had turned up at the factory fifteen minutes early each day so far, then continued to work beyond his hours until Big Henry, the foreman, came to send him away. Despite this, Norman did not possess a psychotic enjoyment of labour. If anything, he was impatient for the moment he would be sent home every time he turned up. The bodies of the foundry moved ceaselessly about the inferno. Their limbs regurgitated the actions that had been pressed into them, loading the furnaces, heaving the molten liquid into moulds. At least five of the elder workers were scarred by burns, abrupt pink canyons that ran up their arms. To become a wheezer was common. Some men had developed a permanent squint. On leaving the foundry, Norman would pat himself down to confirm that his entire body was still there and functional, to confirm that he was not, in fact, a floating pair of arms. Every day he would be thankful he still had his hands. His father's stump would hover over him as he slept.

No, Norman hadn't masochistically taken to the foundry, but he had *taken to the idea of a new suit. A weekly visit to one of the milk bars that had started popping up in the city. A pair of second-hand Oxford shoes if possible, black as a bat. This may have been asking too much. If he were to have any hope of this, he would need to push his way into Big Henry's favour. The foreman would have to consider him indispensable, inhuman, mechanical. He was seventeen, almost eighteen then, and money was necessary. Besides, he was secretly courting Jack Wrigley's girlfriend Florrie that evening and, as it stood, he could not take her to see* The Prince and the Showgirl *because bastard Big Henry hadn't coughed up the extra tanner required.*

Jack stubbornly refused to take Florrie to the picture house, due to his loud hatred of anything American. He hated the United States almost as much as he hated the Germans, largely because of a belief that the Americans considered themselves to be the saviours of Britain during the war. Jack hadn't met an American. His father had during service, he would argue, and as his father had taken a dislike to the soldier in question, Jack had decided that the USA was the land of the glory-leeches. He devoted himself solely to the betterment of British industry, even from his place at the foot of it, and would hear nothing of glamour or hedonism. For him, to sit and watch a Hollywood production for over an hour was comparable to torture and would result in the foyer of the picture house being vandalised. This, very simply, meant that Norman and Florrie could go to The Prince and the Showgirl *without fear of being caught.*

Mardy bastard Big Henry was, for not slipping him the extra tanner after all his additional unnecessary toil. The foreman had enough to supplement Norman's pay packet with his own loose change. Big Henry had grown up in Hunslet, not far from the foundry, and he wouldn't let anyone forget. After thirty years of worming his way up the industrial ladder, however, he was as alien to South Leeds as any other foreman. No one knew where he lived. The countryside, no doubt; somewhere that had to be driven to. Every time he left the foundry in his Phantom IV, the sweat of his parents, his siblings and his fellow men fell as tyre tracks behind him.

Norman watched as Big Henry hovered over the shoulder of a foundryman. The foreman's eyes followed the worker as he laboured about the furnace. The foundryman's face was fixed in concentration. There was a gleam of angry despair on his brow. He could surely feel the weight of time bearing down on him, making him old and disposable, cutting through him, severing his hands. Big Henry crossed his arms and kept watching. Norman decided he would not confront the foreman for the extra tanner after all.

Instead, he paced briskly back to his parents' house. He changed into his father's demob suit, a drab outfit too large for the underfed patriarch, and crept back into the street before his mother could emerge from the outhouse. He would go to the Lads' Club, and then run to meet Florrie at the River Aire from there. Ned Gould would have a tanner, and Ned Gould was always at the Lads' Club. He and his brother Terry made a good few bob every time they went to Headingley. There were people worth pickpocketing in Headingley. Sometimes the odd posh London sod visiting on industrial business would rent a room for a week over that way. There were a few small-business owners living in Headingley also. If it was a vacant night and the house before them appeared deserted, Ned and Terry could easily break in and be gone with their pockets full within a matter of minutes. They had yet to be caught, and if ever the police started sniffing around, they would store their takings under a seat in one of the locomotives their father worked on down Jack Lane. They never kept more than an explainable amount of money on them at any one time.

There is no way of knowing the exact people and scenery Norman would have passed on his way to the Lads' Club. Only maps of the time and corresponding photos of the appropriate streets can offer clues. Let us say Norman walked through the photographs, marching across the developed film available. He wondered through the sepia, past the discarded Weetabix boxes that clogged the drains, past the blasted brick wall with chalk goalposts upon it, the words MAD DOG scrawled above by some anonymous reprobate. An old man he knew vaguely would have stopped him and asked, "Wuh it a win or a loss at Aston Villa?" The film becomes blurry in places, thick with a smoke that refused to surrender. Great plumes from the neighbouring railways rose about Norman, commanding the cobbled streets. It rose from the mills, the iron and steel foundries, the brewery, the linen works, the leather works, lock works and oil works, ensuring that windows remained closed more often than open and the shirts hanging from the washing lines were heavy with the stench of burning, the blouses pregnant with ash.

At the Lads' Club, the Boys Brigade, in matching coats and caps, were marching around the sports pitch, their conductor striding ahead, hollering. The veins in the conductor's forehead were pulsing. In five years, the boys would be marching into the factories, in the boots their fathers and grandfathers had lived and died in. The fire would lift its head to count their fingers. Left, right, left, right.

Ned and Terry were outside the sports pitch, smoking. They wore shorts and rugby shirts of a large black-and-white check. It was a rare occasion on which they were not adorned in their teddy boy suits, the tailored upmarket type that arrived from London and only clung to the shoulders of those with good money. Ned, an eighteen-year-old scarecrow with a plume of greying hair and a hooked grin too broad for his face, waved

Norman down. Terry, considerably stockier, followed suit. He had a firm, choleric yet ripe face that made him look somewhere between a gooseberry and a gargoyle, hair gelled back to reveal his boxer's forehead, heavy cigar fingers, deformed knuckles.

"Ee", Ned cried when Norman explained why he had come. "Tha must think ah'm made of tanners!"

"Wun't that long ago tha last went Headingley, wuh it?" Norman asked, with irritation.

"Aye, but I dun't carry the money around wi' me. Tha got owt, Turry?"

Terry wrinkled his nose and spat at the floor. "An't got owt."

"Ah'm only after a loan, tha knows", Norman persisted.

"An't that Florrie got a fella anyway?" Ned chimed in.

"Aye, but he can chuff off."

Terry erupted in laughter. Ned howled with him. His laughter sounded like his father's locomotives. It would not have been surprising if smoke had burst from his ears.

"It's that Jack Wrigley fella what goes wi' Florrie, in't it?" Terry grinned.

"So what if it is?"

"What tha gun' do if he catches thee?"

"Never mind that. Are tha gunna lend us the money, or aren't thee?"

"What you want to do", said Ned, "is you want to ask for summet off yer father."

"Tha know me father an't got owt. What am I gunna do now, eh?"

Ned shot Norman a furtive glance, grinning with one corner of his mouth, and strode backwards three paces towards the sports pitch. Casting his eyes over the Boys Brigade, who had now begun shoving and squabbling over something inaudible, Ned counted the staff members outside the building and found none to be missing. He gestured to Norman to follow him.

Five minutes later, the three of them were jogging clumsily towards the Aire, a stolen rowing boat hoisted over their heads. The oars were jumping awkwardly in the boat and every few minutes they found themselves stopping to retrieve one from the curb.

"Stroke of bloody genius!" Norman laughed, tripping on the heels of Ned before him.

Every summer the Lads' Club would take their regulars on a camping holiday to the North York Moors. The rowing boat, when not fulfilling its annual duty of capsizing on Gormire Lake, was kept in the shed at the rear of the club. Every August, the chief executive officer would retrieve it, dust it free of cobwebs and give it a sober slap on the stern, as if to wake it. He, having no wife, referred to the boat as Helen. As it was, the thing had not been touched in almost a year and Terry was cursing, wiping cobwebs from his eyes as the three of them trundled out of Hunslet.

It would be simple. They would pile aboard at Canal Wharf and row down the Aire to surprise Florrie with a boat trip. Ned and Terry would do the rowing as a favour to Norman and because they were looking to cadge some extra cigarettes from Florrie. They would glide south until Skelton Lake became visible, then they would heave backwards up the river and return the boat to the club before the chief executive left for the night. That part would be easy. The chief was known to take his meals alone in the club and even if he were to hear the shed being broken into, he would not be torn away from his tea of cold beef.

At Canal Wharf, they eased Helen onto the water. The boat, wetting its nose and turning its head up to the sun, wheezed and floundered as the boys climbed aboard. Terry, his foot tangled in a stray length of rope, flopped into the water and emerged to his friends' hysterics. Ned tugged at the rope, making Terry dance as he attempted balance. "In't boat wi' thee, Turry!" Ned howled. "Come on, Fred Astaire." A flock of pigeons burst away from the waterside. Amidst the dark and looming chimneys, several hollow old faces gazed down. The remaining echoes of a derelict generation, whose youth had passed painfully through them, like bullets at the Western Front.

With Terry in the boat, Norman pushed them away from the land. In the seemingly endless expanse of water, time ceased to exist. There was no glacial Malham Tarn behind them, no River Ouse in front of them to sweep the voyager on to sea. All was flat and still. The Industrial Revolution had never ended. The factories resting their heads at the waterfront were as natural as the river, as natural as boils, mounds that had swollen and risen from the soil. They were blackened with age. The same hermit fed the same pigeons at the same time every day and was seen nowhere else. The same working men sat smoking on the curb. The Victorian slums were immovable, broken-backed. The same people entered them and departed them and were born again within their walls. The North had been ageless before the war. Children had sold their little wares to the pawn shop like their parents. Babies were birthed in stoicism and did not cry. The war, of course, had left a nation to rebuild. The problem with that, a friend of Norman's father once told him, was that the meek had inherited the work. It was built back but could never be the same as it had been. Now the children had turned into juveniles. They had started rioting in cinemas, dressing in codes like cheap dandies, filling milk bars with their imported music, wielding leather belts and cracking heads. Even the river could not resist ambush, the same river that had grown accustomed to inheriting the meek, taking them nowhere in particular, abandoning them downstream.

"By!" Ned cried. "It's reet nice on t'water, in't it?"

Norman smiled wryly. It had not been long since the three of them had presented their arses to the schoolmaster's cane. Now they presented their arses to the whole of Leeds, pale half-moons hanging above the water, enough to make an old woman curse the modern world. They were doing well, considering the chaos of their homes and the mire of their city. Sports captains at the Lads' Club. Starting to make money in one way or another. Perhaps one day they would move to the South, or even just to a suburb in the Midlands, and earn a comfortable living. They would have happy wives and happy children and read happy newspapers with happy cartoons in them. They would wear tailored suits and drive Morris Minors and, annually, they would go on fishing trips to the east coast of Scotland. It was non-negotiable. Their schoolmaster would rue the day he had left streaks of blood running down their legs.

"'Ere!" called Norman. "There's our Florrie there. Steady now. Tek it slow."

Florrie McLoughlin was waiting by the waterside. She looked as if she expected to be caught at any minute. Her deep-set eyes darted from the path to the bridge, then back. Even in the depth of summer she was pale; perhaps because she was infrequently allowed to leave her parents' house, and even then, rarely beyond the distance to which her mother's voice could travel. It angered her. Often, after her parents had gone to bed, she would creep down the street to talk to whichever neighbours were still awake and sitting out on their doorsteps. Her brother knew she did this. He kept her secret for her.

The accents of the McLoughlins were decidedly alien. They had fled Limerick the summer before. It had become a swamp of economic stagnation and both Florrie's father and brother were out of work. This was not the worst of it. If local stories were to be believed, the McLoughlins had escaped Ireland, with no prior planning, in the middle of the night. Florrie's father was a loyalist and had fallen into disrepute with local men from the IRA. Hours before they had fled, a gunman had let off two bullets at their windows in warning. They had not returned to Ireland since, and as Florrie's father, John Joseph McLoughlin, refused to discuss the rumour, it could not be verified whether it was true or not. He and his wife were reluctant to socialise.

As the boat drew closer, Norman could see that Florrie's poodle cut had been uncharacteristically primped. Typically, she would allow her hair to sit where it liked and hiss at any brave-tongued man who sought to comment on it. She had not put on lipstick. She would not allow herself to go that far.

When Norman first met her, she had been in conversation with a neighbour during one of her night-time excursions. She had been holding chips wrapped in newspaper. The fire inside the window had illuminated her, making her float in the dark. "Spare us a chip, pet." She had given him two. Only when the neighbour started cackling did Norman realise that the chips had fallen in the gutter a moment earlier and were coated in dirt. Florrie had cackled too. He knew then he would have to marry her.

They had met twice since, when no one was looking, and exchanged words any self-respecting person would be disgusted to hear. During one of these occasions, Norman had turned up at Florrie's window and she had near dragged him in, knocking over the crucifix on the windowsill in the process. The buttons had been torn from Norman's shirt. Florrie had howled with laughter, falling back on the armchair. By the time her father had stirred and hollered in Irish from upstairs, Norman was halfway down the street with his shirt flapping about him.

The thrill of the affair was only further fuelled by the necessity of keeping it a secret from Jack Wrigley. He was aged beyond his years. At twenty he may as well have been forty. It was as if Florrie was being courted by a man the age of her father. Jack hated music as much as he hated the pictures. He marched around Hunslet with his Staffordshire Bull Terrier, smoking incessantly. Cigarettes were the only thing he allowed himself to buy. "Money in't water, Florrie", he would say. He kept his earnings from the foundry in envelopes, alongside news clippings on Churchill and the war, and stuffed these into places where Florrie wouldn't find them. "Save that for a rainy day." Every day it rained.

"Ayup, love!" Norman stood with his arms akimbo. Trying to balance on the boat, he looked like a drunk man imitating Jesus, spread out against an unsteady sky. Globes of light travelled across the water.

"What in God's name is this?" Florrie started.

"D'yer like it? I thought we'd go on a boat trip down Aire. Beats pictures, dun't it?"

"Got a spare cigarette, Florrie?" Ned and Terry asked in unison.

"Oh, and you had to bring your pals along." Florrie cackled. Her teeth were rhinestones. Rhinestones stolen from a duchess's neck. They reflected the light of the water. The water was contained within her.

"I couldn't well row on me own", Norman said. "I'd be knackered come Knowsthorpe. Pretend they're not here. That's what I do most the time."

"Or pretend Norman looks like me", Ned chipped in. "That's what lasses do most the time."

"Gi' spare cigarette and yer won't hear a sound", Terry pursued.

Florrie tapped her foot on the bow. "Is it safe, this boat?"

"Dead safe", said Norman. "We go on it every year when we go camping."

"Aye", said Ned. "It only capsizes 'alf the time."

With a confidence that suggested it was not her first time on the water, Florrie sprang onto the boat. Her dim reflection, a body of sodden leaves, floated on the surface of the river. She could not swim but still sprang, and sent the boat rocking sideways. Terry's arm plunged into the river. He dragged it out and sprayed the others with gunk. Slowly, they pulled away from the land once more and continued downstream towards Victoria Bridge. Above them, children with grubby half-moon faces trailed behind their grandparents. Men, with clouds of smoke about their heads, walked to fixed, knowable places, brushing ash from their nicotine-yellow white shirts. Runs of young women and their hardened mothers bundled past the men searching for Lyons' tea and Colman's mustard. The day was soon to be on its way out and there was little time to be used before the sun waned.

Ned and Terry were rowing steadily, sharing the cigarette Florrie had awarded them. She and Norman were coiled together in conversation. Squinting upwards, Ned looked towards the clouds, then to the bridge, at a particular man, as if to decipher his face amongst the mass. "That's never yer fella Jack, is it?"

Florrie jerked away from Norman. "Where?"

Norman frowned, removing his hand from the empty space that Florrie's waist had occupied, shoving it back in his pocket like an abandoned thought.

"On't bridge", Ned nodded. "Aye, it's him. Hat too small for his head. Face like a smacked arse."

The cast of the boat followed his nod. Jack Wrigley was marching across the bridge with a "blood and guts" sex-novelette, presumably to try to woo Florrie with, tucked under his arm above a sober newspaper. His bottom lip was stuck out to taste the salty sadness of the evening. His hoggish eyes swam over the faces of everyone before him.

"Christ!" Florrie cried. "I was worried he'd show his bloody face. This is his way home." She swiftly crouched with her back to the bridge and covered her head with her hands.

"Dun't worry", Norman said. He shifted his body to shield her from view. "He won't see us. He can't see owt. His head's too far up his own backside."

"Tha oughta dump 'im", Terry said. "He's a jerk, that bloke." He took a final drag from Florrie's cigarette and tossed it overboard.

"Aye, dun't worry", Ned added. "We're almost under bridge."

Florrie kept her head down. As the shadow of the bridge washed over them, Norman watched as Jack stalked on. He did not look over the parapet. He had no reason to take in the natural world, the commanding expanse of water. He was a man with somewhere to go; somewhere that would not miss him if he were gone. His fists were as loud as engines. He carried a nation of wind on his back. Norman glanced at the Aire as Jack's reflection walked under the bow of the boat. He looked as if he was beneath the river.

May 2017 (III)

When Wayne Dodds arrived, he brought the military with him; or he may as well have. He and Sherry pulled up at the curb, Heart FM heralding their arrival, a cat taking fright from the front tyres of their white Citroen C4 Cactus. Both wore designer clothes. Both wore designer underwear. A Chelsea FC flag was draped across the rear passenger window, its cerulean lion bearing its tongue with its head twisted back. Wayne helped Sherry out of the car, and when she looked up at Norman's house and erupted spontaneously into well-rehearsed tears, he patted her hair clumsily with a firm, meaty hand.

Wayne's hair had not changed since he was at war, almost nine years earlier. He kept the same crew cut, its shape measured frowningly by the millimetre, and never allowed it to grow for more than a week before his Ealing barber was ordered to cut it back again. For a man who was commonly agreed to be ugly, Wayne kept pride in his appearance and would polish his boots vehemently every night before bed. He needed to see himself in them. He carried himself as if any night he may be woken by his colonel and summoned to his front room to fight the Taliban behind the sofa. The pillows would be peppered with bullets and the garden gnomes would doff their caps.

Every summer, Wayne and Sherry would vacate West London to spend the weekend in Alicante or, once every three years, in the Bahamas. Sherry would busy herself on a deckchair with a pulp novel about a woman's choice between her husband and a muscular Spaniard, whilst Wayne strode about the beach in his swimming trunks. His tattoos would be seen whether the bystander cared to observe them or not. On his right arm, a warplane hovered like a moth of ink. It had been drilled into him by his uncle when he was sixteen. An amateur job, it had long ago started to peel. A gilt crucifix was printed on his chest, *BE THE BEST* stamped beneath it in stencil lettering. The depiction on his back was of a camouflage helmet, the words *TALIBAN KILLER* above it, and around it, a smattering of red poppies. He told anyone who would listen that each of them represented a soldier he had known that had died alongside him. He did not tell them that he had been discharged from the army for punching his lieutenant colonel during a dispute about the cleanliness of Wayne's bed and subsequently barred from returning to serve. He had ridden briefly in a patrol vehicle on his first day in Afghanistan and been discharged on his second. He had not worked since.

Sherry, a solicitor at a firm in Hammersmith, who was fifteen years older and four inches taller than her husband, supplied everything and took pleasure in updating colleagues on the misadventures of the "Action Man" she kept at home. Brenda had given birth young and brought her daughter up in Derby. When Sherry was sixteen, Brenda had relocated to Hunslet with an ex-conman she had met at the Working Men's Club, and Sherry had been told to get a flat elsewhere. She had moved to London during the Thatcher years and put in enough hours at several jobs to buy her own council house in the East End. By this time Brenda's lover had vanished, along with half of her possessions, and left Brenda to stew in Hunslet alone. Sherry had then put down a mortgage on her semi-detached house in Ealing, whilst renting out the council house she had lived in previously to an endless cycle of drugged-up art and theatre students. As it stood, she continued to rent out the house in East London and had added another ex-council property in White City to her portfolio, whilst living in Ealing, her mortgage fully paid off, and working as a solicitor to keep herself busy. Mam and I hated both her and Wayne. They hated us too. For the sake of Norman, however, we had always acted jovial.

Sherry and Wayne made themselves at home without pleasantries. Sherry flopped onto the sofa and kicked her shoes off. Wayne examined the framed photo of Norman's father in his army uniform at the foot of the staircase.

Sherry called to me from the living room. "There's a lad, Fred. Put the kettle on. Two sugars for me." I shuddered. She, like Mam, had stripped back her regional accent decades ago for the sake of employment. Unlike Mam, however, Sherry had replaced her Derbyshire twang with a sharp nasal squeal, not dissimilar to a bulldog bat. It bounced off the walls violently, filling the house. Norman, sound asleep upstairs, undoubtedly turned over at the disturbance and pressed a pillow to his ear. Mam sat with her awhile, grinning through gritted teeth, as I boiled the kettle and considered replacing the sugar with salt.

Wayne appeared at the kitchen door. "Got you making the cuppas already? Just be glad you're not married to her."

"I don't mind. I was making one anyway."

Wayne stepped into the kitchen and looked around, as if surveying one of his wife's properties. "Got yourself a bird yet, Fred? Or are you still too busy turning out them articles for the Nottingham rag?"

"It's nice to have a job in't it, Wayne?" I kept my eyes on the kettle. "Are you still unemployed?"

He edged in closely behind me. "A man who risks his life for his country shouldn't need to work when he returns. He's made his contribution. One larger than that of most people."

"I hadn't realised yours was that large", I said calmly. The kettle boiled. I filled three cups.

"I take it one of those is mine."

"I didn't know you wanted one, Wayne. There's no water left now. You're welcome to boil it again." I dumped three sugars into Sherry's tea and, placing the mugs on a tray, carried them out of the kitchen.

That evening, Grandad Norman prodded his double portion of vegetables hesitantly but did not eat. Mam had cobbled together ghoul-pale lumps of chicken, buttered carrots and potatoes, had christened them with salt and pepper, had forgotten to buy gravy. Wayne had changed into a dinner shirt, doused himself in eau de toilette. He brandished his gold-ringed fingers around the jug of squash. Both he and Sherry had complained about the alcohol ban that Mam had imposed. Tough. To guzzle wine in front of Norman, a man who could not be permitted to relapse, would be cruel. Besides, to drink and be merry so soon after Brenda's death could be misunderstood, or perhaps rightly understood, as a non-acknowledgement or celebration of her empty chair.

Within three minutes of eating, I needed a beer myself. Sherry was grimacing at the clump of salt glued to her carrot slice and attempting to poke it off with a manicured nail. Wayne was humming as he chewed. Mam's eyes remained firmly on her plate and Norman was propped up in his chair like a taxidermist's gazelle, a small, boiled potato abandoned on his lap, his gaze fixed on the photo of Brenda on the table opposite. The photo, taken on her sixtieth birthday, showed her sat, drunk and stout, in the Holbeck Working Men's Club. A plastic tiara perched on her messy head, as she prepared herself to sing "Dancing Queen" with her trademark smoker's rasp. The ex-steelworkers told her she had a voice like Janis Joplin. She did not. She had the smile of a truncheon, the face of a bulldog and set-back eyes which surveyed the tables for whatever pints may have been deserted without being finished.

"When exactly will the funeral be then, Betty?" Sherry asked, decidedly having given up on finishing her meal. It was the first time she had mentioned the ceremony since arriving.

"Well", Mam said. "The funeral director said he'd get back to me tomorrow. He's going to go over it all with me. Perhaps next week."

"The sooner the better", Sherry replied. "I need to get back to London, of course. I'm going to be working remotely while I'm up here, but I've got meetings with clients scheduled for next Thursday onwards and it would be unprofessional of me to postpone."

"How about this coming Monday?" Wayne suggested, stifling a belch and throwing down his napkin. He looked at me smugly, aware he had finished his meal first, and nodded at the chicken left on my plate.

"I'll have a word with the funeral director tomorrow", Mam said. "See what we can do."

"Haven't you got work to get back to, Betty?" Sherry asked, seemingly irritated that the decision could not be made on the spot.

"I've taken the last week of the school term off. Next week is half-term. I'd have to see what can be done if the funeral needed to be later than that. I'd wangle it." I became aware that Mam was squeezing my hand under the table. I squeezed it back. She turned to me, smiling. "And our Fred's going to finish a couple of articles and then make the most of some annual leave while he's up here, aren't you, love? You've been working on some great stories recently for the *Herald*."

I smiled gingerly, aware they were neither great nor worth discussion.

"Oh yeah?" Wayne grinned. "Anything that made the national news? A new breakthrough in the Brexit discussions perhaps. A political scandal?"

"Well", I said, taking a slow sip of squash. "It's a local newspaper, and the news differs from day to day, so I don't always write the same sort of thing."

"A mayoral scandal perhaps, if it's local", Wayne pressed. "Or an 'orrible murder?"

"Not this week." I pretended to laugh, but it sounded forced. "An obstruction on the M1", I admitted. "Development plans for a new housing project in Kimberley." I shot Wayne a look that asked whether he was happy now. He nodded that he was, and sat back with his hands on his stomach.

"Speaking of housing", Sherry smiled, attempting to appear amiable. "What's the plan for this place, Norman? I mean now that Mum's gone."

Mam put her fork down abruptly. "What do you mean?"

"Well, you don't want to live on your own, do you, Norman? I know Mum always looked after you well, but now that she's no longer here…" Sherry trailed off. She paused, as if mournful. "It might be better to consider going someplace else. Somewhere you can be taken care of. Lime Hall is only round the corner. I've heard such good things."

Nothing positive had ever been said about Lime Hall, a care home on the outskirts of Beeston. Not long prior, reports had surfaced about the mistreatment of the elderly within its walls — medication being forgotten, meals being inedible and three members of staff found to have been stealing from residents with dementia. The elderly were inmates. They shuffled around the corridors in limp pyjamas, as if they had stones in their shoes. They appeared briefly in unwashed windows but turned away on being seen from the outside. In the winter months, the windows iced over and the elderly were not seen until spring.

Norman, who had until now been vacant, removed his gaze from the photo of Brenda. "I dun't want to go Lime Hall."

"There's *nothing* good about Lime Hall", Mam said, directing herself at Sherry with an intensity that made the woman look away. "Dad's fine here. He'll *stay* here. I can be here whenever, if ever he needs me. You want to stay here, don't you, Dad?"

Norman half nodded, as if he didn't want Sherry to see. He picked up a slice of carrot and slowly moved it around in his mouth.

"But this place must be filled with memories, Dad. Memories of Mum." Sherry referred to Norman as her father whenever she wanted to win him over. She had started doing it not long after Brenda's health deteriorated. She had told him that he was the closest thing to a father she had ever had, that her fleeting visits every few years were some of her most cherished memories. Then she would crawl into him, like a beetle into leaf litter, push herself up against his chest where she could examine his heartbeat. She knew as well as anyone else how kind Norman could be, how open-handed. "Surely you don't want to be reminded of her all the time. It's not good for you. And yes, Betty can be here sometimes I'm sure, but she can't be here all of the time. What if she wasn't here and you fell…?"

"Sherry", Mam cut in, furiously. "He's staying here and *that's that*. Do *not* talk to my dad like that."

"Betty", Norman murmured. "It's alright, love. She's just concerned."

"He's my dad too!" Sherry cried, slamming her hand on the table.

I blurted a single "Ha!" A shred of chicken shot from my mouth and landed on the far side of the table. It was eyed silently by everyone in the room.

Finally, Norman struggled to his feet. "I'm going to get some water."

"Let me get it for you, Dad", Mam said, getting up quickly.

"Betty, no", Norman frowned. "I can do it myself. I'm not senile yet."

Forlorn, Mam returned to her seat. Norman trudged out of the room. No one spoke in his absence. The clock on the wall ticked, its hands jutted and clicked. A minute later, he returned with a half pint of water and sat, scowling, sipping at it. Mam and I finished our meals in silence. Sherry covered her barely touched plate with her napkin. She and Wayne would leave soon. They would stay in the city-centre Hampton hotel until the funeral was done with. I thanked God that there was only one spare room in Norman's house, the room Mam would stay in. I would sleep on the sofa. The clock on the wall licked its lips and ticked. Brenda bared her teeth from the framed photo across the room. She did not sound like Janis Joplin. She had a voice like a house falling down. Wayne coughed and glanced at his watch. It was not until Norman had almost drained his glass that we realised he had not been drinking water, but vodka.

The Man Who Was and Was Not

Norman was a wanted man. He did not know it at the time. No one had cared enough to tell him. Folk who bumped into him in the street paused momentarily, trying to remember what it was he needed to know, before moving on. It would only click when they got home that evening. "Aye, yes. I meant to tell Norman he's a wanted man." They thought to themselves they would tell him at the soonest opportunity, but of course no one can command time as they wish, and so Norman was blissfully unaware at the time of the attack.

It took place at eight, at Holbeck Working Men's Club. What is there to say about the club? It was where dust never settled. Whilst once the reserve of stoic alcoholics, perched on stools like worn battlements, the club had, since the war, become a palace of varieties. It pulsed with the sound of hollering and murmuring, the scuttering of piano keys, of drums. On the weekends, hundreds of members descended upon it, some donned in brushed-down suits, occasionally men accompanied by wives, some of whose wives secretly paid for their membership. The railwaymen, stopping overnight on their way to Scotland, sat drinking in their overalls in their designated blue room, before retiring drunk to their lodges across the street. The fathers and grandfathers of young members were tucked in the corners like ruddy gooseberries, the turn of a folk ballad fluttering on their lips.

The ten-bob acts took their turns on the squat stage upstairs but wheeled around as fast as they had come if they failed to impress immediately. Comedians and singers were heckled into the curtains. Sometimes the compère introduced an act for the purpose of teasing them alone. On the night in question, a fresh-faced comedy duo was performing a scripted bit, one of them dressed in a trawlerman's raincoat. They were attempting a long drawn-out joke about the north-east's fishing industry but were chased downstairs and into the street by a recently migrated Geordie with hairy knuckles.

"I'd love to have heard them get wise about the Shannon Estuary, the feckers." Micheál McLoughlin grinned, turning to Norman. They had returned to the bar on the ground floor, with no vacant tables left to claim for themselves. "Their ears would've been ringing all the way back to their ma's."

Florrie's elder brother, being twenty-one, enjoyed a level of influence over Norman. This was in no way baleful. He liked Norman. He preferred him to Jack. As Jack was closer to Micheál's own age, he was resistant to any outside influence, and certainly the influence of an Irishman. Jack felt this was below him. Norman, however, was more receptive to a brotherly imposition. He had no siblings of his own. He would make a worthier brother-in-law, if a brother-in-law was to be had.

Micheál sank the dregs of his Tetley's and slammed the glass down. He ordered another for himself, and half pints of bitter for Norman, Ned and Terry. Micheál had recently picked up work as a milkman, having worked briefly in the foundry alongside Jack before Norman had taken a job there. He enjoyed his solitary trips around the south of Leeds every morning. The time alone was welcome. There was no master to bark in his ear. He would hum folk songs to himself as he leisurely went from house to house, and the streets would redden behind him as the first light of morning came. After a week, he decided to drive his float everywhere, simply because he could. His boss didn't seem to mind. It was closer to a car than anyone else had. It was parked outside the club at that moment, swarmed by cats.

Ned was already tipsy, already slurring his words. He was wearing Micheál's milkman cap at a slanted angle. "Is it true what they say about thee family then, Micheál?"

"What do they say?" Micheál grinned. He always grinned. One of the traits that made him most popular amongst his neighbours was his general light-heartedness in the face of enquiry. He didn't mind being the alien. He seemed to enjoy the questioning that came as a result of it and took no offense to the curiosity of his peers. He knew that most of them bore him no ill intent. He could even laugh at the ones who did.

"That yus wuh chased out of Ireland by the IRA."

"Well", Micheál laughed. "Wouldn't ye like to know."

"He's a quiet man, tha father", Ned pressed. "Dun't say much on it. It's an interesting story is all. I wondered if there wuh any truth in it."

"Yuh oughtn't ask things like that, nosey get", Norman scowled.

"It's alright", Micheál grinned. "A man can have his curiosity. There's no harm in that." He leaned in close to Ned and placed his hand on the youth's shoulder. "Can ye imagine what would happen to a man if he asked no questions?"

Ned was bleary-eyed. He looked puzzled. "I can't. Can thee?"

"Well, he'd go mad, wouldn't he?" Micheál glanced at Terry. "How many sovereign states d'ye reckon there are in the world?"

"Sovereign what?" Terry asked, and drank.

"One hundred and two, and five de facto. But how many d'ye know an ounce about? Why, I know about Ireland, that's fer sure. I know about the United Kingdom, about England. I know too much about England. You could go to Cyprus, Somaliland or Sierra Leone and you'd still be in England! Everything other than England, you have to learn on your own. That's a lot of existence that stands unaccounted for, isn't it? What do ye know about Yugoslavia, for instance? Well, they won't teach ye that sort of thing at school. Yer done with education by the time yer fifteen, and ye go into the factories and don't come out again. No, I say a world without inquiry would be a world of fools." He drank. "That's not to say that all curiosity can be satisfied. It never will. Think about the solar system. All this talk over the water about sending satellites into space. Will they do it? I don't know. But don't ye want to find out what occupies the spaces we'll

never be able to see? Of course, ye do. Yer human. But it's space. We'll never know the entirety of it. That would be impossible. It's endless. Think about the ocean. It's a scary place. It's like space on Earth. Almost the entire ocean remains unmapped, unexplored. How deep is it? We have no clue. We don't know what's down there. The gates of hell? If I could choose between death by gun or death by drowning, ye can put as many bullets through me as ye like. That's fer sure. Some of the questions we ask we're too scared to discover the answers to. We don't really want them. But our curiosity is what keeps us going. A world without curiosity would be numbing. A man's got to be autonomous in this world. A man's got to ask questions if he hopes to be a man at all. If he doesn't, he's out at sea with no oars to guide him. Nothing to see but the flat surface. He might as well be under the water."

"Aye", Ned nodded, having listened partly. His eyes had wondered to a young blonde woman who had just walked in. Her husband shot him a look of warning and Ned returned to his drink. "So will yer answer the question I asked thee?"

"Ah", Micheál declared. "That's the thing. A man is entitled to his curiosity, but another man is entitled to his privacy."

Norman was unsure of whether Micheál was having fun at the drunk boy's expense. Perhaps Micheál himself was drunk.

"The world is made up of worthy questions. Compact with them. Everything and everyone can be questioned. However, the answers to those questions are sometimes unknown, or forgotten, or incorrect. Many of us learn something and forget it the next day or learn something entirely fictitious and share it as if it were truth, unaware of its underlying falsity. There is meaning, though, in searching for resolutions to the questions you have, even if you eventually discover there were no resolutions to be found after all. It's a noble pursuit to chase the answers to the questions that shape the lives of entire communities and populations. Those are the real questions we have to concern ourselves with. Of course, I know the answer to the question you asked me, Ned. After all, it's a question that's *personal to my own experience. But where's the fun in answering it? The more worthy questions exist outside of the mundane circumstances and histories of specific people."*

"So, you're not gun' tell me", Ned frowned, clearly lost with the detour the conversation had taken.

"This bloke speaks in riddles", Terry said. He looked to Norman as if to ask if Micheál was a raving madman that he had dragged in from the street.

Micheál sat back on his stool, grinning, enjoying the effect he was having. He sunk half his pint in three gulps and wiped his mouth with his sleeve. "I prefer to keep a bit of the unknown about me. Makes for better stories. Like I say, individuals aren't the cornerstone of truth. We're largely made up of falsities ourselves. There are things we want people to believe about us that aren't true. Things that are true that we want nobody to know. We create our own versions of ourselves and parade them in front of others who are doing exactly the same. It's interesting. You'll never know someone inside out, not even your own family. And since the individual really doesn't matter in the context of the most pressing questions, why not embrace the fantasies ye hear about people? Imagine, for a moment, if ye knew everything about a man. Then, if somebody told ye a story about him — say they told ye he climbed Ben Nevis in half an hour with his eyes closed and one hand behind his back — you'd know that's not true. You'd know the fella has a crooked ankle. You'd know the fella's never been to Scotland. You'd know that on the day he was supposedly climbing Ben Nevis, he was actually at home masturbating, struggling to even get up the stairs. Wouldn't that be a shame? Isn't a man more interesting when he can be five different men at once, when half the things you know about him are imagined, or falsely remembered, or absolute deception? You can walk by two folks and they'll each be sure you're somebody completely different. Most of the time it doesn't matter, so let people be who they most want to be. Mythology gives us an emotional and romantic level of truth, and that's equally important as a scientific level of truth. The two have to coexist to make the world bearable. Some things you can know, some things you can never know, and that's how it should be. But I do know one thing, and that's for certain."

Ned leaned forward. "What's that?"

Micheál laughed. "I need a piss." He left his listeners at the bar and disappeared into the crowd.

"Chuffin' 'eck", Terry frowned. "Where'd thee find that fella, Norman? High Royds Hospital?"

"Never realised how much of a mad bastard he wuh", said Ned.

"None of that", Norman scolded. "I know this is the first time you've met him, but you'll get used to him. He's a bit different, but that's areet. He dun't have to keep Florrie and I a secret from his folks, but he does. I owe him for now."

"He must get it from his father", Ned continued. "Odd man, him. Never know whether yer coming or going with him."

"Well, keep yer lips buttoned", Norman hissed. "It's nowt to do with thee, so dun't pry into his family life again."

Ned's eyes had drifted off once more to the same blonde woman, who was now stood drinking a bottle of milk stout by the door of the lounge. Terry said nothing but drained his half pint and belched into his hand. Four men waded through the crowd behind Ned. Ned was still wearing Micheál's hat. The bask of men moved closer. Three of them, chosen for their height, were mammoths that dwarfed the room. Strongmen plucked from folklore. The fourth planted his hand on Ned's shoulder.

"Is he bothering thee, Micheál?" Jack Wrigley asked the boy in the milkman's hat. He was looking directly at Norman. Before Ned could turn his head, Jack had stepped forward and landed a punch between Norman's eyes.

The room erupted. Norman dropped from his stool, knocking an old man down in the process. Jack turned, expecting Micheál's praise, but, to his surprise, found himself being lamped by Ned. The three strongmen started forward, but two were pulled back by Terry and swung over a table. Suddenly Norman was back up and fending off the third, and the old man that Norman had knocked was grappling with Jack, forcing his head into a chokehold. As the two giants splayed across the table clambered to their feet, a steelworker realised they had spilt his wife's port and lemon and preceded to drag the offenders to the floor by their hair. The young comedian in the trawlerman's raincoat poked his head back inside to retrieve his hat and was immediately punched back out.

Norman was, by this time, seeing red. The scarlet curtains. Contorted faces of claret. The bottoms of the pint glasses were ruby with blood, the confetti of glass about him all scarlet. Jack had shed himself of the old man's headlock and, with the help of the third strongman, wrestled Norman to the floor. Kneeling on Norman's chest, Jack's fist rose and fell, methodically. He set about his work as he would in the foundry. He was punching the hierarchy of age into Norman. Men above boys. He was enjoying himself. His fist rose and fell, like the stoic boot that brought retribution to the indulgent woodlouse. He was delivering a parable. The vermin of intemperance would be run out of Hunslet, mowed down where they danced. The milk bars would be gutted. The rowing boats would be sunk.

Norman could feel his brain shifting back in his skull. His nose was broken. The bone was pressing up against his skin. His muscles loosened. He seemed to be levitating. The dark, sickly carpet lay patiently below him. Above, a phantom hand, whether Jack's or his father's, hung like a star. This was the hand blind men followed down the river. In their twos and threes, they followed it — good Christians, good, blind sods — to be hanged, drawn and quartered. Soon, to be handless would be celebrated. It would be expected of all men. The phantom hands were the invisible architects. They constructed the state without complaint or comment. Left, right, left, right.

Then, the third strongman slumped forward. A boot collided with Jack's face. It happened slowly. Norman had entered a space beyond sound. He could hear nothing, yet as his head rolled sideways, he could make out

Micheál, red all over, brandishing a hammer. The crowds were clearing into the fringes of vision. Jack's other two accomplices had vanished, leaving Ned, unconscious, stretched out on the floor. Terry was shaking Norman's shoulders. He shook him like Norman's mother did when waking him for work. "Not now", Norman mouthed, "I'm dreaming."

Micheál was crouched, his hammer inches from Jack's face. He was saying something Norman couldn't decipher. A farmer warning a volatile horse. A soothsayer telling of the blackness on the other side of the moon. Words that can never be known. A steady, unaccountable glow emitted from Micheál. The landscape shifted around it. Moths fell. People scrambled through to the door and disappeared inside the glow. It was a hazy, foreboding sort of thing, but strangely comforting. Norman wondered if he were the only one who could see it. Did Micheál know it was there, and what would he do with it if he found out? Would he try to scrub it away in the bath or would he laugh it off and walk down the street looking like that? Perhaps Micheál already knew about the glow and would be angry if he discovered that Norman had seen it. All sound had evacuated from it. All light succumbed to the vacuum of it. Norman put his hand out and somebody touched it. All was red, then black.

May 2017 (IV)

It was all vapid. Fuck the bastard lot of them.

Lying on the sofa the next morning, I thumbed through the copy of the *Daily Monotony* that Wayne had left behind in the kitchen. A rag saturated with celebrity gossip, spin-doctoring and right-wing reactionary opinion pieces. An early-Noughties pop singer had been pictured working as a travel guide in Spain, sporting a white-hot blazer and shorts. A Polish plumber had charged a grandma two grand to unblock her sink. *I just bought my second home, and you can too!* A man who feared crushing his wife in bed had shed three stone in four years. *The Tory MP who smiled at me.* Vouchers for Iceland and Boots. One bingo advert, two, three. I flipped through to the back pages. Leeds United had finished seventh in the championship, having been slapped by Burton and Norwich City and drawn with Wigan Athletic. Chelsea had won the Premier League, having trounced West Brom, Watford and Sunderland. *Bastards.*

I woke up early every day. It had once been a labour, but now it was a matter of habit. I did not do lie-ins. They made me feel like the day had been extracted out of me before I had even peeled the shaving cream from my face. Between five and seven in the morning was my solitary period. Sometimes I would spend the time flipping through yesterday's news, sometimes attempting to read the classics in an effort to secure holy cultural capital, the ability to avoid embarrassment amongst the bigwigs I might find myself rubbing shoulders with one day. Despite this, *Middlemarch* remained unfinished and *Jane Eyre* barely touched after nearly two years festering on my bedside table. I was no one's fool, however. I had mulled over some chapters of the Williams, Jameson and Eagleton books Norman had showed me in my early twenties. They had stuck with me. I had read my Barthes, my Baudrillard, my Lyotard — in part anyway. I had liked Lyotard until *Libidinal Economy*. After dropping that text (from a third-floor window), I had contemplated trying Heidegger, whom I had heard of but never read and truthfully knew nothing about. After looking up Heidegger online, I decided most philosophers were wankers, and sacked off my morning reading habits for a while. Due to this, more recently during my early hours of solitude I instead planned whatever tripe I would turn out that day at the *Herald*. On the morning in question, I had succumbed to *the Daily Monotony* partly to discover how it had changed since I was a teenager, if at all. Back then, the opening pages of the newspaper, exhibiting photos of topless glamour models, would be torn out by grubby hands at the off-licence and paraded around school by a pandemonium of boys, echoing whichever bawdy phrases they had found in the paper, memorising them. The topless section had been replaced with one or two photos of lingerie models, but other than that it remained much the same kindling.

The other reason I had picked up the *Daily Monotony* was due to my insatiable need to feel angry. I had realised that I hadn't been truly seething for several months, and perhaps was not furious more often than a few times throughout the average year. It was not that there was nothing to be angry *about*. There was an abundance of that, and it was important to measure out just how much vexatious material I exposed myself to, so as not to overdo it. No. The rarity of my fury was, if anything, due to a feeling of inexact numbness which had been gradually making itself at home under my skin throughout the latter part of my twenties. Now, at twenty-nine, I seemed void of noticeable sensations and emotions for longer periods than I once had been, sometimes for as long as a week. This was a popular numbness. My housemates had also felt it from time to time, and it was becoming increasingly autonomous within their bodies also.

I lived in a rented ex-council house in Bulwell with a taxman who worked by Nottingham train station, a bouncer at the PRYZM nightclub on Lower Parliament Street and a barista who had made cappuccinos in Costa, Starbucks and Caffè Nero for most of her adult life. The taxman and the barista had been to university but the benefits of their degrees in sociology and fine art were yet to kick in. This was something that caused them disgruntlement but little noticeable anger. It made me somewhat glad that I had sacked off university myself. I had spent the decade since leaving sixth form in a string of meaningless retail and bar jobs, signing onto jobseeker's when the work dried up, spending the majority of what I earned on cheap lager and, occasionally, spirits. I had stopped smoking when I racked up two grand's worth of debt to my landlord, despite this being the time I wanted cigarettes the most, and finally had landed a job at the *Herald*, scarcely able to believe my luck at finding salaried employment in a field that interested me. Since then, however, that interest had gradually waned, as more and more stories of human boredom found themselves designated to me to report. This was when the numbness had become discernible.

It was perhaps a numbness born from stasis, but surely this was due to my own stasis, having never left Nottingham, rather than the stasis of the city itself. The city and the country, after all, were always transforming — transforming so swiftly and yet so gradually that you could be forgiven for not noticing the changes until they had taken place. The defilement of anything recognisable. Buildings, icons and cultural reminders were flattened overnight and replaced by unsullied new builds, by images of a surgical cleanliness, by mirages. Evidence of such a project could be found across the country. Even in Hunslet the landscape had been restructured. It was no more Norman's land than that of the southern architect. Density had made way for space, for sterilisation. In place of what was there were cul-de-sacs, apartments rising in price, motorways, corporate branding, supermarkets and shades of bleached grey, cream and beige. The red bricks had been carried away without a trace. The problem here was that these transformations, even if sinister, were seemingly mundane. In the de-characterised terrain, eventually unrecognisable to itself, the nefarious had become prosaic, revealing itself in such dull ways that it was not worth the hassle of anger. It did not feel the need to hide. The wicked could be seen whenever you took your bins out, and you would yawn at the sight of it. Despite incessant erosion and remapping, an air of predictability hung thick in the air. *Well,* you might think, *if you're going to burn it all down, at least make it worth stepping outside to see.*

I flung the newspaper onto the armchair opposite and turned to the TV. Beryl Blanc, the pop star responsible for forty glitzy songs with "love" in their titles, was holding her new lip gloss. A sensual sigh rose in exhalation and the words *Oh-So Blanc* ran across the screen in joined-up script. Next, two green-haired disciples from the latest post-punk, post-electronic outfit appeared on a trainer commercial karate-kicking the air. An indiscernible instrument wailed. *BE SUBVERSIVE,* the brand demanded. *Be subversive so we can absorb your dissent and sell it back to you as products.*

I rose, yawned, sat down again, then decided against it, and switched off the TV, for the day had started, cars were coughing into life and the postman was already being chased by a dog.

At Salter and Son Funeral Directors, Mr Salter sat, chameleon-like, his pasty greening skin blending into the faded botanical wallpaper behind him. He was, if anything, the last of the Victorians. His pallid jacket hung from his malnourished body like a cloak. His eyes were colourless. Anything he ate was barren of flavour. He had wandered out of a flat world and, when his side profile was seen, he seemed near flat himself. "You can see her if you like." He gestured to a door at the rear of the office. Norman, hungover and still unwashed, chewed his saliva and nodded.

Brenda's funeral was to be on the coming Monday. She would be set alight at the Cottingley Hall crematorium. It would, in fairness to Sherry, be best to have the service as soon as possible. That way, she and Wayne could vanish quickly and leave Mam and I to our own devices, leave Norman to his own home, leave the lights to be turned on again.

It would not help Norman to see Brenda again but there was little that could be done to stop him. He walked like a man possessed towards the door and the younger funeral director, assumedly the "son" of Salter and Son, his face that of a permanently frowning toad, moved aside. Mam and I followed.

Brenda had her eyes closed, thankfully. She did not look at peace. Her face, whilst resting, appeared clenched in frustration. She looked like she could erupt at any moment, shouting at the ceiling, making it tremble above her. She was not pale. Spray-on tan still stained her fleshy body. Her red nail varnish was chipped but not quite gone. If she was, at that moment, in conversation with the afterlife, it was not obvious whether she was staring down hell or heaven. Norman shuddered, from emotion or fear. Mam put her arm around him.

"She's with God now", the son of Salter lied.

There was a moment's hush. Mam mumbled something, the Lord's Prayer. Then Norman removed her arm from him and whispered to her. "Let me just... have a moment alone."

Mam nodded and we withdrew. We waited in the office. The son of Salter poured Mam a glass of warm tap water. Salter busied himself with paperwork at his desk, seemingly having forgotten we were there. I studied the burgundy, the russet, the artichoke green of the botanical wallpaper. The walls were decked with flowers. Flat flowers, flat prayers and flat yesterdays barely remembered. On the other side of the door, Norman could be heard in low tones, telling Brenda a story. The narrative itself could not be made out, but Norman began it as he began most of his stories. "There once was a man..."

We walked through the city centre on the way home, flagged on either side by the multinational fast-food chains, the American sandwich rackets, the mobile phone conglomerates, the internet moguls, the faux-French coffee giants and the sportswear empires. Shoppers in their thousands, a phantasmagoria, passed through, stacked high, the colours of their clothing smearing the air. They were indistinguishable, melting into one another, emerging from each other's limbs, vanishing behind each other's heads.

Waiters, waitresses and chefs with thick Yorkshire accents exploded out of the Italian restaurant to smoke, compare tips and mock their manager. Angry boys sauntered in puffer jackets in twenty-five-degree heat, their faces childlike beneath the anonymity of hoods. Bronzed girls gathered at the McDonalds to plan a getaway to Zante and reality-show-made gym lads crossed the road to talk to them, leaving at the bus stop a red-faced man in a Hawaiian shirt littered with St. George's Crosses. A bucket hat and a string vest shot past on a bike, drum and bass tumbling from a portable speaker. An open-top BMW was stuck behind a malfunctioning Renault Clio at the green light. A megabus sounded its horn, its mascot waving embarrassedly at the scene of disruption. A man stood like a flagpole, three scarves draped over him, murder hanging from his face.

The gutted and refurbished Kirkgate Market watched on, its towers and turrets sweating under the sun. Inside, the stench of raw cod swam from Eskimo Joe's fishmongers to the Phone Clinic, to Baobab Tree and Brown's sweetshop, clung to the wigs of Dimples Hair and Cosmetics. The sun's heat seemed to intensify every year. This was something to be celebrated. Should the bricks of the ex-industrial buildings one day melt away, the bustling crowds below would receive them as rain, would strip down to let the dust flow over them.

– SAFETY MESSAGE:
PLEASE DO NOT ATTEMPT TO PUSH THESE DOORS OPEN
        – Radical exit.
                – U Ok, hun?
– I hold up the scales of the last salmon.

   — I have got the shell of the last oyster.

   — Down, boy, down! It's only a busker!

— A lot of policies that really went out of fashion in the 1980s.

— LEEDS. THE FOODIE CAPITAL OF THE NORTH ☼

   — A Northern League team have had their pitch rolled up and stolen overnight.

— Shame it wun't Garry Monk they fookin' pinched.

   — OFFICE SPACE TO LET.

   — *The Sun*, in which you wrote this article, had to provide a translation of your words for its readers.

— BEAUTFIUL SPACIOUS OFFICE SPACE.

   — How do you confuse a Man U fan?

   — How?

— Show him a map of Manchester.

   — SPACE SPACE SPACE.

   — Broken promise. Three hundred and fifty million.

— The War of the Roses never ended.

   — Broken promise. Yer said we could have chippy tea!

   — We *are* having chippy tea.

— The chips at home in't same!

   — I don't mind asylum seekers. I really don't. But they're stealing our Polish folks' jobs!

   — GOT A HUNCH? WE'LL MATCH YOUR FIRST BET! BET £2 TO MAKE TWO HUNDRED! WhenthefunstopsstopPleasegambleresponsibly.

— Commie bastard. He wants to take us back to the '70s. I never did like flares.

   — Less business for bossman.

   — Thank you. *Please* come again. ☺

— Terrorist sympathiser. Makes strawberry jam with ISIS.

   — That wuh the textiles factory me mam worked in, and me nana before her.

Premier Inn now.

— I'm tired of "experts". "Experts" in their ivory towers in London. Self-serving posh cunts.

— Blokes din't go shopping in them days. They had a billiards room above their suit shop to pull the buggers in.

— If you're a citizen of the world you're a citizen of nowhere.

— Oh aye, I used to play on that road when I wuh a lass. Or maybe it wuh over there. Actually ...

— A big vanilla wasteland. Sterilised if anything.

Before we could reach the car park, we were accosted by the Bunny sisters, elderly twins who had tottered towards us on Boar Lane, brandishing supermarket bags. It was Brenda who had named them the Bunny sisters. She claimed they were "bunny boilers", each as desperate as the other to drag Norman away from her. They were both spinsters. They had both, in fact, never lived apart, and had been sharing a flat together somewhere in Hunslet Carr since God knows when. "There's Nunny Bunny", Brenda would say, "and Gummy Bunny." The former wore a bronze crucifix pendant around her neck. The latter had next to no teeth. Brenda enjoyed the fact they had never married and enjoyed the fact that she had.

"We're *so* sorry to hear about Brenda, love", the former cried, holding herself to Norman's overcoat, stroking his arm. They were not sorry. No one was.

"I only saw her last week", mumbled the latter, taking his free hand in her own. "It wuh such a shock to hear."

"Thank yuh, Dorothy. Thank yuh, Ruth." Norman continued walking. He did not want their attention but would not shake them off. They shuffled down the street with him, draped around him like a weighted vest.

"When's the funeral gun' be?"

"I shall wear me blackest blouse."

"I can bring summet t'eat. For the reception. Egg and cress p'haps."

"We could stop by shop again on way home", one suggested to the other, who nodded her head vigorously.

"Well", Norman said, forcing a dry chuckle. "That's dead nice, but we aren't too sure when the funeral will be at the moment. We an't got it ironed out wi' directors. I'll be sure to let yuh know when."

"Oh do!"

"You have our phone number still?"

"Aye, aye", Norman grunted. "Have it somewhere."

A tin of soup dropped out of one of the twin's shopping bags. Norman stopped. I picked it up and handed it back to the woman, who snatched it without a word and returned her attention up to Norman's chin. Norman continued walking, quickening his pace. The car park was in sight.

"You oughta come over to ours someday soon, Norman."

"We can make yuh summet nice! You just say what you'd like."

"Our treat."

"Or if yuh need help getting rid of Brenda's old stuff!"

"I know a young man from church what would gladly take it t'charity shop. I could mention it to him."

"I could mention it too."

"I'd mention it first." One scowled at the other.

"It'll do yuh good to move on now, love. There're other women out there, y'know. Say, Norman. I've always loved the way you dress. Dead smart."

"*Dead* smart. A proper bobby-dazzler!"

Norman was wearing an unwashed rugby top beneath his

overcoat. A pair of sunken grey slacks. He had almost left the house with only one sock on until Mam had drawn his attention to it. The twins' sense of smell was clearly faltering because Norman's breath still carried the stench of vodka. His eyes were bloodshot, his face gnarled by discomfort. He was not the Adonis of South Leeds they believed him to be, not even the man he had been a few weeks earlier, and whilst Norman would have once gladly invited such female attention, his patience was thin.

We reached the entrance to the car park. A young, hungry couple were kissing passionately at the door. One of the twins wrinkled her nose in disgust. "Git a room", she hissed at them. "Grubby buggers." The couple smirked and sauntered off.

"Areet", Norman said, shaking the sisters free of him. "We're off up to me grandson's car. It wuh nice bumping into yuh."

The Bunny sisters looked hurt to no longer be touching him. Nunny Bunny stared down at her crucifix. Gummy Bunny fingered her gums. After an overdrawn goodbye, the twins shuffled away. They disappeared into the manic rhythm of swinging shopping bags, the chattering of teeth, the flicking of crisp twenty-pound notes. The buses were jammed. The retailers were heaving. People were pressed up against the windows inside, their cheeks like pancakes on the glass.

I thought I may have remembered the Bunny sisters from an earlier time, a time in which they were happier. It would have been during my childhood — they would have had more teeth then — but I couldn't quite elucidate whatever memories there were. Perhaps they had bought me ice cream once. Perhaps they had once sat with Norman and me at the Working Men's Club when I was very young. A bus honked and it sounded like Brenda shouting. I quickly followed Mam and Norman into the car park.

The Devil and the Cat

John Joseph McLoughlin brought a knife to the wedding. No one questioned him. No one made eye contact with him. He sat alongside his wife in the pews, running his finger along the edge of the blade. He put the tip of the blade to his thumb and gently massaged his skin with it. He used it for whittling. He was a whittler now. It was a pastime he had taken up without warning. He collected wood from the streets and turned it into miniature Connemara ponies, wolfhounds and crucifixes. He placed them on the windowsill of the McLoughlin house, so the wooden creations glared out at passing neighbours. Declarations. Omens. He had been invited to the wedding only because there was no way for it to go ahead without his permission.

Jack Wrigley had not bothered Norman since the storming of Holbeck Working Men's Club. He had turned up unannounced at Florrie's door the following morning and ended their relationship, making sure there were neighbours to bear witness to him being the one who had brought it to a close. Despite this, he was known as "Black-Eyed Jack" at the foundry for a couple of weeks. No one questioned Norman's broken nose. It seemed to be quietly respected. He stayed at the foundry until the end of the month then quit and began work as a sports coach at the Lads' Club. His father's phantom hand could not haunt him there.

Norman was in charge of training the club's young footballers. A knot of grubby-faced secondary modern reprobates would pile in from across South Leeds and Norman would drill them mercilessly. He'd make them run until their skeletons could have overtaken their legs. "Got a soft underbelly, lad? Christ, tha couldn't hit a cow's arse with a banjo playing like that."

Having been born a matter of months too late, Norman had narrowly missed the call-up to National Service. He would have enjoyed serving in the armed forces, if only briefly. He created the same environment on the football field that he assumed would have existed in the training camps, fashioning local troublemakers into athletes skilled enough to try out at any first division club. One day, Jack Charlton and Billy Cush came to watch the boys play a five-a-side match, along with a quiet man in a nubby tweed blazer who Norman understood to be a scout for Leeds United. When they departed, they left Norman a match-worn Leeds shirt in the office. It was a V-neck of rich blue with a lemon trim. The city's coat of arms was luminous on the chest. The electric-yellow owls. The golden fleece hung from a rope. Pro Rege et Lege. *Norman sprinted home to show his father and wore the shirt every day religiously for the rest of the week.*

Norman and Florrie had continued to see each other for a further six months before Norman proposed. He had bought a ring at a pawn shop, using the money he had put aside from his own earnings and an occasional pound slipped to him by Micheál. Micheál himself seemed never out of pocket. Norman had thought there must be a small fortune to be made from milk.

When Norman had met Florrie's parents, as he knew he would have to, he found them insufferable. John Joseph McLoughlin was a harrowing man whose glassy eyes followed house guests wherever they went. There was something heavy and knowing about his eyes, as if he could see under a person's skin by looking at them, as if he knew what they would say before they said it. He picked his mouth at the dinner table with an overused toothpick. He collected morsels of food in his beard and let them live there for days. He had become something of a bogeyman to the local schoolchildren. Whenever a small child got on their toes to peer in horror through the window, he would run at them, caterwauling in Irish. "Go n-ithe an cat thú is go n-ithe an diabhal an cat." Micheál, laughing, translated it for Norman. "May the cat eat you, and may the devil eat the cat." During his first visit to the McLoughlin house for tea, the man had asked Norman to be blunt about his faith. Norman told him that his family was Protestant. The man had nodded at the table, let his tongue hang and crushed a spider beneath his thumb.

Ma McLoughlin went by no other name. Even her husband referred to her as Ma. She was a muscular woman who said little and concerned herself with chores as if they were acts of penance. Her face was cut from sandstone. She looked gravely on Norman when meeting him, considered him for a moment, then said: "Alright."

Norman and Florrie were to be married at a Protestant parish church in Meanwood. In order to avoid choosing between Ned and Terry, Norman asked Micheál to be his best man. Micheál was surprisingly reluctant at first, for his own personal reasons, but eventually succumbed when Norman had asked him to the point of irritation. "I'll do the bloody duty", he had said, "but I won't make a speech. I'm not that sort of man, and it's not my day to speak at."

On the day of the wedding, the Whitbys and the McLoughlins sat in separate aisles. Before the ceremony, however, John Joseph was occupied with his daughter and Micheál with Norman, so Florrie's mother sat in the McLoughlin pew alone, staring fiercely at the lancet Gothic-style windows, the trendy modern Christ. In attempt to bolster the McLoughlin side of the church, Micheál had invited a mixed bag of community strangers. A shopkeeper. A Scotsman that Micheál had once chatted to at the Working Men's Club. At the back of the church, off-duty milkmen stood pleasantly in a row.

Norman's mother was decked out like a walking bouquet, tulips pinned garishly to her floral dress. His father had loaned a slate-grey suit from the pawnshop. He kept the cuff of his handless arm in his pocket and watched Norman like an elated spaniel from the pews. Behind them, in drape jackets, drainpipe trousers and beetle crushers, Ned and Terry were jostling and baring their teeth at the vicar. There was Uncle Vernon, who Norman hadn't seen in at least five years. Uncle Vernon had been captured by the Nazis and held as a prisoner of war. He had not been the same since demobilisation and moved to a different city each year, as if he could leave his memories of capture behind him. He had travelled up from Birmingham the night before the wedding, for that was where he was living at the time. The next year, he moved to Wigan, then to Manchester, where he set fire to his bedroom and was carted off to Strangeways with his pants around his ankles. There was also Norman's grandfather. The story went that during the Depression he had walked from Leeds to York in search of work, with two other men who had been injured in the mines. When he returned, he was half-starved, without a job or his companions. The two dead men were later plucked from the road. Behind him sat the chief executive of the Lads' Club, who was trying to conceal the sandwich he was eating, three good men from the foundry, Norman's mother's friends and a slew of neighbours who had always existed on the cobbles and would cease to exist when the cobbles were gone.

Norman adjusted the white rose he had pinned to his lapel. The "Bridal Chorus" came, and the congregation rose. Florrie walked slowly, arm in arm with her father, flower girls trailing behind her. John Joseph's face was marred by barrenness, a destitution of emotion, a begrudging acceptance. He did not look at the beaming congregation. He looked like a man leading a sheep to the slaughterhouse. He would be ignored that day. Despite his misery, he walked with the white rose of the future, the new heraldry, the romantic promise that the townsfolk had come to see.

Florrie's dress was tea-length, laced, waxen white. She was rapturous. She had spent days floating around dress shops in the city centre. Norman's mother would not rest until she had found the perfect fit. Every embellishment of the dress was to be considered thoroughly. Florrie's mother had come along once. She looked out of place in a dress shop, being someone who had given up on love and come to celebrate wrath instead. She told a nearby bride-to-be that she had knobbly knees and looked like a harlot, then went home when the shopworker asked her to leave.

Norman span to Micheál, his mouth wide in adulation. Micheál, looking at his shoes, was still.

Florrie had put on lipstick with some reluctance. Norman's mother had insisted. It looked peculiar on her face, like a birthmark on her lips. That was a large part of what made Florrie appealing to Norman; her complete lack of desire to pander to pleasantries and customs. She was rarely on time, wherever she went, and when she finally arrived, she wouldn't apologise. When she cycled to Beeston, she swore at policemen. She refused to support anyone but Limerick AFC and would break into Irish curses to disorientate the hopeful men that approached her. She clipped her toenails on the sofa and belched loudly after tea, louder than any man in the room. She let the plates pile up in the sink, and smoked in bed, talking to Norman about Marilyn Monroe. She had been bullied by Jack. He had wanted her two-dimensional, categoric and unconditional. He had been so close to compressing her. Now, she stood in her fullness, in her unadulterated naturality, in Technicolour.

Florrie's father left her at the altar and went to examine his knife in the pews. The parish vicar stepped forward. The widows in the pews remembered their husbands who had died, still suited, in the trenches. The bedraggled and the lonely and the unloved looked on. "That", they would say, "was a union of a brand-new England." "The lucky, beautiful buggers." "They belong to an England that only the young can believe in." "An altogether more roseate England." "An England where flowers are not shot in their beds." "Do you think the Lord kept us alive deliberately so we could see such a union?"

"I do."

"I do."

After the ceremony, the cake was cut. Florrie chopped it straight down the middle, like a log, like a lumberjack. The reception swelled forward. Norman's mother fed his father. Ned smeared his face with icing and, imitating an Arctic monster, chased two toddlers down the aisle. Florrie's parents had seemingly gone outside for air, or, at least, could not be found in the hungry crowd. There was no time to be distracted by this. Terry stood atop a pew, singing in baritone slur:

Take the scorn to wear the horn.
It was the crest when you was born.
Your father's father wore it
and your father wore it too.

Taking the cue, the crowd joined in the chorus, stomping, swinging, extending their arms:

Hal-an-tow, jolly rumble O.
We were up long before the day O,
to welcome in the summer,
to welcome in the May O.
The summer is a-coming in
and winter's gone away O.

Florrie leapt onto a pew and started dancing with one of the bridesmaids. They balanced chaotically, howling with laughter. The vicar rushed to beckon them down as they sang. Norman was clapping to the beat and urging her on when a breath drew close to his ear. A whisper.

"She's yours now. She was always yours."

Norman turned. Micheál was crying. He clapped the groom on the shoulder and offered a pained smile. He was swept away.

God bless Aunt Mary Moyses
and all her power and might O,
and send us peace to England.
Send peace by day and night O.

The sun often captures the briefest of moments. Without warning, it imposes itself on scenes at random and makes angels out of the most common folk. At some point, everyone has walked in heaven, and the luckiest will saunter through it again. Sometimes the sun arrives just as it is most needed, sometimes when there is no use for it. It often hides behind the clouds the moment people notice it. It is best celebrated spontaneously, before the specks of light give birth to rain. Before the dance slows. All of a sudden, knees are hard to lift, and the dancers are embracing for need of staying on their feet. The sun captures the colour and the glory. It is best to snatch what is available whilst it is there. It is best to be a thief, for when the sun decides to pack up and leave, there is only yesterday on the doorstep. Many stand outside their houses feeling foolish then. For maudlin are the slow and joyous are the fed.

Hal-an-tow, jolly rumble O.
We were up long before the day O,
to welcome in the summer,
to welcome in the May O.
The summer is a-coming in
and winter's gone away O.

May 2017 (V)

I couldn't write. It wasn't working.

The monotony of my reportage had finally caught up with me. The world had become flat and predictable. There were two guns to my head. They were held by the great boring heavies of travel disturbances and building plans. I could not write about anything else. My hands had grown numb and impotent.

I was, I thought, less of a person than I had once been. I was a multi-pack white shirt, ironed with swift abandon, a tie that came unfastened as the day wore on, a pair of suit trousers (*two for £20 at the supermarket — a bargain*) and an invisible body. Imagine a uniform floating in the mirror. The shirt cuff rises but no hand is there. *Nice to meet you. I was Fred Whitby.*

My writing had once been meaningful. Before reporting, I had written short stories and poems. They were unexceptional little trinkets, I suppose. They had been scribbled on the back of napkins and till receipts, serving as reminders of my autonomy during shifts at work. Still, I would stuff them in my pockets for safe keeping and read them back when I needed them most. Now, this. I had hopped over the gate to find the whole field barren. The harvest had been taken.

Someone must have crept in whilst I slept. I was convinced of this. I would never have consciously let myself be robbed. Whatever was left in the field had been bundled into a car in the dead of night. The bandits were likely to have headed south, to share out the spoils amongst the home county hacks.

Perhaps they had buried the bounty at sea, so no one would know it had ever existed. *The bastards.*

Day by day, I noticed that I was becoming indifferent to language. My own was empty and I had little energy to learn another. Words on a page were suddenly no more than branchless trees, littered across a snowscape. How to break the ice?

Whenever I tried to write outside the prosaic form of a tabloid, a cloud of plasma entered the room and laid down its coat. It hung about me for a while, stroking my neck as I attempted to think. It clogged my head. Then, eventually, I would sit on the plasma like a sofa. I would surrender and put everything off until tomorrow.

It was not long after Brenda's first death that I had decided to keep a journal of sorts. The writing within it was not to be extensive. It would not be imbued with emotion. My numbness ensured that there would be little risk of that anyway. Instead, I would try to be spontaneous in my journal, and care not for the quality of the writing. Freewriting, almost. The words would act as a pickaxe, no matter how blunt, and surely they would chip away at the ice. Remnants of the day. Simple descriptions of objects. Character sketches of strangers that moved off the page as swiftly as the subject departed from sight. I built metaphors like the rooves of houses but (having laid no foundations beneath them) ran as soon as I let go of the pen. It was a start. Once the frost had broken, I would push my head into the cool water beneath.

To be active also helped. The morning after our visit to Salter and Son, I began using my morning hours to go for walks, to Knowsthorpe on one day, then as far as Beeston on the next. Few people were awake at this time, only the irascible larks who worked at dawn and dragged themselves to bus stops when no one else was around. Some things never change. On one of my outings, I saw a man injecting himself with a syringe beneath a pylon. When he spotted me, his eyes widened and became ox-like. He retreated into the surrounding shrubbery, and I could feel him watch me as I left. In the ink-blue mornings, I would survey and write swiftly about the fences and the washing lines. The shopping trolleys outside front doors. The peeling letters on the signs of the off-licences. Crude stock photos of vodka and rum and brandy and gin and whiskey and port and beer and bread were glued over the windows of the shops so you could not see in. I felt a sense of growing satisfaction in forcing myself to do this. It was a gradual process.

I was not ready to write subjectively — about my opinions on the things I was observing. Like so many days, there was not much taking place that required opinion. When eventually I began noting down the unremarkable comings and goings in Norman's house, my scribblings read as hastily as the following: *Grandad sleeping. Sherry "checks in". Isn't happy that Mam opens the door. Leaves.* There was also: *Grandad in kitchen. 3.02am. Looking in cupboards. Gives up at 3.08am. Goes back to bed.*

I preferred to write as a ghost, or a wall. There is not much to know about a wall, and a ghost can be present at one moment and gone the next. Neither can be satisfactorily interrogated. It would take time before I was able to write subjectively again. The numbness would have to be banished first, and, even then, I would refrain from opinion for a little longer. Whenever I had written subjectively, I had always written about events in retrospect anyway. I could not trust myself to write subjectively about the present. It was a moment that was still unfolding, and so opinions and emotions were subject to change at any turn of the wind. I was better placed to review an event or experience with an understanding born from hindsight. Hence, there were times in my early twenties that I would not be able to subjectively address until I was well into my thirties. There were also events that were too uncomfortable to be tackled until much later. Like feeding a rabid dog, I did not dare get close to them. Despite this, they crept up on me sometimes, after a long period of being dormant and forgotten. When they did this, they became scarily present. They had to be locked away again swiftly.

The past was of more comfort. It seemed, at this time, easier to dictate (*more fool me*). The world itself appeared less real at a distance. It ceased to be material and rose instead as vapour. The past was a collection of images, a story. It was shards of glass, piled up, in need of sorting through, organising and reorganising. In Norman's house, reminders hung from the walls. They cluttered the hallways and poked their noses through the doors. Items that signalled memories, false memories and mythos. As I described the relics, I gradually started to jot down the stories associated with them — or as much as I could remember. There was, before me, a foliage of both reflective and transparent glass. When all the fragments had been coalesced, in crosshatch pattern, they would form an object part mirror, part window. It would be enough to make an observer seasick. All these scattered shards of a man.

One morning, Wayne arrived in his Samsung Chelsea shirt, the one they had won the Champions League wearing. He sniffed around the spare room and swept his hands over the top of the fridge, looking for anything of value that Brenda had left behind. He came away with a few unfinished cigarette packets, a jewellery box containing cheap necklaces and metal rings, some change located at the bottom of a drawer and a

Seventies golliwog that Norman could never convince her to throw out. He unearthed several photos but left them in their place. The subject of one photo was Brenda's father, a miner of the Pinxton coalfield. "Don't get me wrong", Wayne said. "The miners were *real* men, *massive* cocks. But they were thick as pig shit." He drove off blaring clubland classics.

In the afternoon, Mam and I decided to take Norman to the North York Moors. "It would do him good", said Mam, "to take in a bit of nature. He's always been fond of the Moors." Norman was neither for nor against the idea. He mutely clambered into jeans that had grown too large for him and slept on the way. I steered us north, through Boston Spa and Wetherby, past Ingmanthorpe and Flaxby, until we reached the A168 and turned east. On Sutton Road, the country rose on either side. The corroded barns, the farmhouses, the wheat fields and the pylons clambered about and fell away. Mam pressed her finger to the window. "I wonder who lives there. It must be weird to lives miles from your neighbour." She invented the daily lives of the locals, what they did in the evenings, whether they had a television, whether they got lonely. I nodded. The rustic folk, where they still existed, almost certainly had televisions. As we drove further, Peugeots and Hyundais began to poke their noses out of pebble-dash driveways. A few solar panels gleamed. These were not the dream pastures of Romantic poets nor the sites of toil of the labouring man — they were more likely the private land of finance workers and their families. Something of the mystery seemed to have gone from the pastoral, or at least had been capitalised on — but then, what hadn't been capitalised on, and hadn't the countryside always yielded to some form of human profit anyway? Even if deromanticised, green earth was a rare spectacle for us. Usually, there was no time for it. The country was an afterthought.

Finally, we pulled up beside a concealed gate, at the Moors, and woke Norman. The path we followed was narrow and we could see no one along it. Mam was happy. The work of man was anywhere but here. We headed up through the cow-wheat, the juniper and cloudberry, and the woodlands swept down to engulf us. England, like a highwayman, crouched behind the hawthorn. None of us spoke for a while. Norman put his hands in his pockets and jumped when a sparrowhawk took off behind him.

I had been to the Moors as a child. Norman had taken me almost every time I visited him. Back then he had seemed able to name each plant, each bird, each tree. He had christened them as we walked. He had told me fairy stories. Naively, I had believed him, and went to sleep dreaming about gnomes that kept pet wood mice and hobgoblins that ate Marmite butties. I was a man now. I stopped to urinate behind an oak. Mam was cross that I could not wait. "The trees don't care", I said — and, indeed, they made no complaint.

Still, some of what Norman had told me as a child retained a shade of truth. The Moors existed outside of time. The same light that garlanded the hazel understorey had heralded the hunters and gatherers, the Beaker people, the settlements of Angles and Saxons. Their hands had aged on the sword and their faces filled with rain. They lay atop one another, beneath the acid soil.

We reached the foot of Whitestone Cliff. A lake was ringed by clouds of trees. It was still and dark, with not a ripple to disturb it. A merlin headed west, its reflection vanishing from the surface of the water. I pulled up a log for Mam and Norman and dropped onto the bank.

"Lake Gormire, this, isn't it, Dad?" Mam drew the scenery in through her nose and dispelled the city from her mouth.

Gormire is a place populated with stories, Fred. Perhaps I'll be able to tell yer all of them one day.

"Aye", Norman said. "That's the one."

"You used to come down here all the time, didn't you? You'd tell me about it. You'd come here with the Lads' Club on holidays."

The moor grass rustled. Norman watched. "Aye, to the Moors. Aye."

It's left over from the Ice Age, this lake. Glacial erosion. Over twenty thousand years, lad. Think of all the folk that have touched the water, just like we are now. By! I'll bet knights and kings have done the very same.

"You had a mate called Ned", Mam continued, "and a mate called Terry. What was that story you told me once? You were camping, but it must have been windy. One of your tents flew into the water. You all jumped in after it. Terry came out covered in leeches. I'm not telling it properly. What happened after that?"

Once there wuh an abbot. The abbot of Rievaulx Abbey he wuh. He had this fantastic white mare, Fred. You wouldn't believe the speed of the bugger. It wuh the fastest thing in the land and beautiful as anything. It wuh celebrated far and wide. But there was a knight who was jealous of the abbot, yer see. Sir Harry de Scriven, his name wuh. He wanted to ride the white mare himself. His own horse, Nightwind, wuh no comparison.

"I can't remember", Norman said. He smacked his lips and closed his eyes.

One day, Sir Harry came across the abbot at a local inn. They spent the afternoon drinking together, until they were perfectly pissed. As the evening drew close, Sir Harry told the abbot that a nearby farmer was desperate to see him, that he'd forgotten to give him the farmer's message earlier. But this was a lie, yer see. The farmer didn't exist.

"You must remember coming here though", Mam persisted. "You told me Moors stories all the time. In Hartlepool. Let me see which ones I can remember. I'll start them. You can finish them."

"I remember coming here", Norman said. His eyes remained closed. His fingers gently searched the log he sat on. "But vaguely. I remember little details. The smell of the place. The unique sounds yer hear on the different crags. I get a feeling. Dunno what it is. But when it comes to stories with people in 'em — that's more difficult. I remember telling the stories more than actually living them."

Why would he lie? That's a good question. It's because Sir Harry was so desperate to climb atop the abbot's white mare. He suggested that the abbot should ride Nightwind to the farmer. The sky was stirring up a storm, and Nightwind was stronger and better able to cope wi' weather. That's what he said. He offered to ride alongside him on the white mare, so as the abbot was not alone on his journey.

Mam was crouched by the lake. She scooped up a handful of water and created a rivulet in her palm. "It's still just like it was", she said. "Just how I remember it being. Here, Dad. Come and see."

I blinked. Norman had stooped to drink from the lake. He bowed his head to the water and drank like a horse. I blinked again. Norman was stood at Mam's hip. He poked the rivulet in her palm with a cautious finger. "It is", he said. "Just like that."

But as the pair of them travelled along through the storm, gradually they turned their ride into a race. The abbot on Nightwind. Sir Harry on the white mare. Well, Sir Harry was sure he would win. He had the most agile beast in the land beneath him. But, suddenly, to his surprise, the abbot wuh ahead of him! Sir Harry had no clue how he had done it. He flogged the white mare desperately. He had to stay level. He could not concede that the abbot wuh the more gifted rider. He wuh in such a state of frenzy that when the abbot disappeared, he had no clue where he'd gone, and, even worse, he didn't see the cliff edge swiftly approaching. That very cliff there. See it? Directly overlooking the lake. Well, as he drew nearer, he could hear laughter. It echoed all around him. The abbot wuh laughing at him, standing at a distance. Horns had grown from his head, and a horrible red tail wuh swaying about him.

Mam was tight-lipped. Something had spooked her. She was nervous to ask, but nerves had never stopped her before. "Mam liked it on the water, didn't she?"

Norman stood silently, gazing away. The breeze fluttered against him, against the dwarf cornel. "Your mam loved it on the water", he said. "She couldn't swim but she loved it on the water." His eyes grew wide and aware, almost wild. Like a small boy, he looked around him in wonderment and confusion.

Sir Harry wuh terrified. He could do nothing to slow down. Suddenly, the white mare had galloped over the cliff edge and both knight and horse plummeted to the rocks below. The abbot rode over to survey the scene. Satisfied that Sir Harry was no more, he thrashed Nightwind into a fever and together they leapt down into the lake. Great plumes of smoke rose over the Moors and the water itself wuh left hot and dark. Even now, Fred, centuries later, the lake is still yet to cool. Touch the water. Feel how warm.

A body of twigs and leaves was floating on the far edge of the lake. Noticing this, Norman started. He stumbled forward, possessed, almost falling. "Love!" he cried. He was waving his hands.

Mam shot me a look and we quickly went after him.

"Dad!" she called.

"Grandad!" I shouted.

We followed him down the bank, but he was starting to run. "Love!" he cried. "Can yer hear me, love?"

Norman ran into the water. At the edge it was up to his knees. He splashed about to regain balance. "It's me, love! It's Norman!" I thought for a moment that he was going to start swimming. He would have had the chance had I not jumped in after him and took him by the shoulders. He wheeled around. He had no idea who I was. I had no idea who he was. His eyes were not my grandad's.

It was harder to pull him from the lake than I had thought. Norman still had his strength. He had, if anything, grown in strength. He freed himself twice, and it was only when I had dragged him to the bank and Mam had taken his arms that we were able to successfully return him to land. Still, he struggled against us. "Florrie!" he yelled. The collection of twigs and leaves broke away.

Nana had loved it on the water. She couldn't swim but she loved it on the water. All these years later, and Norman was still on the water — but sinking.

Blackbirds

On the morning of 14 April 1960, the milkman did not come in Hunslet. Micheál McLoughlin was an uncle. Several days earlier, weighing 7lb 1oz, Betty Whitby had been born. Micheál had waited in the hospital for over an hour, until the halls were abnormally quiet. Eventually, Norman had walked alone into the waiting room holding the baby. Florrie had not called for Micheál. Florrie would never call again. She lay still. Her eyes were closed but her chest did not rise and fall. It was at this moment that Micheál knew.

His delivery schedule was pointless now. He had, however, been close to attempting it — attempting to continue, attempting to live. No one could say he hadn't tried. Loading the bottles onto his float on the morning of the 14 April 1960, he had almost forced himself out on his milk round. No. He couldn't do it. Not even God could make him. What was left? The alternative. Fearful though it was, that was all that was left. The only viable choice. He would leave work and go home to collect the object beneath his bed. The hate object. The instrument of chaos. Why not? What did it matter now? Life was cheap. Florrie had been killed by the Lord in an English hospital, surrounded by English doctors and midwives, below an English sky. It was so sickening it was almost laughable. If even God thought life was cheap, if even God did not care what chaos he sowed, why should Micheál feel bound by morality? If He whom Micheál worshipped was a true destructor, let Micheál, too, destroy. He drove his float home, collected what he needed and steered slowly away from the milkless houses, up towards the city centre.

MacNamara had travelled over from Liverpool the evening before. He had come swiftly when Micheál had finally tracked down a phone to use to call him. MacNamara was also from Limerick, but had lived in Liverpool for five years, having left Ireland shortly before the McLoughlins. Micheál met him in a crowded pub near the station. They talked all night and took the quietest route back to Micheál's house. When they arrived, John Joseph didn't lift an eye. He carried on whittling a crucifix in silence. MacNamara hugged Ma McLoughlin and slept on the sofa that evening. He had gone before Micheál woke up.

It was closing in on seven o'clock, and the south of the city was stirring. Drawing the float to a standstill on the bridge, Micheál considered the Aire for a moment, with a decided sense of finality. A robin was hopping along the parapet. The factories and derelict buildings, from Hunslet Mill to Kirkstall Power Station, absentmindedly sniffed at the riverfront and paid him no mind. Smoke was settling on the water.

Micheál pushed on. He drove until he reached the town hall. There, he steered his milk float up onto the pavement and allowed the vehicle to rest at the foot of the great stone steps. Few people were around. Two cars shuddered along in the distance. A nervous young woman met a sharp-faced old man under an OXO Cubes advertisement and went off with him down a neighbouring street. Micheál lit a cigarette and tapped on the steering wheel. He looked up at the town hall before him. Its colonnaded clock tower stared down silently. His eyes followed the turrets, then the Corinthian columns, one by one, along the façade, counting them, picking them off. The figures of the classical tympanum joined the clock tower in staring. They passed judgement on every human who dared come close, and laid waste to the vulnerable as they pleased. Even the Portland stone lions, crouched on their platforms, seemed to breathe. They were, however, unable to pounce. They were part of the architecture, and acid rain had bleached streaks of their faces a permanent white. Micheál grinned at them, knowing they could not get him, knowing that they were confined to silence. Was this the material testament to power? A municipal palace sweeping its hand to boast the carcasses of houses, the satanic mills, the empty men of tainted streets. It may as well have gestured to air.

Then again, air could not be built upon. Air could not be purchased or conquered, only borrowed, and air, in leaving the body for good, always had the last laugh.

"Mr Milkman", a voice chirped.

Micheál looked down. A small girl was stood to the side of his float.

"Mr Milkman, could I please buy a pint of milk? It's for my mum." The girl held out a podgy hand with a coin in it. The thumb of her other hand was stuck in her mouth. Her eyes were wide and hopeful. The child's mother stood by the road, attending to a baby in a pram.

"Of course you can, my pet", Micheál said. He fetched a bottle of milk from behind him and handed it to the girl. He gently pushed away the hand that offered the coin. "No cost", he smiled.

The child gasped with excitement and clasped her hand shut. Then she tottered away to her mother.

Micheál lifted himself from the float and slowly ascended the steps to the hall. As he climbed, he picked out one of the keystone heads and looked square into its dead grit eyes. The head did not move. The stone did not blink. At the top, Micheál faced the deserted entrance and hummed to himself. He hummed one of his native folk songs, the ones he hummed every morning on his round. His eyes searched for a suitable place — a place to lay down his hate object — the hate object he was reaching for in the pocket of his coat — but paused.

"Mr Milkman?"

The same girl had followed him up the stairs. She was out of breath and panting slightly. Micheál had not even heard her call after him. She tugged at his sleeve.

"Hello again, pet", Micheál said.

"My mum says I can't take the milk for free. She says milkmen need to earn a living, but she says thank you for being so nice." Again, the child held out the coin.

Micheál almost wept. He saw the girl's mother watching from the pavement, holding her sleeping baby. He waved at her, amiably. He paused *for thought, considered his waving hand, then the child, then considered the object his other hand held. He frowned, settling quite suddenly on an alternative course of action. Then he crouched down by the girl and looked her straight in the eyes.*

"Listen", he whispered, closing the child's fingers around the coin. "Your money is of no use to me. I can't take it. But your mother has raised ye well. There are a lot of folks that do need every coin they can get. Now, can you keep a secret?"

The girl nodded and put her fist to her cheek.

"You tell your mother that ye paid me for the milk. Hold onto the coin for yourself. I bet you can get something nice with that from the sweet shop."

"Are you sure, Mr Milkman?" the girl asked, hopping from one foot to the other.

"You bet I am. Now, what are ye going to get from the sweet shop?"

"Chocolate!" the girl cried.

"Chocolate!" Micheál gasped. He was beaming. There were tears rolling down his cheeks. "Well, that sounds good! Make sure ye enjoy every last bit of it."

The girl hesitated for a moment, then she leant in and whispered. "Thank you." She turned to go but stopped nervously at the head of the steps, so Micheál held her hand and walked her down to where her mother was waiting. He wished them a pleasant day and returned to the foot. It took a minute at least for the mother and her children to vanish from sight. Micheál waited. He needed to know they had left. He would not reclimb the steps after all. He was too tired for that — too tired for hate, too tired to leave his object and run. When he was satisfied that the mother and her children were at sufficient distance, Micheál looked to the sky, at one cloud in particular, and did not remove his eyes from it — and then he slipped his hand into the pocket of his coat.

The explosion was not as large as MacNamara had told Micheál it would be. It fulfilled its primary purpose — or at least, what its primary purpose had so suddenly become — but did little irreparable damage to the land. If Micheál had remained at the head of the steps the impact of the bomb would have been incomparable. Due to where he stood, however, only the lower regions of the steps were torn asunder. A parked car was jettisoned into the road with the milk float. The ground was scorched, and a lamppost was ripped from the pavement. Glass bottles erupted in the air like fireworks and the surrounding statues were drenched in milk. An approaching policeman was caught in the blast, but other than that no civilians were killed. The early morning light dappled the smoke and suppressed it. Wings took flight from the clock tower in swift succession. It looked as if Micheál had exploded into a cloud of blackbirds, into a song of sky. Micheál had turned into a plume of words, a trail of history and ash which fell like ink upon the earth.

May 2017 (VI)

It was the day of Brenda's funeral. There was sun in Yorkshire — highs of twenty degrees. Faces like ripe tomatoes clustered at Norman's window, none of whom were mourners. They were off to Hunslet Moor Park, to play football in the shadow of the high-rise council block, to let ice cream paint their happy chins. Knots of sticky chests and limbs. Even I, disappointed a funeral would mar the day, had my shirt sleeves rolled up in the hope of catching the sun. "Too casual, sod", Mam said, as she donned her darkest blazer and submitted to the inevitability of sweat. I wore my work uniform. It felt almost ironic, myself dressed as a journalist, whilst I secretly recorded snatches of the day in my head to hurriedly copy down into my notebook later. I wore sunglasses. No one could see that my eyes were dry.

For everyone else, crocodile tears were the code of the day. One passing neighbour wept as loudly as a fallen duchess in a Victorian melodrama. She clasped Norman at his door. He could not remember who she was but hugged her back anyway. Her husband, a man with a tattoo of David Batty on his calf, pulled her away and told her she could have been actress.

> — Well, I'm glad she's gone. She wuh a disease on the whole community.
> — What community?
> — Dun't start with that crap again.

– She wun't wholly bad. She wuh only human. She wuh as liable to moral failings as anyone else.

  – Helen, no. There's moral failings, then there's her. She wun't just caught down pub wi' someone else's husband. She wuh a monster.

   – She once spat at our Tony.

– Bet he liked it an' all, the grubby sod.

  – You have to hand it to her. She wun't daft. Yer have to be clever to be that bluddy wicked.

   – You quite fancied her, didn't yer love? Is it the austere thing you liked?

– That's a bluddy lie, Linda.

  – She'd have stolen money from charity box if yer'd given her half the chance.

  – Woulda gone park to pinch bread off the ducks.

– Can't stand folks that think they're a cut above me. I work hard as anyone else. Harder in fact. Just to give me wages to buggers like her what's too lazy to work.

 – Well, she only wanted Norman for his money didn't she?

   – Does he have much money?

– Oh, few grand maybe.

  – Must become better acquainted with the bloke.

   – She wuh a bluddy succubus. She'd suck the soul clean out of a man.

– Of course, you would have liked that.

  – I bluddy wouldn't, Linda!

– Face like a farmer's arse.

  – like a melted welly.

   – like a bulldog licking piss off a thistle.

– Woulda never had folk like that in my day. Folk used to look out for one another.

    – Your day? Christ, man. Archaeologists
       are digging for your day.
    – Taking five-pound bets when they put her in the
       fire the devil comes up in smoke to collect her.
– Still believe in the devil, John? Didn't have you down as
religious.
    – I'd believe in bloody Ganesh if
       there wuh fiver riding on it.

At ten, Sherry and Wayne arrived. Valentino and Ralph
Lauren. Ray-Bans. The corridor to the kitchen was a catwalk.
When they thought no one was looking, Wayne photographed
Sherry for social media. He tried from multiple angles to hide
her double chin, then, finding this hopeless, suggested she
held a large flower up to sniff for the photo.

Not long before Salter and Son arrived, Norman descended
the stairs. For the first time since Brenda had died her final
death, he had made a noticeable effort with his appearance.
He had ironed his shirt and hidden the mustard spot beneath
a National Association of Lads' Clubs necktie. His black
suit, whilst a little large, was buttoned smartly and a pair of
brogues had been pulled from the bottom of a wardrobe
and polished with all the attention of a cobbler. He looked
a skinnier version of his former self, and at the same time a
boy on the day of his christening, ready to be doted on by a
congregation of adoring grandmothers.

"You look lovely Dad", Sherry beamed.

Mam sneered.

Norman helped himself to a cold slice of toast. "Ta, Sherry,
love." Crumbs dropped down his shirt front.

"She loved you so much", Sherry said. "She'll be looking
down now and smiling."

"Or up", I muttered.

Wayne turned. I gave a grin.

"Yes, well she always did like special occasions", Wayne blurted. "She'd be wearing her blue number today. The one with the frills."

"To her funeral, Wayne?" Sherry touched his arm.

Wayne left to pretend to check on something in his car.

"Where's what's-his-face wi' hearse?" Norman swallowed. "It's dead warm for wearing this suit all day." He refused to take it off, however. It was the second time he was to see a wife buried and he would not be any less respectful for the latter than for the former. It was a matter of principle. He sat in his armchair sweating. Sherry showed him a litany of photos of Brenda, each increasingly grotesque. I was put off my breakfast. Mam escaped to make a call to Salter and Son.

Finally, the hearse arrived. The funeral director and his deputy had become, if anything, paler than they had been the week before. I wondered if they secretly applied make-up for events. This was their theatre, and the professionality of their sombreness would be paraded all the way to the crematorium.

The drive was slow. My forehead was wet. A fly came in the window and shot around our heads until Wayne crushed it between his finger and thumb. Sherry looked at him, aroused.

Outside, folk applying sun cream stopped to watch. A small boy pointed and clapped, and his mother quickly shoved his arm back down. Passing the Station Hotel, a retired union rep gave Norman a thumbs up and cried with happiness. The electric fans in the open windows breathed a collective sigh of relief as we rolled by. South Leeds was at peace with the inevitability of death and even more so with the deaths of certain people.

A polite several attended the service. They sat apart and didn't know each other. I didn't know them either, but they patted Norman on the back as we arrived. It was an unremarkable service. "You Raise Me Up" by Westlife rang out, too loud. A slideshow of more grotesque photos flickered above the coffin. Brenda grimacing, with an ice cream melting on her fist. Brenda at Christmas, frowning intensely at a stocking. Brenda with a dog that had bitten her no longer than a second after the camera flashed. Sherry wailed. The vicar read a few Bible passages and the Lord's Prayer, for the sake of tradition. *Amen.*

Eventually Norman was called to the podium. Wayne patted his pew to egg him on. The sound echoed around the chapel, and he stopped.

"What to say about our Brenda?" Norman mused. No one replied. Surely, he was not asking the congregation to help describe her. He looked out over our heads as if he had completely forgotten who she was, then continued fumblingly. "She wuh a woman. A short, blonde woman." He coughed on his sleeve. "A good woman. You'll have to excuse me. I'm not too handy at things like this." A pause. He spoke slowly and carefully. "I wuh married to Brenda for almost thirty years. I met her not far from here, in Hunslet. Quite out of the blue, actually. She wuh known round the way for being able to belt a good tune. Wuh in her thirties at the time and a sight for sore eyes. It felt like it wuh meant to be, yer could say. I'd never planned on returning to Leeds. I grew up round here and I wuh living in County Durham at the time. The fact that Brenda lived in Hunslet, and that she wuh good enough to put up wi' me — it felt like a sign. Felt like God wuh saying summet."

The vicar smiled and nodded, happy that the Lord had been mentioned.

"Over the last few decades, I've barely been apart from her. We wuh inseparable. She wuh like a grandmother…" Norman halted for thought. He knew he could lie. It was allowed. At a funeral, a man could lie brazenly and only a bastard would call him out. "She wuh like a grandmother to the community. Loved by many." Another cough. Swiftly, he became animated. "She always had, what d'yer call it? What's the phrase? A thirst for life! She wuh bloody buzzing with it. Why, I remember a few year back, she come to me. She says: *Norman*, she says, *am off to watch birds*. Quite spontaneously, aye. She come home that evening and she'd only seen pigeons, but she'd had a bloody go! She tried to learn Spanish once. Tried for two weeks. She wanted to go to Cuba. She sat in the living room practicing as if she were going t'shop. *Paquete de cigarillos. Paquete de cigarillos.*" Another cough. "Oh, another thing. When we got a computer, she'd play online bingo for hours every night. I din't have a clue what she wuh up to, mind. She won £20 once and she wuh charging round the living room, waving the note like mad. Knocked over the goldfish bowl we had at the time. She did what she wanted, did Brenda. She din't care what anyone thought of her. If someone wuh rude, why she'd just laugh in their face. A thirst for life. That's what Brenda had." Norman drummed the podium. He considered where to lead the speech, turned a few words over on his tongue and swallowed the ones that couldn't be uttered. "Few folks, yer know, they didn't see eye to eye wi' her on couple matters, but that's areet. She wuh *my wife* and that's all that matters. Aye, that's alreet. That's alreet. She would've been thrilled wi' turnout this morning.

All the folk she liked most under one roof." One of the polite several in the pews checked his watch. "I want to thank yer all for coming. Now, I don't know what Brenda's up to today — wherever she is, on whichever cloud — but by God, I hope she's won the jackpot."

Wayne patted his pew again. The sound echoed around the chapel.

Leftover

If there was one thing that was definite, it was that John Joseph McLoughlin and his wife were not right in the head. Perhaps they were secret drug addicts. Perhaps living in Limerick had buggered their brains. The common consensus was that they were either crazed or sinister, and all this because their daughter had married a Protestant when they themselves were Catholics.

They must have felt they had no choice. It would look suspicious for them to stand in the way of Florrie's wedding. Whenever asked by Leeds folk, they had proclaimed themselves to follow the Church of England. Why had they lied? They must have wanted to distance themselves from republicanism, and the suspicion they would be treated with if it was known they were Catholic. If they were anti-republican, they must have hated life in their homeland. Yet if Florrie had told Norman that she was Catholic, he wouldn't have cared. His faith was not as ardent as that of his parents. He would have probably converted to Catholicism for her or even abandoned it all and lived as an atheist. Becoming a pariah, however, would have done neither of them any favours. Nevertheless, was this not the new England they lived in? The stigma of intermarriage was no longer fit for purpose. It was a dog that could be put down in the street at dawn.

It stands to reason that the inevitability of a Protestant marriage was what pushed the McLoughlins over the edge. The acceptance that their daughter was no longer their own, but belonged to England, bound by a vow of faith to the bastardisation of their beliefs. Florrie must have converted to Protestantism before the wedding and kept it secret from Norman. That would be the only logical way she could have gotten around it. Or perhaps she had acquired a dispensation from a Catholic ordinary. Was there even a Catholic ordinary in Leeds, and if there was, wouldn't the husband-to-be have been required to attend? Norman didn't know. She must have converted. She must have. Perhaps her parents had felt pressured to convert themselves. Even with its new modish façade, England, hegemonic as always, conquered everyone in the end. The McLoughlins had likely gone mad with surrender. There was, however, no way of ever knowing. Florrie was dead and Micheál was dead, and John Joseph and his wife were nowhere to be found.

What then was their connection with the IRA? They could not have been militants. They could not have been republicans. They must have been resistant to the IRA at first. Yet even the most assured allegiances are subject to change. An object under force can take on a different form in the blink of an eye. The schoolmaster bends his cane slowly, teasing it. He enjoys the power he has over the item. It keels over in a great arc until it can take no more, then it snaps. Suddenly, it is a cane no longer. It is mere fragments of itself, and so loses its meaning.

For Micheál, Florrie's passing must have been the last straw. He had died a terrorist. As the rumours went, his bomb had been delivered by an undercover republican living in Liverpool. MacNamara had been arrested and would likely hang. That was just what it was. The policeman killed in the blast had been named and mourned. He had a wife and two children and lived in Harehills. He enjoyed beef on Sundays and listening to sports on the radio.

When the culprit had been named, a slew of suburbanites, authoritarians and quite ordinary workers from north of the Aire descended on Hunslet, searching for the McLoughlins. Their anger was not necessarily stoked by the death of the policeman (in fact, the workers amongst them hated the police), but by their awareness that, on another day, a relative of their own could have been killed in the blast. So, they peeped over garden walls and loitered in snickets, interrogating locals as they made their way to work.

The police turned the McLoughlin house over in the hunt for explosives. They found nothing but left John Joseph with missing teeth and a black eye. After this, he and his wife locked themselves in, fearing for their lives, with curtains drawn and furniture piled up against the door. When finally their address became public knowledge, the windows were put through. Jack Wrigley anointed himself captain of the mob and spent his evenings rallying hatred in the working men's clubs. After a few days, a steel worker was arrested for trying to burn the McLoughlin house down. It was at this time that John Joseph and his wife went missing — and were never found.

Norman, too, had barely left the house. He stayed hidden inside with his mother, guarding Betty, sleeping by her cot when he managed to sleep at all. Folk asked after him. Folk demanded to see him. His father stood out on the street waving his stump. "How d'yer think the lad feels? His wife died not a week ago and you's won't give him some peace! He dun't know owt about the bleeding bomb. Let us be, yer bastards!"

One afternoon, Ned and Terry crept in through the back door to deliver Norman his pay from the Lads' Club. The chief executive officer had offered to continue to pay him in secrecy whilst he was not at work, for the sake of the baby. Ned and Terry seemed almost oblivious to what was happening. They spewed jokes and rolled about on the sofa, smoking, until Norman's mother scorned them and threw their cigarettes out the window. They too were far from concerned about the death of the policeman. They practically celebrated it. Norman's father told them not to return until they could show some respect.

The next morning, the Whitbys woke up to find the front of their house had been vandalised. Messages were scrawled on the bricks in charcoal and chalk. IRA BABY/GOT ANY BOMBS?/ POLICE KILLER/MICK-LOVER/DIE/DIE/DIE.

At lunchtime on that day, the chief executive officer of the Lads' Club came over. He helped Norman's father sponge the remaining words from the wall, then sat in the armchair and declined a cup of tea.

"I think it's for the best, Norman, that you get out while you can. There's lunatics round here what need a bit of excitement and they're not going to let this go. Now, there's a Lads' Club in Hartlepool. The fella what runs it is an old pal. He's aware of what's happened, but he sympathises with your situation. Plenty of us do. We know you had nowt to do with that bomb. I've told the fella that you're a good coach. You do your job efficiently and you're great with the lads. If you're willing, he's agreed to take you on in the same role you currently have over in Hartlepool. He's even offered to put you and the baby up in his house until you've enough money to rent somewhere. I want you to seriously consider it, Norman. I think you need a new start. I think this is the clean break you need."

That evening, Norman cradled Betty in his arms and took, for her, the necessary step. She was smaller than awareness. She would not remember them departing under the nose of the dark. When she was old enough, Norman would find a way to phrase it. It was an adventure story. A voyage into the coal-blackened stupor of the night.

They headed northeast from Leeds Central station. Norman wore his knitted balaclava rolled up to his forehead. He concealed his mouth with the lapels of his coat. The owl-like man at the kiosk had pushed them a ticket, swelled with yawning and settled back to the business of dreaming. The occasional train worker, in a limbo of steam, sleepwalked from carriage to carriage.

Norman figured they would be in Hartlepool by eleven. It was lucky that Betty was not awake for the journey. He thumbed the envelope of money in his pocket. Notes from the chief executive officer. Coins from his father. Notes of his own. A single suitcase lay on the floor of the carriage. A life shoved into and enclosed in a case.

On the other side of the window, the dim furnace of Leeds flickered. Lamp posts like miniature lighthouses slipped away into memory. Backs bent, broken figures shuffled home to lumpen dwellings. An assortment of stars and other things, nameless things, hung from the sky. Soon, the only glow on the Earth was lunar, and even the moon was a quiet devil that walked between clouds.

Norman held an armful of innocence. An untraceable quantity of soot was on his palms. He had aged twenty years in a week. His hair would be grey before long, and he would assume the role of chief that his father had occupied before him. Unlike his father, he would be a chief with both hands. He would stuff his pockets with sunshine, stuff them with the ocean and carry them back to his daughter in a house near the coast. It would be a different life. No one would know them. In Hartlepool, father and daughter would be artists. Norman would sit with Betty before a blank canvas and say, "Well, love. What is it to be?" Betty would point and Norman would paint. "Canary yellow, aye, and fuchsia pink. Something bright, eh? What a lovely dress." He would paint her on the canvas. Together, they would construct her from scratch. Then, at night, Norman would take the paintbrush to his own face. None of the locals would know of Norman Whitby. He would be someone quite different.

We create our own versions of ourselves and parade them in front of others who are doing exactly the same. Had he not done what he did, Micheál would have made a wonderful uncle.

Betty opened her eyes as the train thundered. She did not cry. She looked up to the twenty-year-old boy that held her. "Where did yer get them big blue eyes from, love?" Norman asked. He feigned shock. "Did yer get 'em from Miss Dolly who lives down lane? Why, she said she'd run out! All t'other babies' eyes aren't half as big and blue. Ooh, yer lucky sod."

Betty's face lit up.

"Got yer nose", Norman said, and he took her nose. "D'yer mind if I just leave it on me face for a while?" He pressed his fingers to his own nose and looked at his reflection in the carriage window. "Yes, I think that'll do nicely. It suits me, does your nose."

Betty reached around in the air.

"What? You want it back? Yer not missing owt without it. You oughta *catch a whiff of fella in the next carriage. Safest place to hide money would be in* his *house under t'soap. I'll tell thee that for nowt."*

Betty reached.

"Oh, you have it back then. Cheeky bugger. Looks better on you anyway." He put his fingers to her nose. She beamed.

On the other side of the ruinous night, a horn sounded. It could not be seen where the noise had originated from. The train pushed on, closing the distance. Behind it, in succession, fell fragments of starlight, specks of luminescence escaping grasp and depiction, the minutes and the hours, the days, months and the years.

JUNE

North Sea

There once was a man who lost his wife

and couldn't find her!

Well, he wuh dead sure she'd just been with him. She must have crept away when he wun't looking, to play a trick on him perhaps — to jump out and scare him. The couple wuh at Bridlington beach for their holidays. Happy as owt. It wuh a sunny day and city kids who'd never seen the sea wuh piling out of the Wallace Arnold bus. The man and his wife had been paddling, gingerly treading about the sea, not sure what to expect of it. Neither had been to the coast before, yet the wife, gently, edged closer into the water and told her husband she wanted to swim. Surely now wuh the best time to learn. Well, there seemed no harm in that. The husband knew enough about swimming to coach her, even in a body of water as expansive and as alien as the North Sea. He would hold her hand the whole way through. "Love, tha can squeeze it as tight as tha want."

After a while, they were shoulder deep, and the man told his wife to start kicking. "Look, love. Like this", he said, and he demonstrated to her the way to push. His feet jerked back and forth in the water. She attempted it briefly, but a small wave knocked her, and she fell back, yelling. Her husband steadied her. The wave fled. "That's alright, love. Now try again."

There wuh no way out of it. By now, they had drifted too far from the land to return on foot. To swim would be worth it. Both of them knew that. Why, if all worked out well, they could go swimming again. They could go swimming as often as they liked (within reason), particularly now the husband had a few quid coming in. Again, the wife tried kicking, and this time it worked. Her head bobbed as the water rose and subsided, her hair limp on her shoulders, her face edged in concentration.

"That's it", the husband cried. "Yer doing it now!"

Steadying, she rose and pressed the world into his palms.

Then the real waves came. They marched forwards, as if to reassert themselves. At pace, the couple wuh lifted on the lip of the water and dropped, lifted and dropped. The size of the waves wuh increasing alarmingly. They wuh violent. The whole British Army would have been unable to suppress them. The sea refused to let the couple go. The sea wanted to trap them forever in that moment.

The wife wuh spluttering now. She wuh swallowing water. Holding her against him, the husband scrambled for the beach. His hands became shovels. He wuh digging up the seaweed, digging up the earth, trying to push the entire sea behind him. He wuh screaming, waving. No one wuh coming. Where wuh the coastguard? No one could help. Where wuh the land? Everything wuh water. Over half of the human body is water. He looked down to where he held his wife and found that he held only water. His wife had slipped away in the waves.

The husband paced the foot of the beach for hours. He knew that sometimes folk washed up on the shore. It wun't impossible. Perhaps his wife would return, unconscious but alive, carried in on the tide — reborn.

It wuh getting dark by the time he finally surrendered. He seized a pebble and flung it at the bastard sea. He roared and his voice was lost in the wind. The pebble sunk without a trace. Another pebble. A larger one. Then a brick that had fallen from the promenade. Each vanished as swiftly as its predecessor to populate the bed of the lost.

Retreating to a tea room, the husband sat shaking, unsure of what to do. He drummed the table with his spoon. He kept his eyes on the window, in case of a miracle. He listened to the holidaymakers on the tables around him, the faces of the women red and happily exhausted. Their families had come to visit them for the day. When they took the summer home, their neighbours would be crammed impatiently into the holidaymakers' kitchens, in wait of their return, and to celebrate with them.

"Yer the fella what's having trouble finding his wife."

The husband glanced over. An old dear in a headscarf had sat down beside him.

"Aye", the husband said. "How could tha tell?"

"I seen yer", the dear said, "shouting down beach. She went in the waves, din't she?"

The husband didn't reply but turned his face to the window.

"Dark hair", the dear mused. She drew his wife in the air with her finger. "Fair skin. Not one for make-up. A lovely face, oh such a lovely face — when tha see it tha just know she's full of life. Am I right?"

"How'd tha know?" The husband stared, cautiously.

"I seen her", the dear muttered.

"Eh?" He started, jumping to his feet. "When? Where?"

The old dear glanced over her shoulder. She gestured the husband to sit. She ushered him in. "On a boat", she whispered.

"A boat?"

"Aye, a rowing boat. I seen her on it when yer wuh shouting on shore. I did call to thee, but tha wuh inconsolable, and that's understandable. I thought I'd tell thee now. She's on a boat and she's safe. She wuh waving to yer."

The husband remained still. He listened to the stranger out of politeness, then comfort, as her voice rolled gently against his ears. There wuh something melodic about her that couldn't be placed. It wuh likely that she had been sat in that tea room always, perhaps predating it, predating the entire town. She told the husband that his wife was happy. There wuh no need to worry, as no ill would befall her now. Yet no level of searching would bring her back either. Some people go to sea sooner than others, and as it happens, often the most adventurous go first. Without warning, they pick up their bags and push their boat to the water. They take all manner of things with them but leave just as much behind. Things such as love are both taken and left, so as both the adventurer and the folk at home can hold onto it. People carry love on their person at all times. It can't be gotten rid of, even when you want to shake it off or call it by anything but its name. You have to learn to live with it, this love, because it means no harm, even when it injures. Plenty of folk wish they could have it, to keep at their bedside, to take out with them in the mornings in their pockets. Even alone in the wind-tarnished moorland, the empty plains grow occupied as the man with love walks through. It is the last word before the candle goes and the smoke that remains once the flame has extinguished.

The husband was shaking with a love old and new. He didn't know what to do with it. He didn't know how to speak. He suddenly found he was crying uncontrollably and the old dear clasped his hand within hers.

When Norman told her the story of the man who lost his wife and couldn't find her, Betty, overnight, became a lighthouse. As a toddler, at least twice a week Betty would insist that Norman walk her down the Hartlepool coast. "Want watch sea. Want watch sea."

A string of boats would line the water's edge, but these were steered by fisherman. The wife of Norman's story was never accompanying them. One day, a fisherman washed up on the shore and was identified by the unique knit of his guernsey. Fishwives stitched secret codes into fabric. The banded patterns on each man were his family. Each man wore his family boldly, venturing out into the polar void.

The sands were blackened, and even in snow, sea-coalers trudged about the coastal shelf, dark sacks on their shoulders, picking at the earth. Sometimes young men would ride horse-drawn carts through the water's edge, loading the coal into pyramids on the carts, waving their caps and balaclavas like cowboys in the rain. The smoke of the refractories along the coast hung over everything. Betty wondered how the wife of Norman's story could see in such conditions.

"Don't worry, pet. She eats carrots", Norman told her.

"Is it smoky over the whole sea?" Betty asked him.

"Not so smoky the further out tha get."

"And what if the lady meets a shark out there? Sharks are big and they eat people up."

"Don't worry, pet", Norman replied. "She wuh always good with animals."

"But what about pirates? There are pirates at sea. There's Blackbeard and Captain Kidd, and they've got swords that are long and sharp."

"Aye, but that's no problem. See, both of them are fond of the lady. Why, when the pirates come across her on the Atlantic, they invite her up to their ships for tea. She helps Captain Kidd organise his silks and satins. She braids roses into Blackbeard's hair. They have a lovely time. There's no danger there."

"What if the lady discovers a new island?" Betty continued. "A desert island. Do you think she'd stop for a while?"

"Well, she has before, pet! It wun't deserted, but I know she made home on a new island once. She found it strange at first. There wuh lots of new people, quite different to the ones she'd known, and she thought they all spoke funny. Before long, she started to like the island, and the local folk grew to love her. The island wuh a wonderland compared to some places she'd been before. A lot of people she'd known wuh angry, but on this island folk wuh just knackered. So, to cheer them up, she used to talk brightly to everyone and help out the islanders with chores where she could. She got a lot of attention from the local blokes. Every day fellas would bring flowers to her door. Daffodils and daisies and lilacs. By! Her house looked like a florist's every summer! But, as lovely as it was, she wuh never one for sticking in one place too long. One day, she set sail and wuh never seen again. That's no bother. She's out there having new adventures every day."

"Perhaps on another island?"

"Perhaps on another island."

Betty would stay up long after she had pretended to go to sleep. She would sit with the lights off, drawing pictures of the fantastical voyager. She drew the lady with long dark movie-star hair, arms that emerged *from her waist, a face as round as a shilling — and there was a smiling sun in the top right corner — and in some of the drawings there were happy dolphins, and in others companionable pirates with flowers in their hair. There were mermaids and singing sailors with Union Jacks on their chests — and in others, the lady was the queen of the sea and octopuses and whales danced around her in the marble ballroom of her underwater kingdom — and in one drawing, Betty and Norman had come for tea, and they were all sat at a table with roseate cheeks. With their forks in their hands, their smiles outsized their faces, because it was time to eat, and they were all very hungry indeed.*

June 2017 (I)

"Did you know", my ex-girlfriend once said to me, "every time you take a photo on your phone, someone at Apple sees it?" I did not know. That night, as she slept, I deleted all revealing photos I had ever taken for her, imagining the Californian office workers that had already laid eyes on them, but taking comfort in the knowledge that they must see pornographic images every day.

Darla had a crescent moon tattooed on her thigh, and a black cat on her stomach where our baby had grown for a time. She studied English literature at the University of Nottingham. That's why she liked me — because of the "fun little stories" I would scribble in my spare time. She used to carry around copies of *Ulysses* and *Swann's Way*. She read them aloud in my bath while I shaved at the mirror.

"Why not write like Joyce or Proust? A novel on involuntary memory, or a modern take on one of the epics?"

"I can't", I'd say. "I'm not European enough. Besides, I've never read an epic, and I have no memories to involuntarily recount."

"You *can't* remember, or you *won't* remember?"

"Love, I can't even remember what happened last night."

Darla used to read me the characteristics of my star sign. "You're sometimes reserved, sometimes very social. You're hard on yourself, making you sensitive to criticism." She'd recite them from her phone in the local Wetherspoons. I smirked them away but quietly I enjoyed being so neatly categorised.

Her readings made me feel decidedly less autonomous and individual and, therefore, less responsible for my own life and, thus, my freefall into the anxiety of the world.

"Your present is 'the Sun'. It represents the universe coming together and agreeing with your path and aiding forward movement into something greater. Your future is 'the Hanged Man'. It represents ultimate surrender, sacrifice, or being suspended in time. Wait. That can't be right."

Our star signs being incompatible, she left me and took with her the baggy of Northern Lights I kept by my bed and three punk revival vinyls that she had impressively managed to conceal under her coat. I didn't begrudge her. The takeaways from my relationship with Darla were twofold:

1. We are living in the post-truth age. I should not trust anything, even myself.
2. Moustaches are coming back into fashion, and maybe I should consider growing one.

The former point is valid enough. It is an age of deceit and apprehension. It is a country of pretence and of simulacra, saturated with false images, with manufactured meaning. A one-way mirror of a country in which folk are watched silently, their movements, allegiances and words tracked, collected, stored, shared.

I know, loosely, a man named Bulwell Paul, or (to those less affectionate to him) Mental Paul. Sixty-odd. He wears a drab olive trench coat swamped in pin badges. Princess Diana. The Palestinian flag. A pig in a police helmet. He produces homemade newspapers with two other lonely men that haunt the Horseshoe Inn. Some of their beliefs are valid, some commendable, some conspiracies, some reprehensible. On

Fridays, Bulwell Paul hands out his papers on the Nottingham trams. "Free People's Paper. Get the truth! Don't be afraid of the truth!" A Portuguese man once tried to strike up a conversation about Baudrillard's philosophy of truth, much to Bulwell Paul's suspicion. He accused the European of being a government spy and growled at him until he went away.

It is an age of scepticism. It is an age of paranoia. Drones hover outside bathroom windows. Pirates hide in junk emails promising Bitcoin profit, tax rebates, sexy Ukrainians. Bots. Scams. Leaks. Fake accounts. *CYBER CRIMINAL HOLDS SCHOOL TO RANSOM*. My anxiety is growing gluttonous with it all. I am becoming as jittery as a man who has drank for four days straight. I check the windows are locked twice before I sleep. I sometimes think it would be best to carry a small blade on my person. When I wake, I check my phone to see what new catastrophe has taken place that morning, and smile that I am not part of it, and know that one day I likely will be. I am worried that soon I will run into the streets at dawn, perhaps in a chiton, like an Ancient Greek messenger, and shout at the windows, clashing bin lids together. "You, deceived! You think you are protected, but your personal data is sold to the highest bidder! The truth, the truth! You poor soft bastards."

Deano would have joined me had he not vanished the year prior. I knew Deano well for a period of three months. He was a friend of Darla's. He had worked at the Pelican Club until his manager caught him smashing a bottle of Pinot Nero over the table of a rude customer. On Fridays, he'd let me pinch LSD from him, and, in exchange, I'd let him talk to me about UFOs and the Illuminati and how the Royals are secretly reptiles. He riffed on conspiracy theories like a venerable guitarist. When I was sober, he was a lunatic; when on hallucinogens, a genius.

Deano was sick; he wore double denim. He had a tattoo of Myra Hindley on his left calf, and one of Rose West on his right. When I asked him why, he simply grinned and tapped his nose. I didn't know what that meant. I found out recently he had a fetish for being whipped by dominatrixes. I can't ask him if it's true because no one can get hold of him anymore. He retweeted an Ayn Rand quote and disappeared overnight. Part of me, a large part, is glad he's gone. I needed a break from the drugs.

Still, I think of him when I see a menacing headline. *FIVE SIGNS OF THE RISE OF FASCISM IN THE BRITISH STATE. I WENT ON HOLIDAY TO THE CITY OF LONDON AND ALL I GOT WAS THIS SHITTY CAPITALISM.* This unreal, indifferent, sci-fi hypercapitalism. Spacecraft capitalism, interplanetary capitalism, can't-have-a-bacon-butty-without-contributing-to-it capitalism. My thoughts are not my own. My sentiments are manufactured in marketing districts. The word is out. Delete all evidence. Tap the nerve. Many folk die — many self-sacrifice — on the battlefield of mass-produced illusions. Symbols and structures of meaning inflated by propaganda. Their bodies exist forever in cyberspace, still fat with passion, to be replayed, reread and re-enjoyed at a click. *YOU ARE NOT AS SMART AS YOU THINK.* It is an age of the constant present, that is to say, it is the age of the non-age. Time has fallen off its linear trajectory. It is reprocessed, reproduced and revived in infinite cycle. Time has been detemporalised. Time is not itself. I am not myself. I am not quite real. I am the sum of my productivity. I am the sum of my knowledge storage, yet everywhere totality is impossible. I must be more mechanised. I must buy more and sell more. My phone is a sweatshop. My work shirts are from Bangladesh. My food is faux-Indian and faux-Italian. My TV is Japanese. I can never keep up with where my car is being made. I watch American sitcoms about sweaty divorced men. You read British novels, like this one, about sweaty anxious men. When the Euros are on, I support Brazil over England. I am very cultured. I am multinational. I am the corporations' basset hound. I didn't vote for Brexit or for Remain. I spoilt my ballot. I enjoyed being to the detriment of both parties. I read fake news regularly and, secretly, deep down, enjoy sensationalism. It is a guilty pleasure. It is an escape technique. I don't like that, nowadays, everyone's a copper. I don't like that, nowadays, everyone's a snitch. I don't like how capitalism is so fucking intelligent.

As for the latter takeaway from mine and Darla's relationship, I never did grow a moustache, although it is not too late. I am without distinctive style or subculture. I wear hand-me-downs. I don't mind this. It is normal. It has recently been a time of relatively little novelty. My housemates wear the mullets and Chelsea cuts of their parents. Third-wave skins and fourth-wave mods saunter to post-post-punk gigs in gentrified bodegas. £6 Guinnesses splash on Doc Martens as unapologetically talentless drummers thrash, drunk on Buckfast. Am I nostalgic for the past? No. Am I hopeful for the future? Double-no.

It seems to me that the great future society, the painted land of manifestos, is now consciously or unconsciously considered a mirage. Why? Because the future once imagined, in the times of our predecessors, has already arrived, and now we see it for what it is — a detemporalised space which knows no end for it knows no time. We who have known no different are sick of the future-present. We are, then, reproduced images of the past, of our parents, of that which was never experienced, of a past-present, of a present which retained still a future of promise, not because it was romantic, or because it was stylish, or even because it knew itself more, but because it was not this.

There must have been some cut-off point between the past and the now, or at least years of systematic erosion. Those clever capitalists at it again, taking our own trousers off the washing line and selling them back to us. Clever, clever bastards. Where do they get off? Perhaps I should have done a degree in economics.

Sometimes, I think of those I grew up with and wonder if they too have had similar thoughts. Would I be able to sit and eat tea with them, or would the knives have to be confiscated first? When I first said I was a socialist, my friend Weird Craig laughed at me. He laughed all the way home to his council house and told his unemployed father and his father laughed too. Perhaps not all of them vote Tory. A lot of them do. I imagine they too are searching for meaning, in their own way, at their own pace, perhaps more successfully than me. I think of the times we knew no different kind of folk to each other, and had no one to hate in any serious way. Christ, I can't even remember some of their names. Where did all the poor buggers go? Some are in prison now, but I think a few have become builders.

The Londoners left. As soon as the funeral was done, Sherry and Wayne were gone, and the South and North were separate once more. The wind, a disconsolate sorcerer, had waved its hands and everything was back as it should be. No more "Blue is the colour". No more Shepherd's Bush real estate gossip. Mam surveyed the house to make sure nothing was missing. All seemed in place but for a decorative plate which had vanished. A bottle of vodka had found its way into the kitchen cupboard. Mam emptied it into the sink.

We walked Norman daily, to nowhere particularly, just to ensure he exercised his legs. We lost him one afternoon in the Morrisons by the Penny Hill Centre and found him walking into the car park with five plums bulging in his pockets, none of which he had paid for. He was thrilled to discover them and bit into two at the same time. I paid the exhausted cashier the £1 owed.

"Maybe", Mam said, "we oughta get him a rescue dog. He had a dog called Arthur when I was in my twenties. He loved that dog. God knows he could do with a new best mate." So, the next morning, we took Norman to the dog shelter. He pointed at a pug and said "Fat." Next was a particularly dishevelled Lakeland terrier. "Looks like Ken Dodd", he remarked and laughed to himself. A Bullmastiff leapt up, barking at the bars of its cage. We all jumped out of our skin. We left soon after and abandoned the search for a dog.

That evening, Mam sent me around the off licences and supermarkets with photos of Norman. "Please don't sell alcohol to this man", I said, and left a photo with each.

Most shopkeepers did not know him to look at him, particularly the young Lidl and Morrisons cashiers. They shrugged and put the photo I had given them aside, or into a drawer alongside pictures of other old men. On Low Road, a shopkeeper binned his photo as I left. Another told me that he would not refuse service to anyone. "Business is business", he said, as he thrust the picture back into my hands.

The man behind the till at a shop further down Belle Isle Road, a plump Anatolian who introduced himself as Berat, told me he had been serving Norman for years. "It's always sad to see the fall of good men", he said as he propped the photo up behind the counter, next to a candle and a small crescent-and-star flag. Having covered the immediate ground in the area, I trundled back towards the Oval, storing the remaining photos in my bag.

When half-term break ended and school resumed, Mam arranged to take the remaining three weeks of her annual leave in one fell swoop. She had twenty-eight days of paid leave in total but, unlike me, Mam had not touched her time off all year. Like cans of peach slices, of beans, of soup, she had kept them aside for inevitable slumps — slumps such as this.

I was entitled to the same twenty-eight days. I had, however, (unknown to Mam) already used nearly all of them, since my sick days had long ago been spent. One week in December I had faked having the flu. On an earlier occasion, a five-day rainy holiday visiting Darla and her parents in Portsmouth. The occasional instance in which I was hungover and had to call in complaining of fantasy food poisoning or an ear infection. Holiday days vanish all too quickly. Now I had taken leave to come to Hunslet, and when the time came to return, it felt cruel to leave.

Mam and I had come to save Norman and walk him into the life that waited beyond Brenda's curse. We had not yet succeeded. If anything, the curse resisted suppression. It still hung about the house in the walls, in the furniture, wailing through the night. It was not a malediction that could be easily forgotten, and to help Norman make peace with it would take a lot longer than initially thought. I could not leave Mam to shoulder the burden alone. I would need another two weeks off work and had perhaps only four or five more days of paid leave at my disposal.

I decided to call the chief editor at the *Herald* to explain. The man was a jobsworth. There was not a newspaper in circulation that he did not examine every morning. He voted Conservative. He ensured that the political articles he published were saturated with Tory bias and half-truths that weren't half as subtle as he believed them to be. The work of the most protected hacks under his wing smacked of his rotten agenda. To sit in his office was to bathe in the stench of stale coffee and aftershave. His wife, God help her, would be wise to cheat on him.

"You've taken a lot of time off, Frederick. It's starting to become inconvenient."

"I understand that. I do entirely, but I can't help the situation I'm in." I put on my best standard English work voice. "If I could have these next two weeks — and I of course understand that most of it will be unpaid — I give you my word that I will not take any more leave. Not until the next annual rollover."

"Well, yes. There's next to no days of paid leave left to be used. You do realise that in the past I have done you favours by allowing you to request paid leave almost at the drop of a hat. When was it you told me you wanted time off to visit Leeds? Was it two days before you left? Really, we would expect at least a week to two weeks' notice. Now you are asking for a further two weeks only a number of days before you are expected to return to the office. This is unprofessional, Frederick. In fact, I would be tempted to categorise it as misconduct. It is, at the very least, becoming absenteeism."

"Well, I think that's a tad strong, considering I've called…"

"I used my words *appropriately*, I think you'll find. Listen, you have been an effective member of staff here at the *Herald* when you have chosen to be, but far too often you have chosen to put your colleagues through the trouble of having to cover your duties. You clearly have no interest in your professional responsibilities, so I regret to inform you that I'll have to serve you your notice of dismissal."

I did not reply. I kept the phone at my ear. It felt like a gun, and I caught myself breathing. The air rushed in and then shuddered out. It was uneasy on the crags of my teeth. *The bastard. The filthy, self-important, scheming Tory bastard.* Outside, on the motorway, horns sounded like passing ships. People were travelling up to the city centre, down to Wakefield, west to Bradford or Halifax. A party of workers. They would clock in and spend the day waiting to clock out. They would complete their duties to the best of their abilities, so no one could accuse them, but check their phones discretely and creep off for cigarettes when no one was looking. They would sit with their inertia in toilet cubicles with their shoes off, wishing they could remove their feet. Some would consider quitting so they could be free to chat up and be declined by that co-worker they liked. Some would consider quitting so they could be free to use their time exactly as they saw fit. Yet they knew that without money their days would be spent wanking in front of the daily *EastEnders* omnibus, so quit they did not. The youngest would save whatever the landlord left so that one day they might have a place of their own, in the suburbs or in some dead commuter town where the pub was God and they could grow fat with pride. Some would decide to quit drinking to save that little bit extra. On Fridays, they would go straight home to collapse before televisions armed with bowls of microwave rice. Big Daddy Capital kept them alive even if alive was all they'd be. They were the lucky ones.

"You're of course entitled to payment for your remaining days of *paid* leave", the editor continued. "This is your date of notice, but your contract will not be terminated until…"

I had stopped listening.

"You'll be sent a letter outlining…"

I would not listen.

"We've enjoyed…"

"Fuck off, cunt!" I shouted and hung up.

I went to throw my phone across the room, but knowing I would regret it, lashed at the air and fell back on the sofa, my legs kicking like a swimmer's. If Mam and Norman had come back from the Penny Hill Centre then, they would have seen a man touching thirty throwing himself about the front room absolutely naked. For I was, after all, shorn — stripped of my financial independence. Whatever progression I had made or was due to make was gone. I was back to the great zero, that vast blank land from which escape was never certain. I unzipped my jeans to check my penis was still there. *Ah, praise God. They have not taken that.* Yet still, I felt like less than a man. I was a half-formed thing. I was a Neanderthal. Disgusting. Dangerous. Futile.

In many ways, being sacked is like leaving prison. Your boss, the screw, collects you from the place you have spent your years. He tells you that you have served your time and will no longer be required. You are suddenly free. The clothes you once wore in the outside world are returned, and once led to the door, you are released back into nature. You are no longer a mechanism subject to the force of the authoritarian body you have for so long inhabited. You are an independent animal, without guarantee of food or shelter. You stop in the woodland to pick berries and eat. You consider robbing the trees for everything they have. You will need as much free food as possible now that you must fend for yourself. It will, however, rot before long and bacteria will turn it inside out. What then? You will have to grow accustomed to the most minimal and degrading basics of existence. You cannot socialise anymore. You may as well grow your hair out now that you cannot pay the barber. Can you still attract love? Neanderthal indeed. Perhaps this is what you have always been. Perhaps such an ending was destined.

I could not tell Mam or Norman — not yet. I would have to play the part of the employed man. I would tell them I had been granted the extra weeks of paid leave, then confess it all to Mam when we returned to Nottingham. Until then, it was important I did not arouse suspicion. I would need to look entirely Homo sapien.

I sprang to life and rushed upstairs to shave. The blade left a nick on my chin, and I applied a tiny square of toilet roll to plaster the blood. That was OK. I would look like a man who was in a rush, perhaps to get to work! I ran wax through my hair and jogged downstairs to polish my boots, despite the fact I had never worn them to the office. I found myself putting them on and tying the laces and checking my appearance once more in the mirror. Bags, pomegranate in shade, crouched under my eyes. Not to worry. They were nothing a sensible night's sleep couldn't fix. Then I sat in my boots, pants and shirt, with my hair waxed and a bloody chin, staring at *BBC News*.

There again came the numbness, spear in hand, creeping through the bushland, Neanderthal hunting. The clock in Norman's front room would not tick. It appeared to be broken. Had not all clocks been broken for years? I laughed madly. The façade of progression houses, in its margins, a sinister stillness, a stillness which refuses to yield or fade. How can one topple what cannot move? There was more chance of drinking the ocean.

The Penalty Spot

So that decided it. A 4-1-4-1 formation. Lamb in between the sticks. Stanley and Jim "Gnasher" Nash at centre back. Barlow, the nanas' favourite, in defensive midfield, ripe with feeding, a shade of gravy on his cuff. Left back, Briggsy. Right back, Hogg. Centre midfield was occupied, as always, by Ingram and Cairns. There was no getting rid of them. Now, at twenty, both were too old to become professionals in any meaningful sense. Before long, Norman would have to replace them with younger lads who stood a real chance of being scouted.

It would be Wallis at left midfield. Salmon would need to be drafted in on the right, despite injury. Salmon had torn some muscle in his ankle, probably kicking a bus stop. No problem. He could run it off. The striker irrefutably had to be Pilcher. He was the first name on the team sheet and the most trouble of the lot of them. Big bastard, clothes-line-robbing Pilcher, already known by the Durham Constabulary at fifteen and a week, but by God he could leather a ball for his country.

This was the bask of tearaways Norman had been left with. Shoulder-length-haired, flared-jeaned, tooth-picking, arse-scratching tearaways. He loved them like sons. Sometimes, in the pub, Norman would be pulled aside by teachers who would question how he could love the bastards. The dynamically flawed, Norman would tell them, are far easier to love than the seemingly perfect. The seemingly perfect are just as flawed but they hide it cleverly. At least a man can get the measure of the brazen.

Norman had been a sports coach at Hartlepool Lads' Club for fourteen years. His hair had grown ashen, as if chalk had been rubbed down the nape of his neck. He was the firebrand of Rodney Street. When he walked into the Working Men's Club he was greeted by cheers, and at school, Betty remained under the protective watch of two older lads, whose fathers worked and drank with Norman. He had won the favour of the Hartlepool folk. They admired his suede sheepskin winter coat and, even more, the fact that it was his only winter coat. They admired his enjoyment of simple things and that he was forthright with his thinking. He had voted Labour in '64 and '66. He was secretly intrigued but publicly sceptical about Wilson's brand of science-fiction socialism. The first bellows of the Space Age were ringing across the globe but were heard only distantly and with loud reluctance by the traditionalists at the Lads' Club that paid Norman's wages. He kept those old buggers sweet and made jokes about Alec Douglas-Home's skull, which pleased people of all ages.

Norman, to the people of Hartlepool, was a torchbearer for the mythos of man. A man is expected leave his mark on the world if he hopes to have a life of meaning. The Russians and Americans could chase each other around the solar system, leaving their marks on moon dust for as long as they wanted. What the local people respected about Norman was that his mark was that of a man both lucid and earthly. He was one of their own, reared in bombsite and slurry. He bound his own personal furtherance to the furtherance of his neighbours. When he heard that the Nash family were to be evicted from their house, he had paid the landlord off for a month from his own savings. During the miners' strike of '69, he had travelled to the coalfields to picket alongside the colliers of North Yorkshire. In '72 he had joined bands of flying pickets at local power stations. He was a collectivist. He coached the young to be proud of their class and to get stuck into any bastard who tried to get in the way of their advancement. As he walked the sodden streets of Hartlepool, Norman left ripples in his wake.

In privacy, he balanced between the dyed-in-the wool stoicism of his father's generation and the hedonistic revolution of youth. He was in his thirties by this time and was not ready, like so many his age, to act like a man of fifty. He drank sea-coalers under the table with an older man's *flair, but cleaned the house on Saturdays, raised his daughter alone, became a dexterous cook, collected LPs by the Beatles, the Kinks and T. Rex.*

He had courted a few women during Betty's childhood, only one of whom was memorable. Rita something. She had a pixie cut, like Twiggy. The whole street said she looked like Twiggy. She had all the glamour and mystique of a Vogue model. She had not long before been voted the National Union of Mineworker's County Durham Coal Queen. As such, she paraded around Norman's house in her sash and tiara on the days of her public events, much to Betty's awe. Whenever Betty tried to play with Rita's make-up, however, Rita would pinch her, hard enough to make Betty cry. The warmth of the woman's eyes would drain and be replaced with something sinister. "You foul little cow", she'd hiss at the child. Norman caught her in the act once and threw her out without a second thought.

"It's just me and you, kid", he'd tell Betty, and so it was.

If the date can be recalled accurately, Hartlepool were due to face Stockton-on-Tees in the next round of the annual Lads' Club Association Cup. It was June. Norman travelled by foot to the pitch. His banana-slug yellow Hillman Avenger remained at his door, for he preferred to walk or jog to work, so as to keep himself in shape and so as not to differentiate himself from those at the club who could not afford a car. In his coaching duties he modelled himself, as if a Greek terracotta figurine, upon two men. The first was Don Revie, the incumbent Leeds manager and legend of the West Riding. For Norman, the way Revie suppressed the individual egos of his players and celebrated, in equal measure, all staff who laboured thanklessly for the club, right down to the cleaners, justified his position as the benevolent father figure of Leeds United.

Revie was the figurine of the manager; the practical person visible to all; the man that paced the six-yard box as if it was his private study; the hard physicality and tactility of the clay. The shadow cast (separate from the materiality of the figurine but extending from it all the same) was the socialist collectivism of Liverpool's Bill Shankly. This philosophy was

Norman's faithful companion. It wandered with him and sat alongside him on the grass when the day's training was done. These were the parts that built the man, the pages left to be picked up by the next.

As Norman arrived at the Lads' Club, Lamb and Briggsy were sat atop the goalposts, sharing a cigarette, their legs dangling. Hogg was circling the turf attempting wheelies, like a warbler learning to fly. Gnasher and Pilcher were scurrying about the mud, sparring, their blue sweatshirts thrown aside for the sun to mould. These were the sportsmen of the great tomorrow — but only if they were scouted. Perhaps not even then. Those that weren't scouted would end up in the pits. That year, Hartlepool FC had finished eleventh in Division Four. Leeds United had won the First bloody Division. Norman would have to get some Yorkshiremen up to have a look at his disciples if they were to stand a chance.

"We'll turn thee into Hunters, Clarkes and Bremners yet lads", he clapped. "You, Lamb! Hands like feet. Hands like Nosferatu. In goal for penalty kicks!" He walked a football twelve yards from the goal line.

Lamb, who surely had one foot already in the pits, stood with his arms spread, vacantly looking out, his tongue hanging to sample the air. Betty, who had come straight from school, settled down on the grass at a distance to watch.

"Lamb! With any hope lad, we'll improve on last week." Norman handed the ball to Pilcher, who set it down. "Read the kicker! Read his motion pattern. Watch his eyes. With any thought, you can decipher which way he plans to go. Then BANG! Off like a bullet. Commit. Nothing half-hearted. The ball is scared of thee. It's a rat in the kitchen and you need to capture it." He turned to Pilcher. "Do yer worst, son. Get into him."

The striker retreated, brushing his hair from his eyes, then charged and shot out his elephantine left foot. The ball sailed in a direction that defied Lamb's instinct. He had not expected Pilcher to use his weak foot. It careered into the top corner of the goal and the net bulged.

"Good man, Pilcher! Shoddy work, Lamb! Be ready for all manner *of attack. A good striker will catch thee off guard. He may use his weak foot to throw thee. He may hop on the spot before he strikes, to make yer dive early. A good goalkeeper must be a learned as an academic. He must interpret the minds, temptations and tricks of his fellow men. He must understand their decisions before the men can be said to understand them themselves. Another try!"*

This time, Wallis stepped forward. He hopped before kicking, as he had just heard Norman describe, then attempted to plant the ball firmly down the middle. Lamb rebalanced, after stepping right at the hop, and caught the heavy leather in his freakishly long fingers.

"Better! Now Salmon."

The rest of the lads took turns to keep Lamb under the cosh, some more successfully than others. The lashings, leaps and recoveries were the patchwork of their lives. Small achievements and failures fell unpredictably and at random. They would be harvested by the sinking sun and forgotten by the time sleep came about. One man's triumph was another man's undoing. That was a given. Every defeat called out to the future triumph of redemption. These were the truncated pinnacles that served as mountains.

As the day's session was drawing to a close, Norman caught Gnasher kneeling beside Betty. His palms and neck were caked in mud and his right eye, bruised from a flailing header, bulged like a turnip. His bike was at his feet. He whispered something to Betty, and she laughed.

He'd better not lay a finger on her with those grubby hands. *Norman watched like a hawk as he collected in the stray footballs.* He'd better jump on his bike and fuck off home. Must think a lot of himself, Gnasher Nash, assuming he can hold a candle to our Betty. Why, a toerag like that leads astray every lass he chats to. Look at him. Teeth like a donkey. Our Betty's cleverer than that. She'd be right to show him the finger and tell him to hop it.

Betty did not show him the finger. She laughed at his jokes and looked him in the eyes. At fourteen, she obviously felt like an adult. A husk of sick churned in Norman's stomach. The day would soon come when she was eighteen. She would take up her bags and leave him all alone. What would he do then? Who would he talk to, and protect? It was natural, of course, that Betty would become a woman one day, and it would be wrong to infantilise her, but could he not hold off the years that rolled on so swiftly, even if just for a while? It seemed only a day since they had walked along the coast, imagining the lady who sailed away to sea. Time was a predator. It stalked and caught up with all eventually. Norman looked it in the eyes. What all-loving God could allow Jim "Gnasher" Nash, of all people, to be the harbinger of such a prophecy? The little bastard would get pissed and lose the bloody thing.

It was not that Norman opposed the magazine cut-outs taped to Betty's bedroom wall. The pop singers in the magazines were altogether clean and harmless. They looked like they brushed their teeth ten times a day. They were the sort that would listen to a lass's father and bugger off when instructed to. Lads like Gnasher were not fit for Betty. The fact that he was daring to try it on after Norman had paid off the Nash family's landlord was disrespectful beyond belief.

Whilst Betty remembered he felt guilt later, and in fact apologised to her at some point or other, on that day Norman strode over, barking. He dragged Gnasher up by his ear and, clipping him round the back of the head, sent him to do sixty press-ups in the mud. He was banned from the following training session, and his younger brother was drafted in to take his place. The boy was far too soft and came away bruised. The day fell away when the night whistled softly. It gave way routinely, usurped by a moon now conquered by men. These were men of distant lands, men beyond reality. The moon had not even flinched when they walked on its surface. Hartlepool lost one-nil to Stockton-on-Tees in the annual Lads' Club Association Cup.

June 2017 (II)

Mam had painted every day — once, no longer. Landscapes mostly. The Skegness coastal shelf. Sherwood Forest. The River Trent from the perspective of Trent Bridge — the lock, the football stadium and the waterfront flats skittering away into the distance, becoming brushstrokes. The floor of our front room had looked as if it were a painting itself. Electric pink, calypso blue and buttermilk white, like miniature archipelagos, had dried on the wooden floorboards, never to be wiped up.

When I was a teenager, she had painted, at request, one of our neighbours, then her daughter. The portraits were grotesque, unintentionally, I'm sure. Even on a good day, our neighbour's face was throddy, hanging like a lump of beef, and so difficult to depict majestically. In paint, she came out a haggard Queen Victoria, her chin buried in her hands, diamanté tracksuit bottoms clinging to her elephantine thighs.

Our neighbour's daughter did not want to be painted. She pulled faces throughout the sitting and dribbled ice cream down her chin. Mam painted the little girl as she was, impish, with her tongue out, fingers pulling at the sides of her mouth, chocolate sauce smeared across her cheeks. Her mother was disappointed she didn't look more cherubic. She didn't ask for any more paintings. Mam happily returned to landscapes.

She had not painted as much recently. She was chasing her school's upcoming Head of Art vacancy, and so had taken on as many additional responsibilities as she could to endear herself to the cold head teacher. On Tuesdays, she ran a sewing club, a still-life club on Thursdays. She orchestrated school trips once a term to local galleries, and marked her students' work long into the evenings, planning lessons through the weekends until she was forced to stop. She had always been a workaholic but now even more so. When she found time, she hibernated and slept loudly, and dreamt that the horses of age were running through her head.

"Of course, they all died young in those days", Mam said, pointing to the watercolour. She had found it in the attic, in a tattered folder she had kept as a child. She had thought it lost years ago, and, having uncovered it in Norman's spare room, had been sat, leafing through the pages for a while before I joined her.

Dating from the early Seventies, the watercolour rendered the Hunslet Grange Flats in pale, washed greys and browns. Mam had stood on her toes to paint it, peeping over the wall of a second-floor walkway. The work of a child, the pebbledash concrete panels of the building looked as if melting. The colours hung like stalactites in the air. Further down the walkway, a dim salmon-coloured oval, a lady's face, hovered at the door of a flat. A poorly painted hand beckoned the artist in for dripping bread.

"They must have been in their early sixties", I said.

Mam nodded. "She was always very lively. She took a lot of pride in that flat. Redecorated it all the time. She wanted to keep it vibrant and happy and warm looking. I remember her showing me her jewellery box every time we went over, and if I was really well behaved, she used to let me pick a little necklace or bracelet to take home. I've still got them somewhere. I need to find the buggers." She paused. "*He* was always quiet. I remember being scared of him because he only had one hand. Gangsters chopped it off. I've told you that haven't I? Poor man. He watched cowboy films and spent a lot of time sleeping."

The flats were demolished, and never emerged from the wreckage. They were not a mile from where we sat, beneath the new builds and the playing fields, their heads turned up to the streets in the sky that had, since, become walkways of air.

"It's hard to know exactly where they lived before the flat — when your grandad was young. Those streets will have been torn down in the Sixties, during the slum clearance. I don't think he'd be able to locate where his childhood home was now. It could be where the Lidl is or where the Penny Hill Centre is or where the motorway is — but the flats will have been built when I was little, then they were knocked down when I was in my twenties. It was a horrible place really. It needed demolishing. Stolen cars used to get dumped on the grass to rot and all the walls weathered away and started turning black. Boys used to hang around on the stairways to rob people. Nana's handbag was stolen once but she *still* refused to leave the estate. She didn't want to leave Hunslet. I suppose it was all she'd ever known."

It was getting on. Mam went to check on Norman. I did my best to scribble down what she had said, no doubt forgetting some of it. I etched the most significant details about my great grandparents into the paper, then supplemented them with family stories I already knew. I was almost angry at them for dying in their sixties. Had they hung around for another ten years I would have been able to meet them and conjure up real-life impressions of them from my infancy. I would have known the exact intonations and quirks of their voices. As it stood, they would always be characters, never fully realised, three-dimensional people. They had become the opinions and memories of those who had known them and remain little more than that.

Again, I examined Mam's watercolour, focusing on the dim salmon-coloured oval at the door. It hovered fixedly, a lonely shape on paper. There was far too little detail to interpret a facial expression. The painted lady could have been anyone. She *was* anyone. She didn't really exist.

That night, we lost Norman.

The moon offered its nightly luminescence, and the world responded with obscurity. All manner of creatures turned out from their hiding places, including those that existed only in dreams, to crawl on their bellies through the mute streets.

Footsteps. Footsteps shuffling in the hallway. Mam listened to them briefly, then sleep retrieved her. Waking again shortly after, she could hear nothing. Groaning, she rolled out of bed to check on Norman, to ensure he was not searching for some hidden bottle. But he was not in his bedroom, nor the bathroom, nor the kitchen or back garden.

I woke with a start as Mam shook me.

"He's fucking gone", she said. "He's nowhere in the house."

Throwing on a dressing gown, I sprang to the front door and trotted shoeless out into the street. Mam followed behind. He was not there, or, at least, had hidden himself expertly in the night. The dry, shrinking shrubs shuddered listlessly. A dejected child's bike lay toppled by a fence and the wooden posts stood as sentinels, refusing to speak. The sound of traffic on the A61, still humming lowly even at this hour, danced on the air. Fearing the worst, I darted to the road but found no disturbance, no body slumped on the motorway. No tyre tracks trailing blood. Dimly lit cars and vans headed south in ignorance.

"Go on", Mam told me, as she limped behind, so I sprinted back down, past the floating houses, to the Oval. My heart ran with me, overtaking my feet. A night fox, seeing me coming, leapt onto a wall and dropped into a back garden, something dead in its teeth. I stopped at the curb, tossing in all directions. No one. Not even a wisp of a person. Not even a half-formed person. Not even a shadow.

The Oval, in the moon, as the moon's lunar mare, was a silver trail leading into blackness. The last standing lamp in an overlooking window extinguished itself, and even the streetlights, where they remained lit, offered no guidance.

I felt as if I was a component in one of Norman's stories, a figure populating a folk tale. I was galloping through the moors, chasing down a hound of myth, a creature sighted but never caught. It was the witching hour.

"Grandad", I shouted.

"Dad", echoed Mam.

I followed the Oval around the bend, until I saw him. He was there, his back to me, a man shrouded, shuffling slowly down the middle of the road. He was shivering, clearly unaware of where he was, his strands of white hair bright, hovering over his shaded head. Naked.

I called to him, but he continued walking.

As I sprinted to catch up, I heard the engine. Then, suddenly, Norman was glowing, filled in his entirety by oncoming headlights. I reached him. There was a shout and a car veered off urgently, honking its horn into the night.

Norman's eyes were closed. He was dreaming, and as I shook him to life, his lashes fluttered to consciousness, and he stared back at me with confusion and disappointment. He went to speak but couldn't. His voice started, then stopped. He poked his tongue out to taste the muggy air, turning only to the roar of Mam's approaching shriek.

"Betty", he muttered. "What are you doing in my dream?"

The Celestial Basement

Ewan had always been gay. Everyone knew that for a fact, yet his father insisted that the whole affair had only come about since Ewan began listening to Queen. He blamed Freddie Mercury for the indoctrination of his son into what he called "a cult of devil worship." At first, he tried to beat the gay out of him, then, when that didn't work, he refused to acknowledge Ewan as his legitimate child. If someone raised his son's sexuality with him, Ewan's father would state categorically that his wife had had an affair, probably with a gypsy, and that his sperm could never have produced a homosexual.

Betty had met Ewan at the local college of art and design, where, upon leaving school, they had both taken courses in painting. He and his family had recently moved down from Glasgow. The first time Betty saw him, Ewan had been sat on the floor of the college with a canvas before him, wearing a tattered safety-pin-covered jacket, his hair shaped into a red Mohawk. He had been studiously detailing the body of a Glaswegian drug addict, in neo-expressionist style, chipping away at the abstracted chest and neck with vivid yellows and pinks.

Betty had asked to paint him, to which he shyly agreed. She wanted to portray the contrast between the new punk movement and the domestic space of the older generation. She took Ewan home and positioned him on Norman's armchair, his lap covered in a granny square crocheted blanket, his Docs planted heavily on the shag carpet, the orange geometric shapes of the wallpaper serving as a homely backdrop.

Norman got along with Ewan. Over the few years that followed, he became aware that he was usurping Ewan's own father as the young man's masculine influence. Norman took on the responsibilities of the role proudly. Despite the boy having no interest in sport, he found that the punk had a keen knowledge of industry, his family having been employed in the steelworks of Glasgow until the recent industrial decline.

Sometimes Ewan would sit to watch Norman write. He would watch in awe, for he could barely write himself. The man would sit at the kitchen table, crack his knuckles and, like a composer, raise his fingers to the air. Then his hands would descend and for hours the house would be filled with the sound of typewriter keys manically struck. Every evening Norman would thrash out stories, as if he had held them so long in his palms, then place them down gently on the table when finished. Occasionally, when particularly proud, Norman would read a story or two aloud to his guest and Ewan would close his eyes to listen, close his eyes so that he could imagine himself in the stories.

Norman's bookshelves became Ewan's stalking ground, although much of the literature contained words too complex to be sounded let alone understood. Ewan preferred the novels to the theory. He preferred Alan Sillitoe to Raymond Williams. He ran his forefinger across the disgruntled spines. A Kestrel for a Knave. *Walter Greenwood. D.H. Lawrence's* Sons and Lovers. *Orwell.* The Uses of Literacy. *E.P. Thompson.* Billy Liar. *The Liverpool poets'* The Mersey Sound. The Ragged Trousered Philanthropists. Felix Holt, the Radical. Germinal *by Zola. Booklets containing translated excerpts from Gramsci's prison notebooks, handwritten by a local trade union secretary.*

When Norman got drunk, as he had started doing regularly, Ewan knew when to take the bottle away, where to find the paracetamol, how to position Norman on his side as he slept, with a pillow behind him to stop him rolling back and choking on his vomit. His own father drank heavily. Most men of their age did. Ewan knew as well as Betty that Norman was desperate — desperate for a wife, desperate not to leave the past behind, desperate not to get older. He had never fully recovered from Florrie's death. He didn't have to mention her for that to be known. None of the women in Hartlepool could replace her, though they tried. Still,

Norman wanted a wife, perhaps selfishly, so that at least he wouldn't be alone when Betty left, and Betty told him on several occasions, "They won't want yer while yer pissed." Usually, that helped the man sober up.

On the night that Betty met Dennis Muir, she and Ewan had been drinking with Norman in the Stranton. At half ten, they moved on in the direction of the Celestial Basement, the nightclub, leaving Norman in the company of a talkative postman who was forecasting doom to follow Thatcher's ascendency.

Every Friday, Betty and Ewan were at the Celestial Basement. On Saturdays they would take a bus to Middlesbrough and tour the local pubs before heading to either the Rock Garden punk club or, if on ecstasy and hungering for the lightness of chart music, Bennetts in South Bank, where pantsuits, tube tops and terry-cloth shirts set the softies apart from the bondage trousers and chains of the anarchists.

At the Celestial Basement, Debbie Harry's disembodied voice rang out to the street. A congregation of clubbers shuffled forward in the queue. Separated into their distinctive herds, youths moved past to their chosen destinations. Revival mods in cheap suits and pork-pie hats, late disco hangers-on wearing bell-bottoms and halter tops, skinheads donned in bleached jeans and donkey jackets. A huge boy with a safety pin pushed through his nose stumbled to the queue to the Celestial Basement with eyes like whirlpools and a stained-green tongue. Cannabis smoke rose in plumes, holding itself to clothes for days to come, clothes to be stuffed under mattresses to avoid the keen nostrils of wandering mothers. Ewan took a baggy from under his belt and dabbed speed into his gums. He gave Betty some, then allowed a drunk girl behind him to snort a specimen from his thumb.

The bouncer, six teeth missing in action, looked celestial himself. The glare from the windows crowned him in a halo of light. He gestured a thumb. Downstairs. The basement. It was, as always, a knot of limbs. Chameleon faces disappeared amongst shoulders, changing colours, mouths like lamps. A vodka. Music was the chest of an untamed animal. A hallucination. The queasy crouched on stools with their heads down. Two gaunt men quarrelled over a girl with gelatine-spiked hair. The floor moved at rapid pace. As clubbers jostled and jumped, the world rotated beneath their feet. Another vodka, a double this time. Euphoria. Bitter crystals. The thrashing of guitars. An agitation. A vexation. A moonstomp. A skinny tie whipping at a sweating back. A bite mark on a neck, puffing up, forming a gummy crater. A tongue in an ear. The rolling strike of drums. A finger bent back to dislocation. A suedehead, frothing salvia, slurred a Paul Weller lyric to the barman, sweeping shot glasses to the floor in starry crescendo. A pogo. A glue bag of dreams. Bottles of poppers pressed to noses like tissues. Another vodka. An adolescent or salmon writhed on the floor. A mutation of teeth and hair and genitals. A worm of energy swarming and gleaming. The wail of a siren. A blackout.

Stretched across the sofas to smoke, Ewan gestured to Betty to investigate the crowd. A young, skinny man with a mullet emerged from the bodies, pressing a roll-up lightly to his lips, his eyes closed as he blissfully explored his own head. The young man carried an air of romanticism about him, his frilly fop shirt open at the chest. He wore bold eye make-up, as if the wings of peacocks. He walked as if on air, and went to flop on a stool by the bar.

Ewan's face lit up. "D'ye reckon he's....?"

"Definitely", Betty said. "Go chat to him."

"Aw, ah dinnae ken. What would I say?"

"Just introduce yerself. Compliment him. Ask to buy him a bloody drink."

Ewan considered. "Aw, ah canny."

"Do it!" Betty goaded. She pushed Ewan up off the sofa. "Quick, before he fucks off!"

He paused.

"Go see what the craic is!" Betty cried in her best Scottish accent.

Ewan rolled his eyes, nodded and made his way over to the pantheistic young man, who had already spotted him and was ready and waiting.

Ewan refused to wear make-up in public. There were nightclubs in London where you could get away with it, certainly. In London, in fact, you'd be lauded. You'd be invited to feature in music videos and magazine photo shoots. There were gay clubs in London where people dressed as Romantics, as dandies, as French aristocracy, and no one blinked an eye, but these were clubs a long way from Hartlepool. The gay man in the North lived in perpetual danger.

Betty watched, through the squirming bodies, as the two became acquainted. They were locked in conversation, the young man stroking Ewan's arm, moving his hand south. He must have a lot of bollocks to be so brazen. *Perhaps the young man was from London himself and was blissfully unaware of the sinister eyes that would follow him along the County Durham coast at night. Then again, there was a chance he* was *aware but took pride in aggravating such eyes. His friends would call him brave. His mother would call him foolish. Perhaps he did not care what might happen to him.*

Uproar. Suddenly, the music came to a juddering halt. Three police officers had appeared. They were wrestling a Jamaican boy away from the dance floor. Two skins were shouting, demanding the boy's freedom. One of the skins lunged forwards and was beaten off with a truncheon. Blood spurted from his nose. He watered the floor with it. Another grabbed his pint glass but was held back by his girlfriend. The Jamaican boy was struggling. The officers dragged him to the stairs, issuing threats to the furious crowd. A fourth policeman arrived at the door.

Ewan was being pulled by the Romantic young man in the direction of the conflict. The young man's eyes were fixed intensely on the officers. He stormed forward, pointing into the face of the policeman by the door. "Fascist cunts", he spat. "Racist fucking fascists, the lot of you."

The officer glanced nonchalantly at the finger. He moved to block the path to his colleagues as they bundled the Jamaican boy upstairs. The policeman was two-dimensional. Why shouldn't he be? His skin looked as if plasticine had been pulled tightly over his skull. He was crafted, unnatural. His eyes were set and unmoving. He touched his moustache as he stared at the young gay men before him — concentrating on an equation, figuring out what he would have for his late tea. Then his contemplation turned into a broad, crooked grin.

"Well then", he remarked, "they've even got queers down here. Mind who yer talking to and get that dirty hand out of my face, or I'll nick you and yer boyfriend for gross indecency."

"On what fucking grounds?" the Romantic young man snapped.

"Let's say I saw you with yer hand down yer boyfriend's trousers. Who's to say I didn't? I'll have yer both in a cell faster than yer can blink."

The young man turned to Ewan for reinforcement but found him deflated. Ewan kept his eyes on the floor and his hands behind his back, as if assuming the position of one already handcuffed.

"Quiet aren't yer?" the policeman goaded. "Nowt to say? You must be the receiver. Yer'd like it in prison, lad. The blokes get desperate after a while, what with no women to keep them company — if yer know what I mean."

Having detected the weak link, the officer began poking at Ewan with his truncheon. The instrument sniffed at the boy's chest, searching for his heart. The pokes turned to jabs.

Betty rushed in. She tugged at Ewan's clothes. The boy had closed his eyes. Half-crazed, the policeman followed, enjoying himself. Pleas from the crowd fell like invisible moths on his ears. He was doing the work of God and the crown. He stiffened at the thought. He deserved to be promoted to the rank of a sergeant. He deserved a knighthood.

Suddenly, the jabbing stopped. When Ewan opened his eyes, a skinhead had torn the truncheon free and was holding it high above the policeman's head. The ugly thing glimmered in the neon light.

It was the same skin who had been struck earlier. The blood trickling from his nose had stained his teeth scarlet. It had landed like rain, soiling the carefully maintained whiteness of his shirt. A spider's web was tattooed across his neck. A dim swallow was on his wrist and a Borstal dot beneath his eye. His hands were those of a man a generation his senior.

"Right", he announced. "I've had enough of this. You!" He pointed to the policeman, then to the door. "Fuck off. You in't arresting no one in here, so go join yer bastard mates. Now!"

The officer paused. Cautiously, he surveyed the room. His colleagues were outside, further than his voice could travel. Now smirks littered the crowd.

Slowly, the man composed himself. He wiped his hands on the front of his jacket, touched his moustache and, without a word, walked through the door and up the stairs.

A cheer rang out. The crowd surged forward to clap the skinhead on the neck. He brushed them aside and went straight to Ewan. "They'll be back in a minute, maybe with dogs. Come with me. Bring yer pals."

Ewan nodded grimly. He wished he had never approached the young man with the frilly fop shirt, yet he fetched him by his elbow and gestured to Betty to follow. The three of them waded swiftly through the crowd as the skinhead led them to the stock room behind the bar. Above a fridge brightly packed with ginger ale and Harps Lager, a small, begrimed window opened to street level behind the building.

Betty went first. Holding her feet, the skin gently eased her up through the window. Once she had confirmed the back alley was empty, he repeated the same action for the others and, finally, slipped through the window himself, with an ability that suggested it was not his first escape. Then, without pausing to survey their surroundings, the four of them sprinted through the streets until they reached the docks and, finding the area deserted, slumped behind a wall to smoke.

The skinhead introduced himself as Dennis Muir, a twenty-three-year-old miner at Horden Colliery who lived eight miles up the road in Peterlee. He had encountered plenty of officers like the moustachioed policeman before. "They're a common breed of dog", he muttered, and spat. "Yer'd be wise to keep away from that club for a bit now. They'll send coppers back every week to try and find yer. They'll get bored eventually, and then yer can go back."

The romantic young man had evidently taken more speed than anyone else. He couldn't sit still. He paced around the docks, humming loudly, until he suddenly departed to try and hitchhike back to his halls at Durham.

The temperature was dropping, and the wind brought the glacial North Sea in on its back. Dennis laid his Crombie coat over Betty's shoulders. He gave Ewan a cigarette whenever he noticed the boy's nerves playing up. He was playing nurse to the young punks who he assumed had only that night entered the adult world of violence.

They sat for a couple of hours until the drugs wore off. Across the black, foreboding sea, hidden from any human eye, was the German island of Sylt, the Wadden Sea Islands of Denmark.

"I've been down pits since I wuh sixteen", Dennis was saying. "Like me father, and his father. It's shite but it keeps a roof above me head. Can't do it forever, mind you, even if I wanted to. One day, the whole industry will shut up shop, probably sooner rather than later."

"What'll yer do then?" Betty asked.

"Ah dunno. I'll have to pick a new trade what'll keep me a while. Maybe I'll be a mechanic or summet. Folks'll always need cars and scooters fixed. I'm dead good with scooters already, like. Yer shoulda seen me fix up this Vespa I got me hands on. Did it right proper. Drove it up coast as far as Sunderland one day, put a brick through Sunderland supporters' pub window. Got chased by a load of Vauxies but I were away by the time I got to Wearside. Were a right laugh." Dennis burst into hysterics, then coughed and recomposed himself. On second thought, he wished he hadn't told that story. Neither Betty nor Ewan seemed to mind.

"Well, how much do yer charge?" Betty asked. "Me dad's got an old Hillman Avenger that could do with some work, and he keeps putting off going to the garage."

"I could do that no problem." Dennis jumped to his feet at the thought. "Aye, I'd have the thing working like it's brand new. It'd go fast as a Ferrari by time I'm done!"

Dennis agreed to visit the following weekend. Despite the manhood he draped proudly about him, the skinhead carried a level of unconcealable crudity and an excitable immaturity that Betty found endearing. He was far from being the absolute man he thought he was, but then most men share that quality. To Betty, women were the men that men thought they were. They were the real stoic labourers, forced to make peace with the volatility of their fathers, brothers, husbands and sons. Still, she would humour Dennis's eagerness to demonstrate his capabilities. There was something she appreciated about his artlessness, and after all, Norman's car did need work.

June 2017 (III)

Two days after the sleepwalking incident, I took the 167 Sapphire into Leeds City Centre. I needed space to work. The Central Library would offer me the quiet and distance that Hunslet could not. By work I meant to write. This had to be done secretively so as not to let Mam and Norman know that I was now recording every occurrence of our visit. So, that morning, when Mam decided to take Norman swimming in Belle Isle, I told her that I had barely slept the night before and would stay at home while they went out.

At the Victorian library, crowned owls of iron lined the railings ringing the Yorkshire stone walls. Even before the town hall bell chimed its tenth, locals were gathering impatiently at the door. Teachers, museum staff, civil servants and the like shuffled around in the sun frowning and tapping their watches. When the doors were opened one minute late, they stomped slowly inside, tutting.

Asking for directions, I took the stone staircase to the second floor and arrived at the Local and Family History Library. A balcony, lined by terracotta archways of bookshelves organised into specialist categories, demarcated a huge rectangular opening. Beneath this opening, on the ground floor, rows of tables and chairs were set out with yet more hollows of bookshelves. An elderly woman was angrily trying to kick-start a computer.

I took on the role of the independent researcher, the DIY academic, of no institutional links, quite unfettered and unconnected. I could not help but feel like an imposter, as if this was not my place to visit. Surely such research libraries were the home of a roaming intelligentsia of which I was not part — writers, historians, sociology professors being guided by expert librarians to the appropriate materials. I was unsure of what I was even looking for.

I had chosen the Local and Family History Library to, I suppose, contextualise some of Norman's stories. Since arriving in Leeds, they had begun seeping back into my mind, damaged in places, and some only half-remembered but still lucid where existent. I remembered, for instance, Norman recounting his first wedding — the names of the guests, their dancing on the pews, the song they had sang. The story, however, had been cut short by Brenda returning from the shop. I also remember Mam telling me about Norman's punishment of Jim "Gnasher" Nash at the Hartlepool Lads' Club, but even she could not recall the names of every boy on the football team.

I figured that such stories were likely to become only more obscure in Norman and Mam's memories over time, let alone my own, and so now was the time to write them out with as much accuracy as possible. Of course, an entirely truthful retelling was practically unattainable, but still, I would do my best. I needed to know, firstly, what Hunslet was like before I was born. I needed to be able to map Norman's stories and calculate the mathematics of the land in each relevant year. I needed objective records to act as the groundwork for these subjective stories.

Perusing the bookshelves, I decided the playbills, parish records and electoral registers on display were of no obvious use. There were, however, specialist books containing photographs, newspaper archives, journals and maps. These were far more promising, so I took down a sample, then a fistful, and within minutes I was sauntering down the stairs to the reading desks with some fifteen books and documents balancing against my chin.

First, I laid out pocket atlases of 1940 and 1947, more recent maps being untraceable on the shelves. I ran my finger along the veins of roads south of the Aire and, deciding they may come in handy, photographed them. Surely not much would have changed topographically between the late Forties and the late Fifties — the starting point of most of Norman's stories. Anything I was uncertain about could be searched online, and if it was undiscoverable there it would have to be omitted or at least acknowledged in writing as a mystery. I snapped another photo of the southern regions of the 1947 map. The elderly woman at the computer scowled at me.

The archival newspapers were useful in small ways. They told me exactly what was being advertised in the early to mid-Fifties and how much things cost. I had hoped to find papers from 1960. That was, after all, when Micheál was alleged to have blown himself up. It seemed like an incident that would have been widely reported, something that could easily be discovered by a brief search on the internet. I was, however, yet to find any proof of the event, and when I asked a librarian if she could help me locate newspapers from that exact year, she told me that if they were not on the shelves, they were not available. Nevertheless, I photographed the articles in the papers at my disposal and moved onto the books.

The first was entitled *Nature & Industrialization*, a Seventies study that covered the blighting of the old Leeds pastoral. The photos were what interested me most. They enabled me to visualise the occupants of the maps, to interpret their thoughts and lives from the geography of their faces, to humanise the characterless paper.

One photograph captured a celebration on VE Day. A throng of women and children and a man playing the accordion gather around a fire in Victoria Square, their mouths forever open in song. Elsewhere, pictures of the Skelton Grange power station, its cooling towers looming above the Thwaite Mills. The Hunslet Mills on Goodman Street. The Leeds Steel Works in Hunslet, closed in the mid-Thirties. Dodos dead in the water.

On another page, a photograph of the very room I was sat in. The reference library, constructed in the style of a medieval great hall. I turned my eyes up and acknowledged the same coffered timber roof arching over like a wing. The cameraman, however many decades prior, had stood behind me, at a distance of perhaps five metres. I looked back to see a gaunt man walking away, staring at his phone. For all I knew, I could have, at that moment, been immortalised too.

Before adding *Nature & Industrialization* to the pile, I examined one last picture, this depicting a crowd of Edwardian children, around thirty-five of them, on the now decimated Copenhagen Street, staring straight at the cameraman. The reason for their gathering was not given. The writer asserted that the street had been named after one of Nelson's victories. Then he pointed out the cottages on one side of the road and the privies on the other. Many of the children's faces were a blur due to their movement. Their heads were a spectral haze. Those of the children who had stood still for the photo seemed to be marked by soot or slurry, their eyes ringed with darkness, their chins crumpled into their shoulders. Torn posters on the side of the closest cottage proclaimed *EMPIRE* and advertised *BATHS! BATHS!!*

Perhaps five paces to the rear of the children, two older boys, adolescents or even young men, stood together looking forward, too distant to be made out clearly. It would be fair to assume that these young men would have been born in Leeds at the same time as Old Massey, the greengrocer that Great-Grandad Jim had lost his hand defending. One of them may have been Old Massey himself. I turned to my notebook and quickly sketched what I imagined the greengrocer to look like, reconsidered, then put a line through the illustration and redesigned. Alongside, I jotted down the following:

> *Old Massey was the Hunslet greengrocer. A dour man of perhaps his mid-sixties, exceeding his life expectancy with little known arrogance for this fact. His first name cannot be remembered or recovered.*

I decided I would return to writing later and opened the next book before me. A ring-bound, surely self-published work called *Flameproof Diesel Locomotives*, documenting the history of the Hunslet Engine Company. The joint managing director, his name given, in his office, his sombre face hovering above the form he is signing. Blacksmiths at work on the forgings, bent and smudged, lit by flames. A worker welding up the exhaust-conditioner, the back of his waxed head glowing. Driving wheels being quartered. A gearbox shaft being miked by a stained phantom hand, disassociated from its body, belonging to anyone. *Many of the Hunslet workers are craftsmen of the old school — absorbed in the job for the job's sake and satisfied with nothing less than the best.*

"Is there any history on the people that worked there?" I asked the librarian, tapping at the page. "Any registers of their names, or studies on their life outside of work? Perhaps journals they kept?"

She shook her head and took the book from me to study it. "We have documents on the proprietors. I know a bit about them myself. In the Victorian and Edwardian period it was James Campbell and his sons. When Campbell died, the chairmanship passed to his eldest son, Alexander III. Edgar Alcock became the works manager in 1912 and passed the role onto his son, John Alcock, after the Second World War." She tapped the portrait of the sober-faced man in the office. "I'm sure we have documents about his children and grandchildren. I could find those if you like. Nothing on the workers. I don't think anything like that survived, if it existed in the first place."

I thanked her but told her there would be no need. I had, after all, been in the library for an hour and Mam and Norman would be home from Belle Isle before long. Leaving the muttering academics to continue their research into empirical events and historical figures of renown, I left the library and headed towards the bus stop on South Parade.

The town hall was not as large as I had remembered it being when I was younger. There seemed to be fewer steps than there should have been. It did not surmount the sky but sat back as if an old hermit in the trees, counting the clouds. I looked down. The pavement had at some point been raised and now covered the lower region of the stone steps which descended from the hall's entrance. I tried to think of whether those steps had always flown into paving slabs, or whether this alteration had taken place during my lifetime. I figured that the raised pavement must at least outdate me.

Still, I felt almost let down that I had grown and now saw the steps from the perspective of an adult. Everything seemed less expansive. Surely a bomb blast, no matter how defective, would have caused significant lasting damage in such a proximity. Yet, the Portland stone lions sat comfortably on their platforms. The steps still visible were undisturbed. Maybe they had simply been restored or the pavement had been raised above the shattered lower steps. Maybe the explosion had taken place entirely beneath my feet.

Then again, perhaps Micheál had not blown himself up there at all. Perhaps he had committed suicide somewhere quite random, less impressive, less metaphorical and poetic, not as worthy of a story. It seemed like something I should have been able to find out, but maybe I would never know, and maybe I didn't need to.

With Norman's mental state seemingly worsening by the day, it would now be a race against time to recover as many stories as possible. The tales he had told me throughout my childhood had been devoid of any real specificity, all too general and open to interpretation. As it stood, my retellings of these stories were no more than objective interpretations of a subjective experience of factual events. In order to do them justice, I needed to garner as much information as possible on the forgotten world they originated from. Yet, after visiting the library, I could not help but feel like I was fishing in a barren sea, as, all around, small lives, like waves, faded into obscurity.

Who am I to point at the ocean and expect it to explain? I do not command history. History commands me.

Scab

The one thing Tony Dunlop didn't want to be known as was a scab. He was a scab, however, and in the Durham Coalfield, his name was dirt. When the miners went on strike in '84, he had lasted no more than a month before caving in and returning to work. Dunlop blamed it on his sudden inability to put food on the table for his wife and daughter. He was keen to tell people that his wife had lost almost two stone in a month.

In the wider community, the blame fell on the weakness of his character, his lack of regard for his neighbours and, amongst some, a secret self-abasing worship of capitalism. Dunlop was a man who seemingly took pleasure and comfort in being under the control of his superiors. He would never stand his ground in a dispute and willingly went to work on any degrading task that was put to him. Rumours began to circle that, since the strike, he had been caught on two occasions masturbating in the pub toilet to a newspaper photograph of Margaret Thatcher. He was not a revolutionary. He was not a communist. He was a scab, and the local union wanted him held to account.

When Bowers and Mead requested Dennis Muir's help in kidnapping Dunlop, Dennis was unsure how to say no. It was less of a request than a command and an outright refusal would make Dennis a figure of equal suspicion. He had agreed, and so found himself that night behind the wheel of a Ford Transit, his head hugged by a balaclava, waiting for Bowers and Mead to bring the scab kicking and screaming from his house.

Bowers and Mead worked with Dennis at the Horden Colliery. Both had faces like half-cut moons, sullied by years of coal dust that could never be entirely cleaned. They sauntered around the village of Horden in jeans and winter jackets donated from abroad, their green enamel strike badges pinned proudly to their chests.

If a miner or his family had a problem, he went to see Bowers and Mead. The pair, ten years older than Dennis, had spent the best part of their working lives building robust relationships with the most influential members of the National Union of Mineworkers. They were certainly the beneficiaries of special privileges, although they never spoke of this to the lower men on strike. No more than a month prior to the kidnapping of Dunlop, Bowers and his wife had been on holiday to the German Democratic Republic. They had kept it quiet, but when it was realised that the Bowers house had been vacant for a week, suspicions as to their whereabouts had quickly surfaced. The holiday was believed to have been a gift from an East German union in alliance with the NUM.

This was no real scandal. It was known that NUM representatives accepted money from a French communist union to fund the strike, and that the East Germans and the Soviet Union organised the shipping of food parcels and clothing to British miners. Occasional gifts such as holidays were sure to be distributed to the miners seen as most deserving. No one could blame Bowers for accepting the offer. This was another reason Dennis had agreed to help kidnap Dunlop. He would have welcomed a holiday to East Berlin. Perhaps tickets to a BFC Dynamo match could be thrown in too, if there were any spare.

If possible, he would take Betty. They had been together for four years when the strike was declared. In that time, they had begun renting a council house in Peterlee, experienced the passing of Dennis's father and made a joint effort to help Norman become teetotal. Betty and Dennis had started taking him for jogs. It appealed to Norman's inner sportsman. On a Saturday, they would meet in the morning at the Hartlepool docks, then pace up the coast as far as Crimdon, or Blackhall Colliery when particularly energetic. Then they would sit on the beach, black with the dumping of mining waste, and eat before heading their respective ways home.

Norman got along with Dennis. On discovering the young skinhead was an eager socialist, he had lent him his copies of the three volumes of Das Kapital, The Making of the English Working Class *and* Homage to Catalonia. *After four months, Dennis returned them all, well thumbed, with pencil notes in the margins outlining the questions about the texts he wished to ask Norman the next time he saw him. They would spend evenings in Norman's kitchen, discussing whatever world affair was taking place at the time. The US invasion of Grenada. The election of Yuri Andropov. Betty painted them as they talked at the kitchen table, Norman reclining in his Umbro tracksuit, his fingers twisted in his greying hair, Dennis leaning forward in his Fred Perry polo shirt, like a boy before his headmaster. Vivid, rough, emotional colours. Magma and aqua.*

Suddenly, the rear of the Ford Transit was thrown open and Dunlop, unconscious and wearing only his boxers, was thrown into the back. Bowers and Mead clambered into the passenger seats. They carried the autumn chill in their weathered hands. Bowers nodded and Dennis drove.

They pushed on silently through the pit village, south of the bruised colliery and into the dark maze of terraced houses. With no jobs to go to in the morning, the folk could have very well stayed up all night, but it was a night like any other. Men and their wives turned in at their regular times, hoping to maintain some semblance of normality; some still in their boots, some with their keys unconsciously in their hands as if they must leave the house early in the morning. A curtain rustled as a restless child was laid to sleep. A dog took heed and scarpered up a ginnel. A starved man in pants and T-shirt stood at his doorstep smoking, looking out to the street with nothing to see but blackness, and abstract shapes in blackness, before retiring inside.

Dennis pulled up at the curb on Eighth Street, outside the Bowers' house, a one-up one-down, end-of-the-road pitman's cottage where the crucifix atop the roof of St Mary's church lingered watchfully behind the chimney. The three of them carried Dunlop out into the road and through the front door.

The room was furnished with yellowing patterned wallpaper. Filthy dishcloths hung over the fireplace. Tins of beans and a loaf of Mother's Pride sat beside the stove, accompanied by a small sporting trophy that would seemingly fit nowhere else. Bowers' wife, hard-faced and permanently occupied with thought, was slumped in an armchair watching the news. On the entrance of the men, she glanced up wordlessly, then pulled her cardigan around her, collected her ashtray from the floor and went upstairs.

When Dunlop finally stirred, he found himself bound by rope to a wooden chair. Three men were scattered before him wolfing down bowls of dry Weetabix. Now away from the eyes of potential snitches, all had removed their balaclavas. Mead noticed the scab's awakening, and launched his spoon at Dunlop's head.

"Here we bloody go. Some movement", he called.

"About time", Bowers grunted. "We almost thought we'd killed yer."

"What the bloody fuck's going on?" Dunlop roared, squirming against the rope, adjusting his eyes to the light. "Gary! John! Fucking Dennis! Where am I? What yer playing at?"

"Eh, eh, steady on now, Tony." Bowers crouched, grinning, to hold the chair still. "Yer better not break that chair or yer'll be in even deeper shit than y'are already."

"Let me fucking go!"

Bowers straightened up and struck Dunlop across the face. The crack of a horsewhip. Dunlop quietened and spat blood.

"Now, I warned yer, Tony", Bowers pointed. "You stay fucking still and don't make this harder than it has to be. Yer going nowhere until we're done with yer, yer hear? Shut up and behave like a man."

Dunlop lowered his head and did not reply.

"There's been word", said Mead, "that yer've been causing trouble in't camp. Slandering the president to anyone what'll listen. Why, you were in *pub t'other day saying Scargyll will bring the miners nowt but misfortune, were you not? What we wanna know, Tony, is what you think you stand to gain from it."*

"The way we see it", said Bowers, "is that yer not just a scab anymore. Yer've gone further than that. We think yer a Tory."

"Am no bloody Tory", Dunlop protested. "I've voted Labour all me life! I've been a union member since '61."

"We think yer a Thatcherite", Bowers continued slowly, taking pleasure in antagonising the man. Like a farmer putting a pig to rest, he knelt beside him, his glassy eyes rolling up at Dunlop's face. "In't that right? Yer a dirty scab fucking traitor, and yer lucky blokes an't strung yer up from lamp post."

"Yer fucking loonies, the lot of yus!" Dunlop shouted. He began wrestling against the ropes once again and Mead stepped in to deliver a blow which sent the scab crashing down onto his back.

"Keep it bloody quiet down there!" Bowers' wife shouted from the room upstairs. "Am trying to sleep!"

The men waited in silence, then Dunlop spoke. "What d'yer want from me?"

"We want to mek sure yer've learnt yer lesson", said Mead, clutching Dunlop's throat, pressing it into the ground. "We want to mek sure yer don't carry on with yer lies about the president, about the union, about decent folk like us. What d'yer say?" He let go of the scab's throat.

Wheezing, Dunlop managed, "I won't say owt. I'll keep meself to meself."

Mead glanced at Bowers. His eyes gave nothing away.

"We have to be certain", Bowers muttered. He was already rolling a cigarette. Once lit, he sat down on the floor beside Dunlop's head and exhaled rolling crests of smoke from his nose. He held the burning end of the cigarette up, glanced at it momentarily and looked away.

"Give me his wrist."

Dunlop screamed for help. Again, he writhed. Mead knelt into his chest and pulled the scab's arm out from under the rope. Enlisting Dennis's help, the pair of them managed to restrain Dunlop and position his arm on the floor with the veins facing upwards. Bowers twisted the cigarette onto the most prominent vein.

The shriek was harrowing. It sounded inhuman. It was the alien screech of a fox echoing through the abysses of the woodland at night. Dennis instinctively went to let go of the man's arm, but Mead pressed his palm down on Dennis's knuckles.

Bowers pushed the cigarette into another vein, this time for longer, and the same shriek echoed about the dismal front room, seeping into the walls, storing itself there for years to come. When Bowers finally climbed to his feet, Dennis jumped back. He sank into the armchair and turned his eyes from the scab.

"Yareet, Dennis?" Mead laughed. "Yer look haunted, pal."

"Aye, no. I'm fine", Dennis insisted and stood up to pace the room.

"We're not done yet", Bowers mumbled, disappearing into the kitchen. When he returned, he held a blunt vegetable knife. Flipping it, he offered the handle to Dennis. "Carve an S into his leg."

"What?"

"An S. For scab." Bowers thrust the handle. "Tek it."

Shaking, Dennis took the blade as the men positioned Dunlop's calf. He stood reluctantly, his palms dampening, and looked down at the helpless scab. Dennis tried to think of Dunlop's wife and daughter, but he didn't know them, so it was futile. Instead, he thought of Norman. Would Norman be proud of him? He wouldn't. Norman had already decried the use of senseless violence. Achieving socialism, he had said, was a matter of inventive solidarity, of a resilient body of labourers able to outwit their rivals in debate and democratically appeal to the minds of their fellow workers. Physical action was, of course, unavoidable at times, but should be carried out with responsibility and humanity, to avoid the chaos of hollow anarchy. Striking was necessary. Barbarism was not.

Dennis thought of his own father. His own father would be proud of him. His own father would have murdered the scab and, with the blood still running down his arms, gone straight to the fridge to crack open a beer. But his own father was dead and there was no sense in impressing a corpse.

Years earlier, Dennis would have set about the task without thought. That was all it was, after all — a task. It was like taking apart a car that had run its course. If anything, Betty had domesticated him and made him soft. He felt the doughy centre of his stomach and was disgusted. He hadn't even been in a scrap for the fun of it in years. He'd broken a few policemen's noses at the picket line but that was an action with political purpose, and also, who hadn't? This was quite different. This was purposeless. It was sadism.

Bowers was losing patience. He clapped his hands and barked indecipherably. Dennis could hear only the vibrations of the room. They were fast and dizzying, heightened in volume. It was as if he was listening to the world underwater. Light, in orbs, journeyed up to the ceiling. Kneeling, Dennis pressed the blade home.

June 2017 (IV)

That night I dreamt of violence.

He had been warned of the Gytrash before encountering it but, more fool him, had not believed in its reality, let alone its power. Albion — industrialist, murderer, father of countless urchins in all corners of the country. He lived on Norman's tongue. His voice was not his own, but Norman's attempt at the accent of a Victorian London dandy. He was born of a moment when, out walking in the Moors, we had stopped to rest at the side of the footpath. Norman, pulling his guernsey up to his mouth as if to hide the tale from the moorland itself, had spoken Albion into being.

Albion, travelling to the steelworks between Middlesbrough and Redcar, had halted for the night at the Bull's Head Inn just south of the Moors. As the weather was fine and the days were long, Albion had decided that in the morning he would walk the rest of the way through the valleys on foot, a trek that would surely take him til dusk.

"Beware the Gytrash", the innkeeper had told him, face ruddy as blood, his piggish eyes swimming in a knowing terror. "The spectre haunts the dales round these parts. Particularly in the evenings, the moorland's not safe. There's folk what've seen it, and some that won't even talk about what they've seen. It tempts the unwary traveller to follow it, off the path, into the woodland. It does not appear out of the ordinary when tha see it. It disguises itself, so at first it appears a quite normal beast. A black dog. A horse. It has even adopted the form of a mule. But believe tha me, once tha alone with it, it has the eyes of Hades, and teeth what could rip tha

chest open. Foolish men have gone missing up there. If tha's to walk, tha's best not to go alone."

Albion had laughed off the warning. The innkeeper was drunk and possibly insane. No sane man could believe in spirits and demons. Albion was an empiricist and man of science. There was more danger in the madman's inn than there was in the uplands. By morning, the innkeeper's raving had been forgotten.

The dog, like a slip of darkness, had appeared in the pastureland at dusk. It had been nowhere, and then it was. From a distance, Albion watched it, trying to decipher its breed. It was more muscular than a greyhound but of a similar size. An oversized Labrador, perhaps. A wolf. It was all but none. It was bleeding from the mouth.

Albion waited as the dog slowly approached. It did not bark. It moved as silently as time. When it finally reached him, it sat on its haunches and rested its bloody jaws on Albion's foot. Albion knelt to stroke it. The dog panted and yielded. What nonsense the innkeeper had professed. That was the problem with northern country people. Their lives were a patchwork of irrational old wives' tales. They would never belong to a Britain with its eyes on the future.

There was something in the old dog's eyes. More blood? No, but it was as slick as blood. The mutt seemed to contain a certain depth there. A watery, attractive sheen, more blue than red, but emerald green in places also, like little globes between its sockets. Yes, there were whole worlds there, mesmerising in their lustrousness, but as Albion went to examine them, the dog moved away. It slowly descended from the path and, panting heavily, returned to the pasture.

Albion, now, was compelled to follow it, for Middlesbrough was near and there was time yet for a small detour. So he took off after it, but as he strolled promptly over, the dog quickened its pace in the direction of the woodland. "Boy!" Albion called. "Come here, boy." The dog did not. It began to sprint. Albion chased it, irate at its disobedience. He hunted the dog down to the edge of the woodlands, and as he reached the trees he slipped between them. In the thick of ashes, it was dark and the pasture behind him was no longer visible. The dog had vanished, and Albion was alone. He cursed and turned back, but then; there it was.

In the eyes of the Gytrash, Albion saw no longer his little globes. He saw his countless urchin children. He saw those he had slain. He saw in the Gytrash the valley of the inferno. Albion had been, and then was not. He had vanished out of existence and logic. He had been a foolish man.

I had come, over time, to disbelieve this story, for how could Norman have known Albion's fate, without witnessing it (generations prior to his birth) or without being the Gytrash himself? I had been naïve in believing him, and even more so in disbelieving him. In my dream, I fantasised. I imagined the Gytrash was my own. I would be much like the men that keep hyenas in Nigeria. I imagined that I was walking the Gytrash on a leash, down city streets, setting it off on plump toffs in Belgrave Square Garden, watched by the statue of Christopher Columbus and the resplendent white stuccoed houses. I imagined walking it to Stamford Bridge and unleashing it over the railway bridge to chomp on Chelsea wide boys in blue Yokohama Tyres shirts. I imagined the stomping line of stoic policemen and the media crew, their cameras held like bazookas on their shoulders, blissfully unaware, as I walked my dog through Westminster. "I'm just showing my dog the House of Lords", I would say. And in my dream, I could hear all the chaos of the world, condensed into an orchestra of sick anxiety, the screeching of cars, the chattering of bone, the roll of boots. I could smell the burning. The rancid, sickly burning. The bonfire. The pressure point. The parched earth rising for sustenance. Yes, I could hear the hungry, angry earth.

I stirred to the smell of smoke. To the sight of smoke. It hovered at the door, having accidentally found me asleep, and being unsure of whether to wake me. Any number of possibilities ran through my head. The oven had been left on. A forgotten candle had been abandoned, unattended, beside a curtain. Brenda was snoring in the bedroom upstairs, a cigarette still lit between her fingers, alive again. Impossible.

I raced to the hallway to find Mam already coming down the stairs, wide eyed, tucking her dressing gown around her. The smoke was coming from the back garden. There was a fire, discernible in the blackness, a silhouette moving about it.

As we rushed outside, we found Norman in his pyjamas stoking the flames with kindling composed of miscellaneous items. The fumes seemed not to irritate him, for his eyes were focused unflinchingly on the task at hand, yet huge plumes of toxins rose to escape and discomfort the sky. Norman's eyes seemed to be holding back tears. He had somehow cut the palm of his hand. Silently, he took up a jewellery box from the pile and emptied it into the fire before throwing the cheap wooden object after its contents.

Unlike his previous night-time divergence, this time the old man was wholly awake. He had consciously selected what he planned to destroy. Despite the influence of the bottle of rum at his feet, he moved in a way that was alert and deliberate, as if a man carrying out his religious and moral duty.

Casting my eyes across the pile, I found a host of car-boot pottery and figurines, an ashtray, several trashy paperbacks, a knock-off Louis Vuitton handbag and bundles of large tasteless dresses, their dank floral patterns arguing with the flowers that wilted in the garden. Norman was burning what was left of Brenda's belongings.

"Don't come near me", he muttered. "This needs to be done."

"Dad, you're drunk", Mam started.

"Aye, but I'd be too scared to do this sober." He lifted a clump of dresses above him and sacrificed them to the blaze. The wood he had gathered to start the fire crackled and split off on the garden tiles, forcing us to step back from the sparks.

I went to fetch water on Mam's instruction and filled a bucket of it at the kitchen tap. I could hear her talking to Norman about the charity shop, suggesting the bin or the refuse centre. As he cast Brenda's handbag to the fire, she took his wrist and pulled him inside.

Extinguishing the flames alone, I found I needed three trips to refill the bucket before the water could finally overpower the fire. By this time, a neighbour whose name I could never remember had poked her head out of her bedroom window, her eye mask stamped to her forehead, squinting down at me.

"It's three in bloody morning", she called. "What's all this?"

"Don't worry", I said, pouring out the last of the water. "It'll be out soon. Sorry for waking yer."

"Your Norman needs help, love. Everyone round here thinks it. Yer can't sort that out on yer own. The way he's acting now — it must be years and years of horrible stuff that's built up in his head. He never chats about it does he?"

I didn't reply but began to search for scraps of debris still lit.

"Yer oughta get him to a therapist or something", the woman continued. "It's gonna come to a nasty end if yer don't. Anyway, don't let him start a bloody fire at 3am again or I'm calling police. Some of us have work in't morning."

When I looked up, the woman had disappeared back inside, slamming the window behind her.

Cursing her under my breath, I stamped out the remaining embers.

Arthur, Aging

"I never liked that Scargyll fella", Brenda said as she plucked a scrap of pork pie from her teeth. "Marxism's a murderer's ideology. Look what happened with Stalin and the Soviet Union."

She was stretched back on her sickly floral armchair, amongst the vanilla and violet of the living room. Armies of pottery and figurines lined the fireplace, the cupboards and the TV counter — barrow boys, rosy-cheeked maidens and shy tabby cats. Dennis was looking particularly queasily at a piggy bank, the pot swine sporting a top hat and monocle with a stately sneer. He felt compelled to smash the lot.

When he and Betty had arrived at Norman's new house in Hunslet, Brenda had been marching around the back garden in a blue shoulder-padded skirt suit, interrogating the flowers. Her hair was up in a bouffant, and as she had stood on her tip toes to peer over the fence, she sneered at the neighbouring gardens she found. Now, she sat attacking a plate of pork pies, grapes and toast. She gleefully pressed her sticky thumb to the crumbs and sucked them at her leisure. Norman and Betty had driven to the hardware shop to collect a new shelving unit, leaving Dennis to help Brenda unpack the boxes that lined the wall. Brenda, herself, had not touched a box but had opted for lunch and looked set to park a Marlboro between her teeth to celebrate.

How had Norman ended up marrying the creature? The woman was a glaring Tory. They must have never had a political discussion of any kind. Either that or Norman had become a desperate old dog and had settled, as could have been foreseen, with the first woman that would devote herself to him and provide him with sex.

The pair had met at a National Association of Lads' Clubs party. It had been held in the Hunslet Lads' Club itself, celebrating fifty years of care for the youth of South Leeds. Norman had not been to Hunslet since his parents had passed, and on returning was taken aback by how the place had changed. The Hunslet Grange flats had been flattened, crushed into an open land of starving grass. The printing works and the Tetley's brewery remained in business, but derelict factories clumped together on street corners, swaying in the wind, soon to be demolished. Committee men in pinstripe suits stood at Balm Road and Beza Road planning industrial redevelopment, tutting at their clipboards. A Morrisons had been erected. Conservationists raged against the likely decimation of the Hunslet Mill. Itinerants' camps had popped up on waste grounds, alongside mountains of tyres which littered the grass beside the M1. Anyone who had ever known anything about the McLoughlins had seemingly died, moved away or simply forgotten.

The Lads' Club itself had moved to a new road. The interior of the old building was a bomb site, scarred by shrapnel, unsafe to walk within. CHRIS, SHAZ, JANET and DES had left their names in spray paint on the wall that followed the staircase inside. Norman visited briefly, accompanied by a young representative of the new club, but did not stay for long as he found there was no nostalgia to be had in the unrecognisable space.

At the party, Norman had been the guest of honour, and had been gifted a semicentennial necktie emblazoned with the blond Hunslet lion. He had taken pride in the esteem his old club bestowed on him and took charge of the evening's bingo. "Goodness me — number three! Knock at the door — number four! Man alive — it's number five!"

The prize — two tickets to Blackpool — had been won by a brash, stubby woman in a spaghetti-strap dress who introduced herself as: "Brenda, thank you very much. Practically a celebrity round here. And who would you be?"

Her bluntness sparked Norman's interest and he found himself buying her a pint of bitter in a nearby pub after the party. Brenda knew the Lads'

Club staff well enough. She kept her nose in everyone's business and never missed a party offering free alcohol, even when not invited. She lived a ten-minute walk away, in a rented council house, on her own since her vagabond ex-boyfriend had scarpered.

"Don't yer think it's lonely living on yer own?" she asked him.

"Why, it's areet", Norman had replied. "I've plenty of friends and neighbours what pop in, and me daughter and her boyfriend as well. Besides, a lass like you must be reet popular with the blokes round here. I can't imagine yer'll live alone long if yer don't want to. Yer must be beating off fellas with a stick."

Brenda snorted. "Sadly, Norman, yer wrong."

"Ay!" he protested. "I've only ever been wrong once in me life."

"What happened?"

"It was this one time, I thought I'd made a mistake — but I hadn't." He grinned away like a Cheshire cat.

Brenda sprayed bitter from her mouth, dampening Norman's shirt. "Eee, yer cheeky sod", and then she asked suddenly: "Why don't yer come back to mine?"

Six months later, having gone on the Blackpool trip together and seemingly succumbed to its romantic power, they had decided to get engaged and move into a house of their own. Norman was to sell up in Hartlepool and buy a new place in Hunslet, where he had been guaranteed the job as the new director of the Lads' Club. When offered the role he had almost ripped the retiring director's hand off. It was his homecoming tour. He was not sad to be leaving Hartlepool. Whilst most folk would be glad to replace the city with the sea, Norman was impatient to divorce himself from it and reinstate himself in Leeds as a new man, a successful man, and a man who had withstood and conquered his past.

Betty was happy for him. Norman could not live without a woman, it seemed, and at least he now would have someone to keep him away from the bottle. She was, however, cautious of Brenda. Despite her obvious crudeness, there was also an icy air of indifference about the woman. She would deprecate those in her company without — apparently — realising she was doing it, and without an ounce of remorse. When Betty had questioned her, for instance, on calling Norman's postman a "hunchback" within earshot of the mail van, Brenda had merely smirked and walked away.

The woman had also made a habit of spending Norman's money. It ran through her fingers like sand. In the pub, she would have him buy her three gin and tonics in the time it took him to finish a half pint of lemonade. In fact, whenever Betty saw Brenda, she seemed to be coming home from a shopping trip, swinging bags stuffed with blazers, pleated trousers and blouses. Norman didn't seem to mind. He almost encouraged it. Whether he took pleasure in spending half his earnings on Brenda or whether he was merely desperate to keep her happy was uncertain. Betty bit her lip, against her better judgement.

By this time, she and Dennis were set to leave Peterlee. Thatcher had won, the miners had returned to work and Horden Colliery was due to fall. The coalfields had frozen over, and the community had crawled back in on itself, to hibernate and, but for all its small dreams, to never re-emerge. Betty and Dennis were to relocate to Nottingham, where Betty would begin her teacher training, and Dennis would enrol in a vocational course in mechanical engineering. They had moved to a rented flat just outside the city centre two weeks prior to Norman's return to Leeds.

"Yer can't smear Marxism with corruption in the Soviet Union", Dennis said calmly, cutting a box open with his keys. "This country were at its best under the socialism that came about after the war. Yer can't deny that — and yer can't deny that the right has caused the deaths of far more than the left either."

"Was that socialism?" Brenda chuckled. "I thought socialism were meant to make life better for all. I were poor in the Fifties. Me father were a miner. He were poor in the Fifties. Yer socialism didn't do much for us."

"He were a damn sight better off than the miners now", Dennis snapped. "*What's left of 'em. I don't see how yer can despise the NUM when yer the daughter of a miner.*"

"*My father were a bastard*", Brenda smirked. "*Wouldn't put the bottle down. Hit me mother all the time. Came home every evening and made everything dirty. Him and his pals were all the same. Not an ounce of ambition between 'em. I'm glad he's dead.*"

Dennis scowled, but for Betty's sake did not rise to retaliate. He began unpacking the box on the floor and was pleased to find the socialist texts Norman had lent him when he had first met Betty. Slyly, he laid them face up on the floor in direct view of Brenda. Das Kapital. The Making of the English Working Class. Homage to Catalonia. *She scoffed. "I didn't know Norman had been shopping for kindling. Be a dear now, Dennis, and put those by the fireplace for later.*"

"*Be better off throwing yer wigs on the flames*", Dennis mumbled.

"*What's that?*"

"*Nowt.*"

An eleven-year-old Manchester terrier wandered into the room. Norman had adopted the rescue dog to keep him company when Betty had moved to Peterlee. He had named it Arthur, after Scargyll, and had kept him beside him constantly when the canine was young and tireless. He had jogged with Arthur down the coast on weekday evenings and, on returning to Hartlepool, sat with him in the working men's club until close. The old dog was reluctant to move as much as he used to.

Arthur sat on his hind legs, panting, watching. Brenda beckoned him, retrieving a biscuit from her pocket, shaking it in the air. The dog edged towards her, treading over the books and almost slipping. He jutted his head up to the biscuit as Brenda pulled it away and chuckled. She repeated the same action several times before launching the biscuit at the door. Arthur turned to retrieve it, but as he did, Brenda reached out and yanked the dog back by his fur. He howled and crumpled.

"*Arthur*", she cooed. "*Yer daft old rat.*"

"What yer doing?" Dennis cracked. "Don't grab him by his fur. That'll hurt him."

"Oh, he's fine", Brenda grinned. "It's just a game we play. In't it, rat?" She let go of the dog who, once more, went for the biscuit and was wrenched back by his fur, between the woman's throddy legs. Arthur, howling again, fell on his side.

"Are yer fucking mad?" Dennis blurted. "Yer hurting him!" He leapt to his feet and stood defiantly over her, then grabbed the biscuit from the floor and fed it to the dog.

"Look at you", Brenda smirked, lighting another cigarette. She lay back in her chair and gazed at Dennis with relaxed amusement. "Getting all uptight? Some dogs like a bit of rough handling. Some dogs live for it. They wouldn't know what to do if they suddenly went without it."

Dennis decided not to continue the conversation. He took Arthur into the hallway then went outside to wait for Betty and Norman to return.

June 2017 (V)

A man is an ocean. A soundless depth of mysteries and impossibilities. A threatening terrain. A natural place.

The North Sea is deep. There are lots of fishes and some fishes have lots of shiny scales. The further in you go, there are ugly fishes too, that wallow under dark reefs and poke their teeth out to feed on the smaller, weaker fishes, and no one knows as much about the ugly fishes because no one wants to go near them. In the Atlantic Ocean, there are also fishes we don't know about because we can't swim deep enough to discover them. Submarines are too expensive for normal people, and it would be dangerous to venture that deep anyway. The North Sea is deep. There are lots of fishes and the human cannot count them all.

I finished my show-and-tell presentation. My primary school peers clapped me.

I sat up as I heard the sound on the staircase. There was a thumping, like a man knocking on the door to an empty room. The thumping stopped.

By the time the ambulance had arrived, we had sat Norman up. He looked annoyed at us, and dazed. "Why have you woken me up?" he asked.

There was a lot of blood. It was coming from his head. Mam explained to the paramedics that he'd fallen. He'd fallen down the stairs and struck his head on the glass table by the door. There was a lot of glass. There was glass everywhere. The paramedics had to tread on the glass to lift him. It sounded like they were treading on pebbles.

We went with them in the ambulance. The neon light threw

itself on our faces, lighting us up, exposing us as we really were. No one had slept. We were dirty and our eyes were red, and the lights were red. The paramedics hadn't slept in days. They rested perhaps on the hospital floor. They had mustered up an out-of-body energy. They moved in colourful blurs around us.

Norman was drunk. He slurred as they pressed the luminous gauze to his head. He wouldn't answer their questions. He did not know who they were. None of us knew who one another were. There was bone. There was a fracture.

There are great fractures in the sea. They're called submarine canyons. They're steep valleys in the seabed that are formed by mass wasting or by submarine landslides.

At the emergency ward, people materialised from the door in scary aquamarine uniforms. I can only remember their aquamarine uniforms. They talked in fast, hospital language. I couldn't understand them. They wheeled Norman on a stretcher.

Inside, the light was blinding. I walked with my eyes closed. In darkness, phosphenes scurried away to hide themselves. The ward was crowded. A green-skinned woman melted into the wall. Children in slings were slumped in seats, nursed by drained mothers. An old man in a leg cast, his foot raised above him, was leaning back against a bed of air, mid-fall. All manner of boils and rashes rushed past. A huge man's face had swollen to the size of a pufferfish, his cheeks and lips rubbery and bright, ready to erupt. Someone attempting to smoke was carried out kicking. All was collapsing.

You cannot talk underwater.

The surf is louder at night for a very simple reason.

I sat waiting. I was alone. Mam had gone in with Norman.

The roar of the world became white noise. Simple noise. The noise was neither here nor there.

The doctors performed their dance. One, fingers entwined, palms rising and falling. The nurse skirted round the bed, her bun coming loose, her hair flowing. The aquamarine waved in and out. Some words were muttered. Hard-to-hear words, filtered by liquid.

The dance stopped. The note rang. Norman had passed from one impossible place to the next. In the operating room, heads bobbed like buoys.

There once was a man that lost his grandad
*   and couldn't find him!*
He wasn't in his armchair. He wasn't in his bedroom or behind the
curtains. We searched high and low, but he seemed to have vanished. How
odd. He wasn't even in history. Silly Grandad. Where had he got to?

He had returned to the sea.
                    He had become a light bulb that will not turn on.
        An unfinished story.
                            Countless more lost.

                                            A fiction.
A component of a dot.
                    A millisecond.

                                        A song.

JULY

Inheritance

There once was a boy who lost his father

and couldn't find him!

He woke up one morning and the man had gone. His father, on any other day, would have been collecting the newspaper — *collecting the* WARRINGTON BOMB ATTACKS, *the* UNEMPLOYMENT REACHES THREE MILLION *from the doormat — but, without caring to leave a note, he had vanished into twilight.*

It reminded the boy of the time his father had pulled a coin out from behind his ear. The boy had not remembered placing the coin there. It had been magic. His father was a magician. He had disappeared in a puff of smoke.

The boy's mother had no idea where the man had gone either. He had mentioned no plans that would occupy him that day. "Don't worry, Fred", the mother had said. "He'll be out looking for work." That's what she said — she would set the sorry bugger straight when he walked back through the door — but her face was a house on fire, and the boy didn't believe her.

By the time evening had laid down its hand, there was still no sign of the misplaced man, and the mother went to ask the neighbour if she had seen him. The boy listened for a while by the back garden fence (No, I haven't seen him. No, I have not.); then, deciding to take matters into his own hands, he stuffed his feet in his trainers and slipped out the front door.

His father was not in his mother's Ford Fiesta. On close inspection, neither was his trademark denim jacket — and that usually hung from the passenger seat like a hood. His father was not in any of the neighbour ladies' cars, like he had been the week before, nor was he hiding underneath them.

The boy marched to the end of the road and decided to head east onto Southchurch Drive, where the parade of shops made for numerous hiding places. Perhaps his father was playing hide and seek with him and his mother had been in on it all along. Clever! If so, his father had made a real effort to not be found. Last time they had played, his father had stood behind the front room curtain and his big, red boots had given him away instantly. The man must have been working on his hiding techniques — working too *hard. He must have been planning this for quite some time.*

The boy poked his nose into the chip shop. Inside, Take That blared on the radio and the brawny chip lady rested her arms on the counter.

"Have you seen my dad?" the boy asked, confidently, as if he might be hiding beneath the haddock.

The chip lady seemed bemused and even glanced over her shoulder. When she realised who the boy was, she adjusted her paper hat and scratched her head. "No, an't seen him. Try the bookies."

The boy went down, past the pound shop and the Boots, towards the Betfred, which was closing for the night. Men in shell suits shuffled out gruffly, discussing Canaska Star's probability of winning the Epsom Derby and England's likeliness of toppling Poland in the World Cup qualifiers.

"Have you seen my dad?" the boy asked the man behind the counter.

The bookie lay down his newspaper. THE ECONOMIC RECOVERY CONTINUES. *"No, an't seen him. Try the Mare and tell him that he owes us a fiver."*

The boy huffed and turned back the way he had come, up Southchurch Drive, with his small fists clenched. When he got to the Grey Mare on Farnborough Road, the landlady was bickering with a dazed student barman at the mock-Tudor entrance.

"Have you seen my dad?" the boy asked the landlady.

"No, an't seen him. Have you seen Dennis?" She turned to the barman. "That is, if you can see anything at all."

The student had an earthy, herbal smell about him. He tugged on his paisley bucket hat. He considered for a moment, then looked over at the empty car park. "No, I can't see him."

The landlady scowled. She threw a parting glance. "Try yer house." Before the boy could explain that he had just come from his house, the landlady had dragged the student inside.

The boy groaned and turned on his heels once more. He continued down the street until he came to the roundabout, where the Clifton Lane A-road carried travellers from the margin of Leicestershire to Nottingham. The cars trundled on relentlessly, their drivers desperately intent on capturing the last glints of sun in their multitudinous destinations. They encircled the roundabout and broke apart, like game birds fleeing a gunman. All the people, not a recognisable face among them.

I could not find him. There was only England. The man who brought home the benefit money. The man boys sang for at football matches. The man whose hard hand hovers in waiting above the rising heads of his disgruntled children.

Every evening I took the bin out, mumbled at the weather and wrapped my dressing gown around me, scowling at the news in my father's armchair.

Every evening, fatherless boys run to England, who waits, arms open, at the end of the street.

July 2017 (I)

At Salter and Son Funeral Directors, Mr Salter sat (as if he had not moved since the last time we visited) chameleon-like, blending into the faded botanical wallpaper behind him. He seemed to not remember us. Perhaps a little over a month was a long time in the bustling business of mourning, or perhaps Mr Salter was well accustomed to forgetting everything he had seen. Either way, his coin eyes glazed over as he recited his script.

"You can see him if you like."

The morning after Norman passed, Mam folded his shirt and left it on his bed, so he would know what to wear when he woke up. She emptied a hidden vodka bottle into the sink so he could drink no longer and, having turned on the sports channel for him, went back upstairs to sleep some more.

I did not write for a few days. Mam and I did little but sit in the front room. We talked. We stared down silence for a while. She looked unmoored on those days, cast adrift. The house felt emptier. It was a person lighter, and the summer sun lit up the shy corners of rooms, confirming for us that Norman was not, in fact, playing a game and simply hiding out of sight. At night, Mam placed his shirt back in his drawers.

There was a sudden amplitude of space. It was a house a person could run through, dragging a whole life behind them, to race out the other end, never to be seen again. What space! When neighbours visited, they were unsure of what to do with it. Even standing shoulder to shoulder they could not fill it. It was an unnatural space. I found myself shivering looking in at rooms that had rarely been occupied anyway. Turning on the light switch, I was an intruder. A thief caught in the act, I span around to explain myself to the vacant hallway behind me. We slept little, Mam and I.

One afternoon, Sherry called up to enquire about the reading of Brenda's will and said, "Oh," when Mam told her the news. "Oh." She paused momentarily. "This is quite a shock. I'll call you back later."

The obituary went out. At any given time of day, a cloud of grey faces amassed at the windows, trying to see what was happening inside. They left freesias, cerise gerberas and roses, spoke without saying much, piled up platitudes, recycled words of comfort and half-remembered quotations long stripped of their meaning by over-usage. A woman offered a prayer but forgot how to end it. One morning, I woke to see the neighbour who had called to me when I was stamping out the fire. Her nose was pressed to the glass of the front room window. I stood in my boxers with my hands on my hips, waiting, expectantly, for her to say something. Noticing me, she decided some things did not need to be said.

Norman too was to be cremated at Cottingley Hall. Even in death, he was chasing after Brenda, into the same chamber, head first with his eyes closed. "So romantic", a neighbour had said. "Will you scatter them together?"

Fat chance. I had been tempted to flush Brenda's ashes down the toilet or, better yet, dump them down a mine shaft if I could find one uncovered. There would be no one to stop me now that Norman had gone. No one alive wanted her ashes, not even Sherry. I would be providing an invaluable service by getting rid of the bastard stuff.

At that moment, the door to the funeral directors sprang open. Sherry scurried in unannounced with a handkerchief conveniently placed to her eyes. They were red. She must have been rubbing them violently in the car to make it look as if she had been crying. Her snakeskin boots clopped noisily on the floor. She sounded like a tap dancer as she pattered to the desk. Wayne too marched in wearing a tight black T-shirt stamped with a white Union Jack and the words *FREEDOM AIN'T FREE — I PAID FOR IT*. His ruddy face, like a concrete block, did not move as he walked. He held himself as if the funeral directors were a Taliban camp, as if at any moment he would duck and roll at the desk.

"Betty", Sherry wailed. "We came as soon as we could. I can't believe Dad's gone." She threw herself on a chair, her face turned to the ceiling — God.

"Fucking hell", I muttered.

"Sherry", Mam scowled. "We weren't expecting you. How did you know we were here?"

"A bird in the shop told us", Wayne replied bluntly. "You could've fackin' told us. We was looking all over."

"You could've told us you were coming", I shot.

Wayne's mammoth hand gripped my shoulder in artificial support, tightening slightly.

"What's being settled here?" Sherry pressed. "The funeral? When will it be? Will it be soon?"

"We've arranged it for the end of next week", Mam said.

"Oh." Sherry looked glum. "It couldn't be sooner?"

"No", I snapped. "It couldn't."

"I suppose it'll give us time to clear out the house."

Mam gripped the edge of Salter's desk, her teeth gritted. "We're not clearing out the house yet."

"Why not?" Wayne demanded. "It'll need clearing eventually. Might as well start now."

"We're only here for a short time", Sherry said. "We'll stay in the Hampton again. We'll help you go through the lot, Betty. From the top to the bottom. No stone unturned. We wouldn't want you to clear the house on your own."

"Fred's here."

I nodded. "I'm here", I said.

"Isn't it time you went back to Nottingham?" Wayne sneered. "That newspaper might collapse without you. Who else is gonna write about obstructions on the M1?"

"I *do* have a job, Wayne", I lied, "you're right. I suppose three of us here *do* have jobs to get back to."

"Right! Enough", Mam barked. "If you two want to take pieces out of each other you can do that in your own time. We're here to organise my dad's cremation. Nothing else! Christ, are you children?"

Wayne withdrew his hand from my shoulder. He stood awkwardly with his arms behind his back, avoiding eye contact. I apologised and focused my sight on the wallpaper. Sherry shifted in her seat. She slipped away her handkerchief.

Mr Salter coughed. "You can see him if you like."

At Norman's, we came across a Hunslet Lads' Club fabric badge. It was black, adorned with a flaxen lion; a white rose, bulbous as an eye wide open, sat within a golden geometric border. I decided I would like to wear it, as Norman had worn it, to carry him on my chest like an appendage. Mam sewed the patch onto my denim jacket, insisting I catch up on sleep on the sofa.

As she sat studiously at the sewing machine in the kitchen, a ghost of steam escaped the kettle in a heaving sigh. It clung to the window, one sticky finger at a time, prodding the wasps and mosquitoes back out into the garden. I was rocking between shoulders on the sofa, dreaming, the same way lads had rocked themselves off the changing room benches of their clubs, faces pale as polar owls, falling about themselves, racing to become men on the leftover football pitches. The kettle steam strolled about the hallway, clicking its heels, making its presence known.

Grandad's fingers, sweet needles, pressed the badge into my chest. I held it, like a boy holding a lamp post as he is dragged to school, like years that grow too large for their own good. I clutched at the steam as it observed me sleep, but it evaded my hands and turned to air. *Now you see me. Now you don't.* As I woke, I was holding nothing.

At some point that afternoon, Wayne poked his snub nose through the front door. Drifting in and out of sleep, I caught snatches of his conversation with Mam in the hallway. "Sherry's in a bad way, poor bird. He really was like a father to her." Then, "How much do you reckon the house is worth?" *The grasping bastard.* I had the mind to hide him. Before I had a chance to sit up, however, I had returned unwillingly to dreams. Yet even there I recalled a song; a song about men like Wayne once taught to me by lovely angry strangers on the terraces. I felt my lips mouthing it, filling the space with it:

> *When I was just a little boy,*
> *I asked my mother, "What should I be:*
> *Should I be Chelsea? Should I be Leeds?"*
> *Here's what she said to me:*
> *"Wash yer mouth out son,*
> *and go get yer father's gun,*
> *and shoot the Chelsea scum.*
> *Shoot the Chelsea scum."*

WE HATE CHELSEA WE HATE CHELSEA WE HATE
CHELSEA WE HATE CHELSEA WE HATE CHELSEA
WE HATE CHELSEA WE HATE CHELSEA WE HATE
CHELSEA WE HATE CHELSEA WE HATE CHELSEA
WE HATE CHELSEA WE HATE CHELSEA WE HATE
CHELSEA WE HATE CHELSEA WE HATE CHELSEA
WE HATE CHELSEA WE HATE CHELSEA WE HATE
CHELSEA WE HATE CHELSEA WE HATE CHELSEA
WE HATE CHELSEA WE HATE CHELSEA WE HATE
CHELSEA WE HATE CHELSEA WE HATE CHELSEA
WE HATE CHELSEA WE HATE CHELSEA WE HATE
CHELSEA WE HATE CHELSEA WE HATE CHELSEA
WE HATE CHELSEA WE HATE CHELSEA WE HATE
CHELSEA WE HATE CHELSEA WE HATE CHELSEA
WE HATE CHELSEA WE HATE CHELSEA WE HATE
CHELSEA WE HATE CHELSEA WE HATE CHELSEA
WE HATE CHELSEA WE HATE CHELSEA WE HATE
CHELSEA WE HATE CHELSEA WE HATE CHELSEA
WE HATE CHELSEA WE HATE CHELSEA WE HATE
CHELSEA WE HATE CHELSEA WE HATE CHELSEA
WE HATE CHELSEA WE HATE CHELSEA WE HATE
CHELSEA WE HATE CHELSEA WE HATE CHELSEA
WE HATE CHELSEA WE HATE CHELSEA WE HATE
CHELSEA WE HATE CHELSEA WE HATE CHELSEA
WE HATE CHELSEA WE HATE CHELSEA WE HATE
CHELSEA WE HATE CHELSEA WE HATE CHELSEA
WE HATE CHELSEA WE HATE CHELSEA WE HATE
CHELSEA WE HATE CHELSEA WE HATE CHELSEA
WE HATE CHELSEA WE HATE CHELSEA WE HATE
CHELSEA WE HATE CHELSEA WE HATE CHELSEA

White and Red

Christmas Eve, 1995. It was match day. The Roses Derby.

Norman swanned into the spare bedroom as the sun broke, swaggeringly sporting a pearl-white 1980s Leeds shirt. Whiter than white; a blue-and-white V-neck collar hugging him, the Lion Cabinets *sponsor printed on his stomach, the white rose of Yorkshire pressed on his chest. He was practically jigging like an Irish dancer. Grinning like a lunatic, he brandished a bacon butty in my face.*

"Up tha get, lad. It's biggest game of bloody season." He slapped a small white turtleneck onto my knees. THISTLE HOTELS *was embossed front and centre. "Get that on. Yer a man today."*

A man at seven. Well, very well.

Snow. That morning, Norman hacked the ice from his windscreen. An Arctic explorer, the fur of his parka's hood pushed up on his cheeks. Carollers were out shuddering, singing of the feast of Stephen on the doorsteps of Hunslet. Mam rolled up the sleeves of my oversized shirt and tucked the hem into my small blue boy-jeans. "You'll grow into the bugger." She had me turn at all angles.

It was my first match. At breakfast, Norman told me all I'd need to know. "Never trust a Manc. If a Manc tries to speak to yer, do not reply. Do not even cast tha eyes on a Manc. There might be some blokes getting rough with one another. Don't worry. We'll steer well clear of all that. But if yer see a red shirt that I an't seen, you let me know, and we'll go the other direction."

The week prior, Leeds had lost violently to Sheffield Wednesday. That day, all was to be atoned for, with the supreme rose to be decided at Elland Road — the white of York or the red of Lancashire.

Norman sprung from his chair to demonstrate a chant, then sat down, then stood up again at the start of each refrain. He encouraged me to do the same with his broad, dimpled grin. I jumped up, and sat down, and jumped up and sat down.

> Stand up
> if you hate Man U.
> Stand up
> if you hate Man U.

We sang, ad infinitum.

Looking back, I can't imagine Norman really did hate Man U, or at least not the average Man U supporter, who was, after all, not dissimilar to him. Deep down, at least politically, he would have recognised the folly of it, but in sport, as in life, a figure of loathing is needed. Without external threat, how can a man truly know his home?

In our shirts, we were indistinguishable from the glacial land. We clambered into Norman's Vauxhall Cavalier and pushed out of Hunslet. A five-hundred-year-old feud sat festering on the dashboard. Richard of York's ghost reclined in the back seat, his own severed head on his lap and a paper crown stuck to the head's matted hair.

We had rattled down the motorway for no more than ten minutes before the frosted floodlight towers of Elland Road — the silent guard posts — rose into view. Pulling up outside the Old Peacock, a brumal carnival had already begun. The scent of fried onions lifted from the burger van. It lingered in the sharp air. Jogging out of the pub, loitering at the traffic lights, flocking towards the stadium were men and boys with white-yellow-and-blue-striped scarves tied to their wrists. Drunk adolescents in white Fila tracksuits stomped through the wasteland surrounding Wesley Street, flags like chivalric capes on their shoulders, pockets full of pennies to lob if the Mancs scored. Whole piggy banks were strapped to their calves. Policemen hung patiently along

Lowfields Road, surveying the underpass tunnel for hooligans, circling the Bremner statue as if to question it, spinning batons between their fingers.

Two red-shirted men, who had arrived from the wrong direction, hurtled abuse as they headed west through the forest of jeers. Across the Pennines, seldom a sentence dare travel. Men turned themselves out from their collective sanctuaries and waged war on behalf of the dead and obsolete. Their blood was older than their weapons and their kingdom. Elland Road, their kingdom, was a crystalline palace sat above the disembowelled coal pits and rhubarb fields of yesterday.

Inside, Norman and I, a cup of Bovril and a pie each, waited in the stands. A man in white hung from the railing a Union Jack with LEEDS UNITED *painted across. On the other side of the pitch, a man in red hung a similar flag,* MAN UNITED *written across it instead. Around the touchlines,* ASICS, McDONALDS, CARLING, NINTENDO, LUCOZADE *and* WILKINSON SWORD *brusquely shouted their logos into the tomorrow of desire.*

Back then, Norman knew Father Christmas personally. He promised to let him know I was after the Rayman *game but kept referring to it as* Rainman *or* Raceman *whenever I reminded him. Secretly, I suspected that Norman was the* real *Father Christmas, having once seen him leave the White Rose Centre still dressed in his baggy red and white trousers. That was perhaps why the match was on early — so he still had time to deliver presents that night.*

The players walked out in their regimented lines. The stands stood to sing of pride and greatness. Full-throated sonorous song boomed around the stadium, lifting the clouds, drowning out all voice of opposition. A man in an argyle sweater covered in pin badges, whose breath stank of rum, leaned down to me and screamed in my ear: "We've been through it all together!" Norman batted him away cordially and swapped places with me so I could stand beside the old lady with the football, like a small moon, reflected in her jam-jar spectacles.

Kick off. The twenty sportsmen threw themselves into free-flowing skirmish, racing up and down the wings, through the centre, poaching the ball from their enemy's mistouches, escaping and booting it up or down field to their target. Their mouths moved silently, like fish, inaudible for the raucous chants ringing from the stands.

At the approach of the fifth minute, Jobson headed at the Man U goal. A red hand rose to touch it. Penalty. A penalty kick for Leeds. Captain McAllister drove the ball to the top corner, out of the reach of Schmeichel, who went flailing on his stomach. The crowd erupted. Roars of protest in the away end. Hands gestured murder. Omens of chaos. Celebrations in the home end. Grins broad as axes. Stand up — if you hate Man U — stand up.

Minutes later, Deane broke free and took his own shot. The ball careered over Schmeichel's head but fell on the crossbar and bounced away. A goal adrift, the reds pushed back, dancing through the midfield, putting passes together. A failed chance in the Leeds box. They were dispossessed. The white shirts had it. A ball nosed wide of the Man U goal. Another, on target, struck the chest of the keeper. Aerial duals fell apart in the sky. On the twenty-ninth minute a red took a touch in the Leeds box and drilled the ball low into the Yorkshire net.

A collective groan rose from the home stands. Norman cursed. Men slumped in their seats with their heads in their hands. The old lady next to me swore at Jesus. In the away end, Mancunians leapt in a wave. The man in the argyle lobbed his shoe at the pitch, hitting a Leeds fan by accident. An attendant climbed the steps to collect him. The chants rose again.

Thirty-five minutes. Yeboah snaked his way through the red defence, scuttled to the right and raised the ball over Schmeichel, who fell as a starfish, into the waiting net. Norman yelped. He hoisted me up. Beer showered the crowd. The stand surged in pandemonium. "He's an engine!" *Norman cheered.* "He's a rocket! They're under the cosh now. We've got 'em now!"

To be a man, you must first don the outer layer of a man. You must proudly exhibit your steadfast loyalty to your region, ideology or kind. You must walk with it, demonstrate it in the way you step, the way you talk and those you associate with. You must remember that not all men are friends. Many want to do you harm, and they will hack you down at the root if you aren't careful. You must tread where many do not dare, and walk above them. You must never forget where you come from. You must look after your fellows.

At half-time, Norman taught me to walk with my back straight, my small chest puffed out like a man stepping forward to present his manifesto. He unzipped his parka to display his Leeds white. I copied him. Men sauntering to the bar beat their chest at us in salute. Norman walked to where the Bovril was sold. I walked how he walked. When he said, "A Bovril please, love", I too said, "A Bovril please, love." I was the parrot at his heels and waited patiently as he stopped to talk to a Lads' Club worker in a white Leeds ski hat. They discussed the declining funding of youth services, then the erosion of the Conservative majority. They occupied the world of men. At the height of their stomachs, I looked up at them standing firm as trees.

"There's not a man alive who can crush Yorkshire", the man in the ski hat said.

> Arsenal 3-0 Leeds United
> Newcastle United 2-1 Leeds United
> Manchester City 1-0 Leeds United

No matter. As we returned for the second half, each face in the home stands was painted with euphoria. The winter sun shot about them. A man with a white rose in his lapel was lifted like an idol, thrust up in a cacophony of cheers. The away fans drifted back into place, offering themselves out across the stadium, never weary of the rituals of war. After the match, *they would meet their adversaries in tunnels and alleys, out of sight of police, and white and red would be scattered like rain.*

Kick off. The seventy-second minute. Palmer ran to the edge of the Man U penalty area. He kicked the ball back to Brolin. Brolin sent it up in an elegant arc towards Deane, who caught it sailing mid-air and headed it home into the red net.

It was over. There was no coming back for the Mancs. Songs ricocheted uncontrollably. Norman raised his hands to the magnificence of the sky. He commanded the choir. He shook his fingers and little clouds fell away into a translucent blue, happy to be finally banished from themselves. He slicked sunlight across the air with his palm, shook it off, rose to paint again. Men were jumping over my head, across the aisles, having waited so long for something to leap for. The romantic with the white rose clenched in his teeth shuddered in the face of the defiant sublime. The old lady next to me was sobbing with elation. At midnight mass, the priest would wish goodwill toward men, with the exception of Mancs. This was the kingdom, the power and the glory, for ever and ever. 3-1.

July 2017 (II)

The next morning, I woke to find Wayne leaning over me, a tiger in waiting. He must have arrived at an unreasonable hour or let himself in through the window when no one was looking. He stank of bergamot, black pepper, leather, tobacco — a White City aftershave. He stank of London. His breath hung like a dust storm at my nose.

"You need to have a word with your muvva", he growled, as if he were about to combust with the vehemence of the sentence. I batted him away like a gnat, and when I had slapped him, I rolled over and went back to sleep.

For brunch, we ate the remains of Norman's Marmite. Sherry turned up from a morning manicure, her pink claws tapping impatiently at the table. She and Wayne had come to look through the house once more, to target the loft, primarily, for anything they had missed during their previous value hunt. Mam had decided to let them get on with it. That way they would leave sooner and, with any luck, never return. She had placed objects with no sentimental value in easily discoverable places — watches barely worn, a stamp collection of reasonable worth, china plates that Brenda had made Norman buy but had never used, a vintage chessboard and items of a similar nature. Anything of real emotional worth had already been hidden in mine and Mam's suitcases or beneath mattresses.

Mam had refused to have an estate agent over immediately. This had aggravated Wayne, who clearly assumed that he and Sherry had rights to a share of a property that Brenda had never paid towards. Seemingly, Mam and Wayne had run into an argument before I woke up, and neither were speaking to each other at brunch.

I watched Wayne as he ate. Observed in magnitude like an ant under a lens, I picked out the slight shrubbery of his nostril hair, the thumbprint of Marmite on his bottom lip, the meat of sleep in the creases of his eyes. *Disgusting*. The way he chewed his food with volume, even a pacifist would want to mow him down.

"Right", he bellowed, throwing down his crust. "Let's get this over with."

Whilst having stated they only wanted to check the loft, Sherry and Wayne in fact worked from the ground floor up and claimed an iron within the first two minutes. They helped themselves to miscellaneous cutlery, then the stamp collection, loading them into the boxes they had brought. "No use for books", Sherry had said in the front room. "And this TV. I don't know how Mum let him keep it. It must be fifteen years old." They ascended the stairs.

The first floor had already been scavenged during their first visit, so they ignored it completely and propped up a ladder to the loft. Inside, a naked bulb hung from the ceiling, and great hulks of boxes covered by sheets sat like hills of dust rising up against the walls.

I stood with my arms folded, watching them go at it. Mam caught her breath on a discarded chair. The first box they trawled through contained nothing but bills and bank statements, the box immediately beneath it nothing but papers. Some of these papers were sellotaped together at their edges as if obscure jigsaw puzzles. *WRITING* was scribbled on the side of this box. As Wayne heaved it to the floor, I collected it promptly and kept it safe behind my ankles. Mam nodded to me but said nothing.

She joined the search party, tackling a separate pile of boxes. Quickly, she slipped small trinkets into her pockets, then carefully pulled out a blue garment coated in a plastic cover. It was brash, tasteless and lined in black frills. Despite the plastic, moth larvae had worn tiny furrows into the fabric. "Oh, look", Mam cried. "*Here's* something you'll want. It's Brenda's wedding dress." She mimed a fond memory. "She looked beautiful in this. Look at how elegant it is. It's like a flapper's dress from the Twenties."

Sherry came to examine it. She crumpled her nose as if Mam was dangling an oversized rat. "The moths have been at it. What a shame. We'll leave that with you, Betty. I never came to the wedding, so I don't have any memories of it. That was when Mum and I weren't talking."

"You didn't miss much", Mam said in earnest and dumped the grotesque thing back in its box.

The search continued for nearly an hour. All manner of tat was unearthed. A figurine of a flamenco dancer and a Solana Hotel mug from Norman and Brenda's trip to Benidorm. Photographs ruined by coffee stains. Empty boxes of spray-tan kits. Tracksuits equally as moth-eaten as the wedding dress. Several of Norman's bronze sports medals, which Sherry put up no fight for, seemingly as they were of no real monetary worth.

A particularly heavy box in the far corner was dragged into the light, and Wayne heaved out a Corona typewriter, still in working order, the keys kept proudly in pristine cleanliness. "Well then", Wayne grinned. "This is something!"

"When do you reckon that's from?" Sherry asked, kneeling beside it. "It's in good condition." She whispered something to Wayne.

"That's from the Sixties", Mam said. "Dad used to write on

that all the time when I was growing up. He used to sit in the kitchen and write after work. Lots of adventure stories about my mam. He used to tell me she was out at sea, sailing around the world, meeting princesses and mermaids and people on faraway islands. Obviously, I found out they were stories when I was old enough. I used to draw the adventures he told me about and he'd write up the stories to go with them."

"Ah!" Sherry cried. "Now I remember it! He wrote a poem about *me and Mum* on here once. Remember I paid for them to have that holiday to Cuba? He wrote a poem about us on *this* typewriter. Something about how *we enabled his ship to sail.* A metaphor, or something. I'm not sure where the poem's got to now."

Sherry was either lying or I did not want to believe her. "When was that? Early Noughties? It won't have been written on this. They had a computer by that time. I've never seen this typewriter in my life anyway. It will have been up here since I was born at least."

"No", Sherry snapped. "It was on *this* typewriter. I remember it clearly."

I sensed what Sherry was trying to do. "We'll have to put that somewhere nice, eh Mam? Maybe on the desk in the front room in Nottingham."

"What makes you think *you're* keeping it?" Wayne growled.

"Because you have no right to it", I said.

"Sherry's just told you", he spat back. "Norman wrote her something on *that* typewriter. We're taking it with us."

Wayne moved towards it. I blocked his path. "What, so you can sell it? Admit it. That's what you want to do. You want to sell it."

"Fred", Mam hissed. "There's no need for that. The

typewriter's staying here. Let's not get into an argument about it."

"Who says *you* can decide if something stays or goes?" Sherry shrieked. "I have every right to it. He was my dad too!"

"Your dad?" I shouted. "Your dad was a conman that fucked off when you were a child. You had fuck all to do with my grandad until you resurfaced when I was a kid. You never visited. You kept him sweet so you could swindle him out of everything he had, just like your bitch of a mother. Even after he's dead, you're here trying to pick his pockets. You're vermin. No one wants you here, so fuck off! Fuck off!"

There was silence. I caught my breath. Wayne caught my neck. I turned to see his fat, ugly eyes. "I think we need to go outside", he said.

He let me go. I nodded in agreement, then followed him down the ladder and onto the landing, ignoring the calls of protest ricocheting from above. We marched down the stairs and, solemnly, out into the road.

A neighbour was in his front garden with his daughter. Seeing our faces, he gave the understanding nod of men and swept the child inside without a word. The cars on the nearby motorway sounded their horns, sparking up a frenzy. England took its seat between the shrubberies, watching with a brittle smile. By the time I had turned to face him, Wayne's fist had already caught my nose.

I stepped back, somewhat stunned by the force of it. Blood was trickling down onto my lips. Wayne spread his arms triumphantly. His grin was the Thames. I could still smell the bergamot and leather on his neck. His belly hung, overindulged, about his belt. There were crystals on his belt buckle. There was gold on his fingers. His foul white teeth flashed themselves mockingly. "Come on then, you puff", he said. "Are you a man or ain't ya?"

I snapped. All that can be remembered is a blur, a berserk flash of colour, a furious drumming of energy and emotion. Later, Mam would tell me that I had caved in, that I was necessarily not myself. *To be a man, you must remember that not all men are friends. Many want to do you harm, and they will hack you down at the root if you are not careful. You must tread where many do not dare, and walk above them.* I, coward that I am, trod where they all tread and walked on top of him. I hated Wayne. His grin. I hated that he had everything I didn't. I hated that he didn't deserve a bit of it. I hated that people like him existed and went about life crushing everything in their wake without fear of retaliation. I wanted to break his neck. I wanted to murder him. It would be worth going to prison to see him wiped out, like a woodlouse smeared across a kitchen table. I wanted him to know how it felt to be exterminated, to be choked into silence and replaced by a strange, unnatural space. As I lifted my head, gasping for air, I became fully aware that I was drowning him. Beneath me, his lungs were heavy in his chest. His eyes were widening. He could not breathe. I was the wave breaking down on him, pleasured and serene.

By the time Mam and Sherry had pulled me away, Wayne was slumped against the curb coughing up red gunk. His face was a knot of wounds. There was blood on his gold and his crystal-studded belt buckle. His arm was gushing from where I had apparently bitten it. My fingerprints were on his neck, long streaked bruises; the shadows of Gytrash claws. I pulled him to his feet. I went back inside.

Sæ

Let us imagine a tree. An ash tree, in possession of enough nutrients and water, planted contentedly in a small brown groove which, for now, represents the earth. Besides this groove, the tree stands against ultimate blankness, if such a phenomenon exists; a space between something and nothing. A space between subject and object. We have given life to the tree, to the groove. We have grown them. The tree and the groove are now our objects.

Let us say a trodden path snakes up to the tree; grass that has turned out like fans under the mysterious footfalls of whichever travellers came before — for there were bound to be some. Let us then imagine the grass that surrounds and gives way to the trodden path, and perhaps four more ashes that lead to the groove. Ultimate blankness is being hidden now. We are creating a forest.

Where is this forest? Wherever you want it to be. It exists outside of tangible place and temporality.

Now that we have our forest, let us create the lakes of the forest, the birds and the mammals and the insects and the plants that inhabit the forest. Now that our nature is as complete as we can make it, let us imagine a man. Where did he come from? He grew out of a leaf, from a blade of grass, he emerged from water.

What does the man look like? We run into trouble here. To imagine the man, we must place him within some context of time; unless, that is, we are to envisage a faceless, hairless body of no discernible size which does not allow us to see whether it walks or crawls. For the sake of comprehension, to allow our brain to create recognisable images, and to enable us to tell this particular story at all, let us place ourselves in the time from which it is theorised our story originated. *The High Middle Ages.*

Due to our shared learning, we can now imagine the man to be bearded, with unkempt hair limp on his shoulders. He is wearing wool, worse for wear, dyed by tree bark, by lichen and by crushed insects to create a pallet of tans, sages and rouges. His face is covered by a frayed hood, which clings to the old cloak that trails behind him. In imagining him in this way, we may in fact be committing the man a grave injustice. He could be imagined in infinite ways, or in no way at all, but as he is not here to protest, let us imagine him as we please.

At the end of the forest, there must now grow a town, for this is where the man is headed. Ah, there it is. Now — let us tell the story.

In this town a body of wattle and daub houses, held together by clay and dung, mounted the hill that rose, like cupped hands, to the moon. Eddies of smoke floated from the holes in the rooves, floating north towards the church. The freemen and their families were home for cena, and a swine was being pushed inside by its buttocks.

On arriving at the town, the hooded man knocked on the first door he reached, at the foot of the hill, and was met by a huge blacksmith, smelling of wood smoke, in dull leather boots.

"Have thee any food to spare?" the hooded man asked. "For I have travelled from far and am weak and desperate."

The blacksmith glanced back to where his family were perched on stools, concealed by smoke, wolfing down porridge. "No food here", the blacksmith barked, and slammed the door shut.

The hooded man tried the next house, where a woman in a sheepskin cloak and wimple balanced two babies like barley in her forearms. This time, however, he could not finish his request, for the hooded man was grotesque and the woman cried out and pushed the door shut in an instant.

The man continued limply up the hill, from house to house, at each turned away before trudging to the next. At the top of the hill, he made for the church and struck his gnarled first against the grand arched doors.

Inside, two priests and their families could be heard celebrating, laughing into warmth, beating their spoons on their bowls of meat pottage. The hooded man knocked again but no one answered, so he knocked again, to no avail.

The man decided to try the final house in the town, which sat back from the rest, squat and unassuming, flanked by solemn ash trees, where a stray cat perched, turning over its prey. At the door, the man was met by a gaunt villein and his wife. The villein's waist-long beard was mottled with mire, his wife's tunic sunken, drained of life.

"Have thee any food to spare?" the hooded man asked. "For I have travelled from afar and am weak and desperate."

The married couple said nothing but beckoned him inside to a hearth that burnt in the centre of the hut. The hooded man sat on the floor beside a silent rouncey whose muzzle rose and fell amid a clump of dry grass. Before long, the couple had brought forth what they could offer; a dark slab of bread studded with acorns and beans, a cup of milk close to turning. The man took them gratefully, devoured the coarse scrap, drained the acid milk and rested his head on the belly of the rouncey for a while.

When he came to, in the depths of early morning, the couple were already awake, huddled together, haggard, in the thick smoke. They had laid a cloth over the visitor, which an animal had been chewing at. As the hooded man started, as if from a nightmare, the wife raised her hand to signal comfort. She lulled his head back down with her fingers.

This couple — let us call them Hilperic and Agnes — introduced themselves, their voices light in amiability but as full as horns. Hilperic worked as a farmer in the fields of the local lord. Agnes was heavy with the couple's first baby. It was spring. The food they had gathered during the autumn harvest was soon to run out. This is why they could only offer bread and milk. Hilperic told their guest that if he would like to stay and rest a further day, Agnes could see what leftovers the priests might offer. Hilperic asked if their guest was a freeman.

The hooded man replied in the negative. He was headed north, to his family. He thanked the couple for their generosity and, as the ruptures of sun were beginning to show themselves in the clouds, took his leave and headed back to the head of the hill.

Already, villeins were toiling in the fields, ploughing, pressing seeds to the earth, chasing intrusive birds to the east; mudmen, so caked in soil they appeared to be growing fur. The priest was out on his morning walk, cheeks fat with tithe, muttering to himself. Glaring uphill, the blacksmith of the night before made a gesture as if to shoo the hooded man away into the trees.

Then, to the blacksmith's shock, the man pulled back his hood to reveal a head as blinding as sun. His lips, eyes and hair were of a gleaming sharp white, and as he tore down his cloak, two celestial wings emerged from his back. He rose a dazzling finger to the town below and, to the attention of all, let his command ring out.

Semerwater rise,
and Semerwater sink,
and swallow the town all save this house,
where they gave me food and drink.

Now we must imagine water. We may begin with the crest of a small harmless wave running out from the trees, lapping down upon the mud, then build upon it; another wave riding upon its shoulder, then a third and a fourth, until a crescent of water the size of a comet overtakes its fledglings and curves into the earth. Suddenly we have a flood. At once, a body of water populated by grayling, eels and bullheads is bursting through the doors of the houses. Men are trying to battle the alien liquid, to suppress it with their boots, but they are swept up, and forgiven, and become floating hats and cloaks on the water's surface. The waves are thrashing violently uphill, and even the priest, thrusting his gilded cross above his head, is erased, leaving behind, in the air, the faint outline of where he once stood. He is replaced by water. He enters that ultimate blankness between something and nothing. An unknowable place. A place it is best not to know.

What of Hilperic and Agnes? They were, as the angel had commanded, unharmed, and as they left home to begin the day's labour they found before them a lake the size of a town; a lake thick with fish, enough to keep them and their unborn child for years.

This is Lake Semerwater, Fred. Named after the town that the flood demolished. Not long before I was born, they excavated the bed and found remnants that suggested an ancient settlement. Outlines and traces. A whole town was down there, under the water. So don't you complain when it rains, my lad.

July 2017 (III)

I drank heavily that night. Sherry and Wayne had left in their gleaming Citroen, down the A61, back towards Ealing with its deli cafés and artisan lager shops. Wayne had not shown his face as he left. He could not have shown it if he'd wanted to. It had been covered with bandages. By the time Mam and Sherry had finished with him, he looked like the mummy of Tutankhamun. I thought it to be an improvement on his actual face. I did not come downstairs to say goodbye.

Despite Sherry's threats to call the police, Wayne had insisted on the law being kept out of it. He was seemingly embarrassed to have been beaten so badly by a failed journalist almost a decade his junior. Besides, if anyone asked about his wounds, he could tell them he had acquired them fighting bands of militant jihadists in Yorkshire with his bare hands. It would do his reputation well in the Conservative Club.

Mam did not talk to me for much of the afternoon. We ate tea quietly, and before she went up for an early night she hugged me but said nothing to accompany the embrace. It had not yet reached eight o'clock. I was in no fit state for premature sleep. Whilst not abnormally energised, I was wide awake, so I wandered to the corner shop and picked myself up a bottle of Scotch whisky.

Norman's photograph was still sellotaped to the tobacco cupboard. "You can take that down now", I said to the shopkeeper. "The photo, I mean."

The man at the till had clearly forgotten it was there. Then he smiled, as if in celebration. "He's given up the drink now then, yes?"

"Aye", I said. "Given it up for good."

"Wonderful news. I quit myself a long time ago. It gives you a whole new lease on life becoming teetotal. People say I look forty, but would you believe it — I'm actually forty-five."

The shopkeeper looked at least fifty. I thanked him and put the photo in my pocket before heading west up Church Street.

The whisky was harsh and smoky on the tongue. It tasted like a furnace, like a wildfire. I gulped it down and decided I would make the most of the evening. I had nowhere to be and no responsibilities. I was a man about town, a bachelor. I would walk in whatever direction felt natural and see where I ended up, and wherever I ended up I would bloody well get pissed there. Perhaps I would walk as far as Headingley. Perhaps I would walk as far as Harrogate. I found a half-smoked cigarette in the gutter outside the boarded-up Sun Inn, placed it in my pocket for later and crossed the Beza Street Bridge down towards the roundabout.

A tunnel beneath me led to the Tunstall Road overpass, but as I approached, I found a gang of hooded adolescents waiting quietly within it, so I passed quickly, and skirted around the roundabout, dodging the cars, then rejoined the pavement that made way for the neighbouring Hunslet Carr.

I had not been to Hunslet Carr since I was perhaps twelve. A drug addict had collapsed before Norman's bonnet. Poor bloke. Norman had performed CPR on him until the ambulance arrived, mumbling "Stayin' Alive" under his breath to find the perfect beat.

It was much the same as it had been then. As I descended the Tunstall Road overpass, dark lines of terraced housing skirted away to the east, then built up to the west as I wandered into the thickening red-bricked labyrinth. The network of marred, melancholic residences met on either side of Dewsbury Road, the vein of the Carr which ran south for miles, escaping the city, leaving its tail behind.

I took another swig of Scotch and headed north. By this point, I was considerably alive with the whisky, and a heat stood in my chest, as comforting as it was sharp. On the low roof of the hospice charity shop, Christmas decorations remained on display from the previous year. An electrical sculpture of Father Christmas and his sleigh stood extinguished of light, dim and skeletal against the reddening sunset. Fake designer rugs hung from the railing outside the corner shop, their Versace and Chanel logos stitched clumsily, and in one case, both branded on the same garish bath towel. As I ambled on, a small boy in a dashiki caught me with a perturbed glance. He stood outside a hair studio. He held his toddler sister on a leash and turned frantically to the window twice as people passed him, as if urging his mother to hurry outside. The Victorian slum buildings had long been converted to flats, of which at least a fifth of the ground floor windows were barred.

"Eh, love. Give us some of that." A call from above. A woman perched at her top floor window watched me as I drank. The glowing light of her bedroom hung about her in the dusk. She bared her missing teeth at me darkly, howled with laughter and spat, and scrutinised me as I continued walking.

Cars thundered past blasting London drill. An old man in a taqiyah sped round a corner, up to the brick outhouses, hollow faced, as if he'd witnessed a stabbing. A blacked-out Volkswagen was parked on the curb by the laundrette. The driver was waiting for someone. He kept his face down, smoking. Vape fumes poured from the window in thick, escalating clouds of butterscotch.

A dog barked. I turned. A Staffordshire bull terrier pounced at my leg. "Fuck", I shouted and leapt, almost swinging my bottle at it. It was muzzled. Its owner, a teenager in a balaclava and a puffer jacket yanked the dog down. "Brutus! Wrong guy." He sauntered off, tugging the angry dog behind him. I waited for a moment before I continued.

As I headed on past the Chinese and the pound shop, what warmth I had garnered from the alcohol was replaced by an intense, thrashing sense of paranoia. This was not my part of Hunslet. This was not an area I wanted to be intoxicated in. For decades, Hunslet Carr had evaded any attempts at sustained redevelopment, and whilst the Oval was a shell of what it had once been, knocked down and reimagined as sterilised suburbia, the Carr still dwelled in a shell long eroded. The new inhabited the old as the old fell apart, an unattended old, too anaemic to contain the weight of modernity. These were not grade-listed buildings. This was a past deemed unworthy of celebration, left to its own devices, left to starve in the hinterlands of the city.

At least architecturally, this was the Hunslet of Norman's youth. Yet, devoid of its factories, its clubs, its common land, and ransacked and pillaged for so many years, there was something sinister about the place, something threatening that I had not wanted to see. It was the closest to the past I could hope to reach, and the closest to the past I would dare to go.

I hated myself for thinking it. I chastised myself for my nervousness. I had been made cowardly and plump by the future. There was no excusing it, but no evading it.

I headed faster in the direction of the Aire, and held the whisky bottle by its neck, ready to weaponise it if the situation arose. As I caught a pride of angry men outside the squat yellow car wash shacks nodding and shuffling in my direction, I switched the bottle to my visible hand to let them see that I had it. Before long, I had passed the plum-and-grey-shaded high-rises, the grey pebbledash council houses, and escaped over the grey overpass back to familiarity of Jack Lane.

To reach the Aire, I continued past the tyre shop, the motorcycle dealership and the autocentre, quiet in nightly abandon, and dumped the empty Scotch bottle outside the gutted colosseum of the old printworks — now a college building. As I walked, characters manifested themselves in the empty windows, walking two apace, looking out on the main road before vanishing into shadows. How strange to know the folk I had attributed stories to had trod the same road I was then, were treading *with* me then, or were perhaps rolling in their graves at the secrets I had revealed and the lies I had told. I would not blame them. I had ventured into their world without invitation and written them back to life without consent. Perhaps they did not want their stories to be told. Perhaps they were happier dead and forgotten.

I would have liked to have written that thought down. I cursed myself for leaving my notebook on the sofa, then shrugged it off as a minor loss. None of my notes would have made sense after a bottle of Scotch anyway, and surely the act of writing peoples' reluctance to be written about was one of contradiction and disrespect. It would be more respectful, if anything, to abandon the project of retelling these stories, particularly as there was no way of authenticating their absolute truth. Did I, in fact, have any right to be the transcriber of these narratives — narratives from a time I had never lived in, of people I had never known? Probably not. Was my reconstruction of Norman's life getting me any closer to him? Perhaps. Perhaps it was making him all the more distant and unknowable.

I needed another drink, so I pressed on, up Black Bull Street and its parade of hotels and luxury apartments, until I reached the bridge that crossed the Aire. To the west, waterfront properties trailed into the distance unapologetically, their windows warm with activity. All images, nothing more, nothing less. Nothing real about them. England's finest fabrication. A champagne cork was let off. It shot out as if from a gun. Music danced down to the water.

I was reminded of a display that I had seen at a museum, when I was younger, with Norman.

> *There was certainly a river, but no salmon in it. If we went on as we were now doing, and if the population continued to increase, the day would certainly come when we should have to meet together, and somebody would say, "I hold up the scale of the last salmon", and another man would say, "I have got the shell of the last oyster."*

I stared down into the blackened water, searching for salmon, for grayling or minnows. The Aire gave nothing away. It kept its secrets well. It commanded respect.

> *A reservoir of poison, careful kept for the purpose of breeding pestilence in the town.*

Now then, this was where the Atlantic salmon had migrated from, fleeing in their masses to the promised feeding grounds beyond Iceland and Greenland. Who could blame them? Many winters passed, and having filled themselves sufficiently, they had returned to the rivers of Yorkshire to breed, carrying with them their loyalties, their sickness for home. This was where the power station had once dumped its waste, where industrial workers had abandoned their sewage, making the water dank with cholera. That would have seen off the fish, if not the poor downstream who caught salmon with blazing forks, or the monks of Kirkstall Abbey who dragged them out with their teeth, half-mad with hunger.

> *If you look in the refuse pits on the grounds of the Abbey, you can see what the monks once ate. Not just the bones of the fish of the river, but the bones of jackdaws, herons and ravens.*

A heron, having outlived its human adversaries, was perched at the water's edge, devouring a small bird in privacy. Were the river a man it would be recumbent, playing dead, unwilling to confess. Its lone arm, a canal, stretched beyond Botany Bay, wormed elusively around the backwaters, clutching vacancy with its fingertips. The bounty of the western coalfields, the knotweed plants of Japan, the wool of Australia, the cloth of Yorkshire, the fury and the barbarism of England, its boats and their boatmen and their forgotten fantasies, the small lives and ready deaths of the centuries, all manner of insignificant things were buried in its skin.

I went briskly across the bridge. I cut through The Calls, past the graffiti, *DELETE YOUR SOCIAL MEDIA, ACAB, ANARCHY IS FREEDOM,* and, at Call Lane, ventured into one of the trendy neon bars that propped up the street. Yuppies milled around with tequila cocktails. As if they had not yet changed from their work clothes, men of my age stood in sharp Italian blazers discussing their fathers and the potential of the untapped property market in the further reaches of the city. Women in Parisian heels brainstormed names for boutique businesses and shared photos from recent Maltese meditation retreats.

Posh bastards, the lot of them. I could have spat. I sized up the men as I waded through, taking in their height, their arms and hands. I could take at least six of them but decided against it, for their sake not mine, and instead slumped onto a stool by the bar, settling for scraping the mud from my shoes onto the polished floor instead.

I coughed up £5.80 for a Danish IPA, making my disgust known, and sat drinking swiftly as the barman, a red-bearded bloke in a lumberjack shirt, watched me. I glanced at him, expecting him to ask me what my problem was, but he took down a glass and began rigorously polishing it, as if hoping to be free of some sudden blemish.

"What's your name?" a woman asked suddenly. I turned to her. The faint waft of Chanel hung about her neck. She was beautiful, of my age if not a few years younger, with a south-western accent and her blonde hair in a perm. "I haven't seen you here before. Are you from Fields and Green?"

"No", I said, bluntly, yet still aware of my attraction to her. "What's Fields and Green? Have I walked into a staff party?"

"It's an architectural firm in the city", she smiled. "What do you do?"

"I'm a writer", I half lied, downing my IPA.

She was impressed, if not taken aback. "What do you write about?"

"How much I hate architectural firms."

The woman left, perhaps taking me for a sombre academic writer. I didn't blame her. I ordered a shot of rum and prepared to head out once more. The masterfully groomed socialites of the city centre fell into one another's arms, bathed in a pale pink light. Their faces were soft with cream and their hands were smooth and baby-like. Not one of them had eaten out-of-date food in their lives. They danced around like singing cats, licking one another's fur. This was what it was to be sucked into the social life of the new city. The buildings had long ago become myths for the yuppies to parade in. History had been dragged into the vacuum of the myth. With no tangible history left, the bricks presented themselves as something other than what they were in reality, images of their past selves, mere images dressed up to deceive, myths with not a grain of truth left within them.

By this time, it was fast approaching ten and there was readily decreasing time to find any semblance of a normal pub, so I hurried back down Call Lane, east towards Bridge End. Outside the French Brasserie, a lecherous Elvis impersonator was badgering a trio of young mothers. On the bridge, a boy with a face like an owl was attempting to uproot a bike from its chain. I gave the Aire no recognition this time and carried on down Meadow Lane, then east again at the A653, avoiding the returning Dewsbury Road to the west. I eventually came to Holbeck Moor Road, its park absent of life, its unsullied new builds shut off at the windows despite the balmy temperature. Apartment buildings stood in embryo state beneath the frames of construction, their grey bricks yet to be painted red, their bay windows and solar-panelled roofs glancing down at the uniform council houses of Gaitskell Walk.

Amongst this, a weathered Victorian building sat back from the road, light soaking in its curtains. Disengaged from all around it, it murmured in the night. I walked to the sign above the door — *HOLBECK W.M.C.* — and went promptly inside. The interior was painted a pale lemon yellow. A reddish geometric carpet snaked through from the bar room to the function room, hiding beneath the shoes of small congregations of locals who sat hunched at their squat wooden tables with pints of Tetley's and San Miguel between their noses. It was not busy. There were perhaps fifteen people in total, at least ten of them retired or knowing that at their age they should be. The pool table had been covered for the night and a plaque commemorating serving members from times long gone hung from the far wall, a reef of red poppies adorning its head. A man of Norman's age sat crouched over the bar, silver running down the nape of his neck, his suede back to me, muttering to the barman.

A few cheery hellos. I said hello to the strangers in return and perched myself next to the old man at the beer taps. "Member or guest, pal?" the barman asked me.

"Guest", I told him. Then, surveying the taps with relief, "Tuborg please, mate."

The barman poured it and set it before me. I paid the £2 and went straight to drinking.

"Where tha come from? Tha not from round this way are yer?" The old man in the suede jacket had shifted on his stool. He glared at me with amusement and curiosity, a hooked grin too wide for his hollow cheeks. The way his grey-white hair powdered his jaw and eyebrows, he looked as if he had walked through a blizzard.

"Nottingham."

"Ah, the Midlands. I like Nottingham. Went a few times when I wuh a lad. Me father used to work on trains. Making 'em first, then he wuh driving 'em. What brings thee round here?"

"Seeing family."

"Where's tha family from?"

"Hunslet."

"Oh aye, Hunslet. Am from Hunslet. They didn't fancy a pint with yer, no?"

"Not tonight. Early night for them tonight."

"Dun't blame 'em. This weather takes it out of yuh. I'd have passed out on sofa if I an't come here but am here every night and have been for God knows how long. Can't hold me back with heat nor hale. What's tha name?"

"Fred."

"Ned", the old man said and passed me his gnarled hand to shake. "Yer seen these new houses what they're building round here?"

"Aye", I said. "Must be good business for the club."

"Is it heck. They dun't come here, these new folk. The club wuh going under a year or two ago. Smoking ban took away a lot of business, then council knocked down the high-rises that used to be here. Started constructing these new builds instead. Brings in a lot of people from outside the area that an't got a connection wi' place. I thought tha might have been one of 'em."

I shook my head. "Still live in Nottingham. Just here for a couple more—"

"Aye, well we wuh fundraising to help save club last year, year before last maybe — whip-rounds, couple stalls set up outside to sell all sorts. New folk didn't even come near. I don't know if it's 'cause a lot of 'em's immigrants. Muslims — can't drink and all that. We had to value the silver trophies we had in here. That's how bad it got. Then there wuh asbestos. Eh by gum. Anyway, it's gradually steadying here now. We're regenerating the place."

"I'm glad to hear it's steadying. It feels like a proper community hub."

"That it is, young man. That it is."

"There's not many other working men's clubs left, is there?"

"No", Ned said, "practically none. I mean, there's still *some* around Leeds. They've changed a lot though. Probably go under."

"I suppose a lot of things have changed round here."

"In Leeds? Aye, it's unrecognisable. It's better now in a lot of ways."

"Better?" I offered him a glance.

He took it gladly and returned his hooked grin. "In a lot of ways. Think about this. I wuh born in 1939. When I wuh a lad, city wuh a bomb site. We had rations most of time but other times we wuh starving. Me father used to send me for a bag of bones from butchers and me mother would make it into a stew. Bones and potato. No central heating them days neither. When it wuh cold it wuh freezing. Had to dress like an Eskimo in yer own house. Baths once a week down slipper baths if yer lucky. Stank like a Gloucestershire pig half time."

"Well aye, living conditions have improved", I admitted, "for a lot of people but not for everyone. I was talking more in terms of community spirit. Solidarity, yer know. There's not as much of it. I'm not from here but I've spent enough of my childhood up here, with my grandad. It's not the place he told me stories about. It's the same in Nottingham. It's the same in a lot of cities, I reckon. Things feel a lot more divided now. The country's a much more individualistic place and that's most obvious in areas where there used to be that hard-headed neighbourliness. Don't get me wrong, it still exists in places — that's why it's nice coming in here — but…" I felt myself ranting. I paused.

Ned held me with his mesmerising grin. He waited for me to continue, and as I didn't, he asked me: "How old are yer, pal?"

"Twenty-nine."

"Yer talk like a man twice yer age", he said. "Tha seem to remember more than me, and I wuh there." He finished his drink. "Another?"

Before I could decline, he had ordered two Holbeck Specials. He waved away my thanks, and when the drinks arrived, he looked at me sternly. "Listen, I can't argue with that. Life in't what it wuh back then, but that's not to say everything wuh better. Why, I had sod all when I wuh a lad! Had to go out robbing when I wuh a teenager. Then I worked me fingers to bone in every factory going. When the factories started closing, I went to work in construction. Eventually I become the foreman of the business. Bold as brass, I wuh. Bought a council house in the Eighties, not far from here, and I've lived there ever since. I did what I had to do for me, and it wun't have done me no good looking out for every other bugger, because I bet yuh they wouldn't do the same. There wuh never a time when *everyone* wuh pally, as much as tha might think there wuh. There wuh always some that done better than others and tha need to be aspirational to make something of thissen. Yer need to be yer own man. That's no bad thing. Now I could tell tha all about what *I* think went wrong — what's happened that's been of detriment to the city — but it's *my* opinion and tha might not like it."

"By all means", I said.

Ned repositioned himself, facing me head on. He thought for a moment. "Right", he started, "well tha had the neighbourliness and the sociability tha talk about when tha had the cobbled streets. In one community everyone wuh as poor as each other. Tha rarely came across a rich man. Tha had to go out of tha way to rob 'em! That neighbourliness wuh done away with by many things.

"*One* — they started knocking down the houses — building the high-rises. Now I'm all for social housing, but at the same time they were building 'em, a flood of immigrants come in. There wuh a huge influx of Pakistanis. Europeans an' all. Eventually, British people couldn't get council houses. Families wuh coming in from overseas with two, three kids and went straight to top of list. Well, *they* didn't have any loyalties to the community. *They* weren't connected to the place like we wuh. The folk what wuh pushed out of their houses couldn't come back unless they'd put aside a decent bit of money. Same thing's happening today with these new builds yer see. *That* helped kill the community.

"*Two* — Most of industry wuh sold off. That's what I couldn't stand about the Blair government. In France, yer can't have a vital industry owned by a foreign company, but how many French and German companies own our waterworks? Gasworks? I knew one bloke from a company in Derbyshire. They made railways carriages. It wuh sold off to a French company who shut the business down. They took the order book to France and started manufacturing the carriages over there. The foreigners wuh buying our companies just to get rid of the competition. When the industry went, it took a lot of that neighbourliness with it 'cause folk had to go work in different places, *if* they could find jobs at all. They wun't living and working together anymore, so they had no loyalties to one another anymore, yer see? That killed off the community too. Now, my father voted Labour all his life — thought it wuh his duty as a working man — but Blair's government wuh what put the dagger in this country — in more ways than in just closing industry."

The old man halted to think. I waited for him to announce the third item on his list, or to conclude his argument, but as he seemed to have lost his trail of thought altogether, I re-joined. "I'd disagree with you on immigration. I live in an area with many immigrants, and they've been active in helping to maintain whatever sense of community there is. Community is as important to them as it is to us. The council house issue is more the result of a failed housing policy, and of course selling council homes off has made the problem far worse."

The man scoffed.

I continued. "As for industry — don't get me wrong, I don't like Blair any more than you. He practically destroyed Labour, but it was the government of the Eighties that *really* killed off industry. More than that! It brought in an ideology that still has a chokehold on the poorest in this country."

"I tek it you mean neoliberalism?"

"Aye. It was Thatcher's government that dropped us in the mess we're in today. Everyone that followed has just added to the ideology she imposed, and New Labour refused to attack it."

"Well", Ned countered, dismissively, "it wuh industry that killed itself off in them days. When the unions got too powerful, industry practically committed suicide. Yer weren't born at time. I wuh there, lad. Unions were pretty much running country. They wuh working to build a communist state. One of my mates, in fact — he worked as a union rep at Allerton Bywater — the colliery. He disagreed with all this strike nonsense what wuh going on in the Eighties. Just wanted to make some money to feed his family. Can tha blame him? Anyway, he told me he went to a meeting with union one evening, and the blokes there who wuh communists talked and talked and talked, didn't let me mate get a word in edgeways. They talked until six o'clock, seven o'clock in morning. By that time, me mate had to get back to work or he'd be losing his job — and he hadn't slept. They'd worn him down. Then what the communists would do was they'd have a vote, and the communists would always win because the people who opposed them wuh all talked out. They agreed to the communists' demands because they had to get back to work. That sort of thing happened all over. Believe me, I know."

"Well—" I went to counter.

"It's not that I'm anti-union", Ned interrupted, energetic with determination. "*I* wuh a union man. The unions helped me. But I *am* anti-communist-unions. Should've seen the Winter of Discontent, lad. That wuh *real* Hell. You'd walked out yer house — there wuh lights down one side of street but none on other. Whole country wuh shut down. Christ! People say Thatcher destroyed the country, but she *saved it*. We would've been like Russia if she hadn't stepped in — don't agree with what someone's doing and tha wind up in jail, or dead! That's what them sort of countries are like. Unfortunately, lad, communism's perfect in theory, but it's ran by *people* so it'll never work. People are greedy. People want to look after themselves. That's just the truth, and it's not a bad thing either! That's the true nature of folk."

Ned sat, staring at me, breathing heavily, awaiting my response. He had moved from the look of an assured man to a look of almost frantic defensiveness. I noticed once of his fists was clenched. "Besides", he said, "couldn't have bought me house if it weren't for her."

A pause. "We'll have to agree to disagree", I said carefully, "on the true nature of people."

"And on Thatcher I suppose."

"I suppose so."

"Very well", he said, returning to drink. "Yer a smart man. I can see that. Just don't fall into the trap of wishing back things what've already gone, things which wuh never good to begin with."

I finished my pint. It was ten to eleven. Last orders were called, but no one wanted to drink anymore. Pensioners took up their coats and shuffled away to the night, saying their goodbyes to everyone they passed. In a decade's time, the doors would be empty, the bar would be empty. There would be no coats to collect, no people to collect them. Everything in sight would cease to exist but space. A disquieting space which populates every room.

"I don't think it's a case of wishing back the past", I said finally. "The past is elusive. It's divisive and you can never be certain what you'll find there. You can never be certain if it's really there at all. I think it's a case of learning from the past, so as to construct a better future."

"Aye", the old man replied, placing down his empty glass decisively. "I think I can agree with that." He climbed down from the bar stool and looked up at me. He was shorter than I'd imagined him.

"What's your surname, Ned?"

"Gould", he said.

I nodded knowingly.

"Who's tha family?" he asked me. "Perhaps I know 'em."

"We're the Whitby's", I told him. "My grandad was Norman Whitby. He died recently."

Ned's eyes broadened momentarily. There was a hint of remembrance in them. He pressed his lips together and thought. "I could've sworn I knew that name — from a long time ago — or perhaps I read it in a story somewhere." He gave up. "Either way, my memory's not what it wuh. I can't remember half the things I want to."

We said our goodbyes and I went quickly towards Hunslet. Lights shut off in the houses as I passed them. Without light, they may well have been barren. All these little houses, empty, in a row.

Checkmate

"A few platitudes highlighted in red", Cyrus said. "Some grammatical errors in dialogue which I trust are intentional, but other than that rather interesting. It evokes, for me, the style of those kitchen-sink writers of the mid-century. Sillitoe and Barstow and the like. You know them?"

"I read them when I was younger", Norman replied, thumbing through his manuscript of short stories, noting the fluorescent slug-lines of Cyrus' highlighter, which had made their way quite freely across the type-print.

"Yes, it does tend to be the case that people grow out of them. Nevertheless, you seem rather taken with the genre, and there is a definite charm to it that I rather like. I wonder, Mr Whitby, what do you read nowadays?"

"A lot of political writing. Theory."

"Fiction?"

"Pulp fiction when I'm after escapism. Cowboy stories. Spy stories. Me wife reads the Mills and Boons. Not my cup of tea, but she makes me read 'em to her sometimes. I should probably turn me attention back to more literary fiction at some point."

"Well, it wouldn't hurt. Have you read the classics?"

"Aye. Not enough cowboys in 'em." Norman smirked. Cyrus did not return it.

"Well, there's certainly some *classics I can get on board with", Norman continued. "I like social realism. State-of-the-nation novels. But there is a fair bit of rubbish out there that has nothing important to say, or, failing that, nowhere interesting to take me — some classics included. If I'm reading or writing, I want to be either firmly planted on the earth —*

so as to effectively engage with and critique it — or to escape reality entirely. Any fiction that falls into the space in-between seems to be full of characters who supposedly inhabit the real world but have problems that are more like fantasies. Their writers are the same. Some of them come across as particularly self-indulgent. I've never got on with that sort of fiction."

"Aren't all writers a bit self-indulgent?" Cyrus smiled wryly.

Norman had come across Cyrus Goodall's masterclasses in the Yorkshire Evening Post. Once a week at the Leeds Central Library for the duration of the summer. Cyrus Goodall, a self-proclaimed "celebrated" lecturer in creative writing from one of the southern universities. It had seemed worthwhile enough, so Norman had sent off his cheque, and every Saturday he made a habit of discretely escaping the house before Brenda could find a litany of chores for him to complete.

Cyrus Goodall had an air of scaliness about him. He had fish lips. He was the sort of man who read the Times Literary Review, but in his car, on the nights his wife would not let him back in the house. Each week, he wore the same mustard cardigan and mustard tie, perhaps also kept in his car, and each week upon the arrival of his students he would feign to be reading a copy of Proust's third volume but seemed never to move beyond the ninetieth page.

Cyrus's pretence, however, was without its desired effect, for the majority of his masterclass students were residents of Lime Hall; pensioners who sat picking at their false teeth throughout each session and seemed to not know the exact purpose of the course for, whilst eager to recount vague stories of their youth, they looked at Cyrus with horror when he asked if they would write them down.

Norman put on his telephone voice when he spoke to the tutor. He conversed carefully with the man, utilising literary terminology where he could, and limiting his dialect in favour of the rhetoric of the knowledgeable student, yet without entirely abandoning his unique selling point — his common touch. He had, at the time, explained to Mam on the phone that he wanted Cyrus Goodall to think of him as the bee's knees — because he bloody well was.

"I am", Cyrus continued, "compiling a small anthology as it happens. *A working title:* The Hard Heart: Untapped Voices from the North. *It will form part of my ongoing research project into the writing practices of unpublished authors in ex-industrial areas, the literary trends utilised by those writers who exist, shall we say, outside of the literary sphere. It seems common to me that, amongst such budding wordsmiths, writing styles of the past are favoured over those of their celebrated contemporaries. Anyway, I'd be interested in including your story "Cautious, a Boat Adrift". It's exactly the sort of thing I've been looking for. Would that be of interest?"*

Norman nodded, eagerly.

"Well, that's fantastic. You'll be joining a host of unpublished writers from as far afield as St Helens and Sunderland. A valuable school to belong to. Of course, I would have to ask for a one-off payment for publication, to the sum of £250. This would be to cover the cost of printing and promotional materials. I must request this from all my authors. In return, of course, I would gladly host all contributors to read a passage of their work each at an academic venue in the south during the month of publication — say April 2001. Does this sound agreeable?"

Norman looked his tutor over. Cyrus's hands were remarkably scaly that day. The dim light of the library meeting room was gleaming greasily on his knuckles. Norman did not want to know where his hands had been.
"I shall have to run it past my wife first."

"I didn't have you down as a man whose wife made his decisions for him, Mr Whitby."

Cyrus sat back with a provocative smile, as if he had executed a checkmate on the hopeful old man. His eyelids shut like guillotines, and he held the silence of the moment on his tongue, savouring it, imagining some classical concerto in his head.

Norman considered the oily tutor. In the past he would have punched him, flat on his slippery nose, but then again not all histories were productive to continue.

Luckily, the silence was broken. Norman's mobile phone erupted into sound, caterwauling around the unostentatious meeting room. This time, Brenda's bat screeches were not of the slightest inconvenience. She would be so frustrated if she knew. Norman kissed his phone as he hurried to the bus stop.

When he got home, he found Brenda stretched across the sofa like a negligent emperor. She was somewhere between sleep and consciousness, dissatisfied with both and showing it gladly. A dead cigarette hung between her ruddy lips. Molehills of ash littered her dressing gown. On the television, Chris Tarrant was asking a contestant for the name of the porcine dictator in Animal Farm.

Norman did not call to her. He edged closer, and as he drew near enough to smell her, he could see that she had chopped off the end of her thumb. How had she managed that? Presumably in attempt to pry open a tinned Fray Bentos pie with a kitchen knife, for both offending tin and mutinous knife had been discarded aggressively on the carpet beneath her.

In my carelessness, I had almost forgotten the tip of Brenda's left thumb was gone. It had been a nub of a thumb since I was twelve. In hindsight, I should have mentioned it earlier. Nevertheless, her thumb looked like the fat end of a truncheon, and she took her possession of one less nail as an opportunity to demand a discount from her manicurist.

Coming to, she aimed the stub at her husband. "Now", Brenda spat, "look what you've done".

Norman lay down his bag. He silently removed his shoes and sat on the sofa. He anchored himself there and delivered his lines. "What I've done?"

"Yer should never have left me alone!" she shrieked. "Yer supposed to look after me. Yer own wife, at home alone fending for herself while you're out gallivanting round the town like a man half yer age."

Norman patiently responded, taking care of each word. "I wuh at the *library, love — as I am every week; as I am for two hours each week — the only time I'm not here."*

"The library", Brenda sneered. "The library, he says! How am I to know yer not out with some trollop? I can smell her perfume on yer, and it stinks. You stink."

Norman watched as a string of saliva swung from his wife's mouth. She had been spitting a lot since the cancer; at people on the television, at dogs, at children. Whoever Brenda had become, she had murdered the woman he had married, or at least given up on pretending to be her. Whatever sickness lived in her had made its home long before the chemotherapy; if anything, she was simply choosing to justify it with her illness. She shrouded herself in her illness. She held it about her like a cloak she could use to deflect all reproval. She smoked her way through treatment.

"You've seen my writing, love. You've seen me *writing. You have no reason to think I'm going around with another woman."*

"I suppose not", Brenda conceded. She fumbled around for her lighter and relit the dead cigarette in her teeth. "Who'd want a filthy old man like you anyway?"

Norman smirked. *"Evidently you, my love."*

"A fat load of good that's done me. Abandoned in me time of need by a rotten husband who couldn't care less for me. If the folk round here knew what you were really like, they'd be sick. Why, I oughta tell 'em. I oughta tell 'em you're the reason my thumb's missing."

Norman smiled, simply, goadingly. *"No one's daft enough to believe that."*

"You think? I think the folk round here are thick as two short planks. Explains why you like it so much. Pigs stay with pigs — all knee deep in each other's shit. That's the way you like to live, in't it? They'd be calling for yer head if they thought yer'd chopped my thumb off."

"Let me get yer a bandage" — Norman rose — *"and a bloody tin opener."*

No sooner had he stood than Brenda had struck him. Norman touched his lip. She had drawn blood. A small rosebud of blood on his fingers. Deciding to make the most of it, Brenda struck him again, then again, and slashed at his neck, until Norman was forced to shove her away, and as he did, he saw she was grinning.

"What are yer?" she hissed. "A wuss?"

Norman went to the kitchen, finding this to be the greater victory; and Brenda, with hatred left to quench, scoured through the papers in her husband's bag, and finding his story, finding "Cautious, a Boat Adrift", tore the narrative to pieces and tossed them, like confetti, about her head.

July 2017 (IV)

On the day of Norman's funeral, I needed drink to wake up.

Coming to, heavy legged, the vein of sleep still behind my eyes, I groped for the bottle of scotch I had concealed beneath the sofa. *Smokey. Chocolatey. Orangey.* Gagging, I sprayed a small stream of liquid onto the carpet and slumped onto my back, staring up at the Artex ceiling. Abstracted waves of paint. Countless fragmentary, immaterial hands reaching fruitlessly for one another.

Mam had not smelt the scotch on me. She seemed to have lost the ability to smell and taste altogether. The insignificant things she had typically acknowledged with appreciation, the taste of health in salmon, the nutty aroma of instant coffee, had dissipated with Norman. She had not slept that night. She stood as a raincloud in the kitchen, poaching eggs, stoically, poking them as if in attempt to make them talk. There was no time to wallow in bed. Salter and Son were to arrive in two hours and, before that, we would have to be ready for the arrival of Ewan.

Mam had not seen Ewan for several years. When my parents had relocated to Nottingham, Ewan had moved to Bristol. There he had opened an independent art studio and garnered vulturous publicity in the late Eighties for facilitating the production of obscene neo-expressionist paintings desecrating Thatcherism, the Falklands War and the insurmountable London powerhouse.

When my dad vanished without a trace, Ewan, for a

few years, had taken his place. On several occasions I had almost called him "Dad", but caught myself before making the mistake. I had not known what being gay meant at the time. Ewan was simply a man, so why not my father? And as a transitory man, he seemed all the more a natural successor to him.

Ewan would drive over, sleep on the sofa for two weeks, then return home for several months before visiting again. While Mam worked, he had busied me with cinema trips and papier-mâché sculpture-making, and before leaving, he would ask what Norman was reading at the time, noting down the titles in his small black notebook.

"Wee man", he would say to me. "Look after yer Ma while I'm gone."

Ewan arrived that day with what was left of his dyed-red hair gelled back, damp-looking, a bask of anaemic coral snakes on his head. His face was roughage, the lines about his eyes as deep set as ploughed land. A miniature Scottish flag sat tattooed on his knuckle, ready to be flashed at Bristolians who mistook Ewan for a Mackem. He wore his own grandfather's demob suit, a size too large — they never fit too small nor just the right size. He hugged Mam for a long time, asked what I was reading and said, "Wee man. Yer not so wee nae more."

Salter and Son arrived with the hearse, in their great coats and top hats, panting dogs in the heat. They would always be there, no matter how hot the earth became. For eternity, they would ride over the hill when summoned, to collect the fallen, never falling themselves. Their black gloves laid the universe on Norman's doorbell.

We drove slowly down fast roads. En route through Hunslet, passers-by harmonised themselves with the shops, the bus stops, the petrol station. They hummed the same song, inwardly, to themselves. No one turned to clap the hearse. It was not garlanded with cries or cheers. The city was a drum that kept on beating. We were translucent, camouflaged against buildings.

It was bin day on Garnet Road. A mother denounced Christ for the splitting of her bin bag. Boiler suits set about bringing a car back to life. By Winston's massage parlour, raddled couples waited tetchily for the years to be kneaded from their faces. The shattered windows in the sky made no complaint and the debris of the wastelands made not a sound, for neither spoke when not addressed by name.

We turned off the A-road into Cottingley Hall, seemingly forgotten by all who could remember. Even Brenda's ride to the crematorium had garnered more attention. It was perhaps for the best. If I were to go, I would be content to go like Norman; leaving behind some invisible quality which, although it cannot be traced to its originator, has enhanced the lives of those who have come in contact with it all the same.

Norman had left such qualities behind whenever he spoke — in his stories, his speeches, his rallying cries, his songs, his promises, warnings, recollections and imaginings. He had stuck out his tongue and, upon it, permanence had glistened. Norman had left behind a dream world in which one must take cover at times when meaning cannot be found in the tangible; a world all the more imbued with meaning (all the more real, even) than that in which we are forced to live. He had left behind the tools for the making of that world, both as a means of individual escape and as a collective project of constructing a better future. He had left behind the means for the gathering of knowledge and taught how to utilise it in times of defence and attack. He had left behind the chance for his tutees, his proteges and his young to run, and to run right past him, and to run and never look back, but to retain their starting points deep in their unconscious and never lose them no matter how far they travelled. If I were to go, I would be content to go like Norman. I would sooner leave behind an overlooked value than a celebrated charade.

Three pallbearers, each a clone of the next, stood at the doors of the crematorium. With Mam and Ewan and I taking a handle each, the pallbearers came to steady the load. We were returning Norman to his own starting point, to where fish are larger than men, to where men need be nothing but rest. So, we carried the coffin like a canoe to water, to cast Norman adrift to the other land, to the land in which Florrie was, in which his parents were, to the land of his stories.

Entering the crematorium, the Bunny sisters became instantly discernible. They were waiting at the doors of the ceremony room, their tears starlike on their faces. It was nice they had come. It was nice that the Hunslet Club had come too, the managing director and the treasurer and the sports coaches and their apprentices, all lined up neatly with their Hunslet ties, the lion of the crest boldly displayed.

In fact, as we carried Norman into the ceremony, I stumbled, for the pews were not as I had imagined them to be. Quite the opposite; they were packed from end to end, with rows of patient onlookers pressed against the walls, in the corners, crouching by the pillars, tip-toeing to glance over the shoulders in front, in some cases sat on one another's laps. Near two hundred faces fell to us as we entered.

> *Take the scorn to wear the horn.*
> *It was the crest when you was born.*
> *Your father's father wore it*

and your father wore it too.

Even representatives of long-defunct lads' clubs outside of Leeds seemed to have made an appearance. There were the matching ties of Hartlepool; yes, the saxe and age-white of Hartlepool in horizontal lines, their wearers falling upon one another in applause. Jim "Gnasher" Nash, his sovereign rings beating the wooden headrest before him, led the crowd to pandemonium. His grey fringe fell madly about his eyes. A pseudo-symphonist, he lifted the applause with his hands, then dropped it, then lifted it again till it was deafening.

Hal-an-tow, jolly rumble O.
We were up long before the day O,
to welcome in the summer,
to welcome in the May O.
The summer is a-coming in
and winter's gone away O.

Cheers and hollers came. They sprang from the neighbours wrapped like wreaths around the pillars. They bounded from the shopkeepers and the ex-milkmen, reverberated on the lips of the pub landlord and the youth club footballers, echoed by the laundrette workers and the union reps. Sunflowers, Peruvian lilies and globe thistles sailed forwards at our feet.

Ned Gould stood amongst the flock; yes, it was him, his suede jacket hunched pensively about him. His flesh hung from his jaw as barnacles. He seemed to have aged years in a week. He nodded to me as I passed. Ned looked as if he'd seen a ghost on that day, and perhaps I was the very ghost he'd sighted. Norman's old friend left without goodbyes. I have not seen him since.

> *God bless Aunt Mary Moyses*
> *and all her power and might O,*
> *and send us peace to England.*
> *Send peace by day and night O.*

What to say about the man of a thousand stories?

— Aye, well I have a story about Norman.

— It wuh in the summer of 1972

— the winter of 2015

— Norman says to me he says

— spring of 1991

— I wuh laughing so loud I woke the dog

— must have been around 2006

— He says "I'm worried Brenda will run off with the fella next door. I'll really miss him if he goes."

— and he could do every Morecambe and Wise bit. The lemon peel mouth, the

— visited our Beth in hospital, as Father Christmas. Of course, she knew it wuh him. Didn't have a beard on

— Fifties then. We'd take a boat out on the lakes in't Dales. Jumping up and down on bugger like it could never sink.

— It wuh Hartlepool Youth versus Stockton-on-Tees Youth. We wuh up against it. They'd won the last match. Once again, they had us outclassed all over pitch. But then, at half-time, Norman comes into the changing room, and surprises us all with this

— I can't quite remember when it was.

Me memory's not what it used to be

— and he had to run the marathon in this great bloody floral

smock — he'd ripped his trousers on way and
that's all the organisers had to change into, yer see —
so he run, laughing his head off all the miles, in this
daft bloody thing and he outran about

— 1986 it wuh
  — I'd just got out of prison. Five years I wuh in. Norman
taught me to write job applications. He gave me some of the
best advice I've ever had. He said
                              — I can't recall exactly how it went
— so he'd turned up outside me house singing "Good King
Wenceslas" at four in soddin' morning. I had to turn the hose
on him
    — paid me mother's rent when the landlord threatened
to chuck us. I owed him a hell of a lot when
I wuh young and I never realised til
                              — I doubt he'd remember me but
— My grandad was many men to many people. He was every
man and not all of those men liked each other. Sometimes it
was hard for those men to live together, share the same house,
the same shoes.
          — My dad used to tell me this story about my Mam;
                that she was out at sea in a boat adrift.
— My grandad lived many lives — not all of them real. Some
of the fictional ones were based on fact, and some of the
factual ones were based on fiction. Some of them may very
well contradict each other. Despite this, he always knew where
he was — until the end.
    — I used to ask him to tell me the same story every night.
I think by the time I'd stopped asking, he'd started
believing the story himself. One of us had to.

– He spent his whole life searching, but he always knew the way home. I think perhaps he was looking for things he knew he'd never find. Memories that it was too late to recapture and ideas that were too distant to come to fruition in his lifetime. He was at peace with that, however, and as your stories have shown, he lived in the present as much as the past and the future. Now that he rests amongst his memories, all that is left is to walk with him — to take him with us — into tomorrow.

    – Are you out there, Dad? On the boat, at sea. Are you waving?

A Few Short Years

13 April 2004: Leeds United 1–1 Everton
16 April 2004: Arsenal 5–0 Leeds United
24 April 2004: Leeds United 1–2 Portsmouth

I abandoned childhood when I was sixteen. I say this, but it would be more truthful to admit that childhood abandoned me. It slipped upstream one evening, refusing to cast a backward glance. By the time I left secondary school, I had decided manhood would be preferable, so I let it in quickly and allowed it to go about its business. It filled out my shoes and distended from my throat. My knuckles grew more gnarled. I had found use for them. They were bruised a lot of the time, as was necessary. In the mornings, I would find my face to be flattening, becoming more pallid. Hair sprouted from my face, but I hacked it back. I didn't have to be a werewolf just because I was a man. There was a litany of minor shaving cuts about my jaw, but there were also countless little etchings, beyond nicks and blemishes, littering my skin, that could not be quite read.

When I got MOT *stick-and-poked below my elbow, Mam had responded for two days with absolute silence. At first, I blamed Weird Craig — my friend and the tattooist — as if he had tricked me into it, but we both knew full well that Weird Craig had simply acted on instruction. "Who would you blame for blowing up a bridge, Fred? The bomb, or the man who commanded the bomb?" I never showed Norman the tattoo.*

In May 2004, I had, for the best, laid a plaster on top of it. "Injured again, lad?" Norman asked me. "If yer getting used to scuffs, I'll have to take thee to the boxing ring next time yer up. You could be a regular Joe Calzaghe."

Brenda scoffed and extinguished a cigarette in her cereal bowl. It floated like a dirty squid in the milk pool. I left my cereal half-eaten. The Leeds match awaited. Bolton away. A loss meant relegation. A win meant there was still the slightest chance of staying up. I got changed — my huge white home shirt; two sizes too big too often — and climbed into the car.

South-west down the motorway, between Huddersfield and Halifax, past Rochdale, cramped into Norman's steel bug — hovering over Manchester, the car turned its nose up, raced on towards Bolton. A battery of Leeds men hung at the foot of the stadium — the frosted tips of the young, the empty shoreline on the scalps of the aging — in their track tops and peaked caps, some topless already, their faces claret and crushed and used by the sun. They talked fearfully and sang.

A man with a St George's Cross emblazoned on his polo shirt, a counterfeit gingham hat and a teardrop tattoo sauntered over to the car. He looked at the Leeds crest stuck to Norman's window. He held eight fingers up then pointed to himself. Eighth. He held up ten fingers, then closed his fists and held up another nine. He pointed to us. Nineteenth. The Bolton man winked and jogged off to the stadium.

Norman grinned. "He's just jealous because I'm far more handsome." We went inside.

Armed with cups of Bovril, the only ones without beer, we needled our way through the wagging mouths, the deerlike eyes of Yorkshiremen teetering at the edge. They brandished brochures. They talked of financial ruin, of necessary violence, of events they had cancelled to be there that day — stag dos, baby showers, mothers' birthdays — to bear witness to the generational demise or victory that waited beyond the stands. An old man in a flat cap bejewelled with Leeds pin badges, near fifty of them, old faces and peacocks and smileys and shields flashing boldly in the solar beams. The men hollered the songs of the ages into each other's ears, beat *their fists on their chests, carried themselves and one another forward into the future. It was as if their own material destruction awaited them; not simply that of their club. Their final pride; their strength to roll out of bed and walk the dog; their ability to show their faces in the places they knew people; the memory and future of their parents and children; their isolated kingdom, their knowable island, their small, budding, promising universe was standing at the brink of extinction. What would be left after that?*

I wondered why they had come (and often still do); to know the job was done, to have the thing over with, these thousands of loyal masochists, their wellness in a net, Norman and I among them, no less guilty, no less innocent. No more, no less. We sang in the arrival of the finishing chapter.

Norman touched me on the shoulder "Whatever happens here today, lad, we'll never be defeated." He thought for a moment. "Just a temporary absence."

The players came out. Plate armour, bedecked with white-and-red tunics. Flanged maces, poleaxes, lances and billhooks. In the War of the Roses, enemies were discernible as each army fought under the banner of their lord. Of course, there was confusion at times, in the frenzy of battle, and men would chop off the heads of their own neighbours. None the wiser.

26'. A penalty for Leeds. Viduka stabbed the ball into the back of the net. The crowd surged forward in sweat and prayer. The rapture of sudden, astonishing hope. The dynamo of tears. Hands arched to seize at shirts. Men dragged each other to life, to witness.

33'. A skirmish on the pitch. Viduka shown a second yellow — sent off. Ten men. A sword wound. The sound of borrowed oxygen being snatched back from lungs. An unsettled limp back to quietude. The misery of worst fears realised. Anarchists and nihilists quietly nodded their heads, looked on with disarray at their less philosophical brothers, at the human sightlessness of anger. We all go down differently.

"Free kick", I roared at the ref. "Free kick, you cunt!" The little fascist

turned on his heels and trotted away, his calves chopping behind him nonchalantly.

47'. Djorkaeff scores for Bolton Wanderers.

53'. Djorkaeff scores for Bolton Wanderers.

55'. Our Harte scores an own goal, giving Bolton their third.

78'. Nolan scores for Bolton Wanderers.

2 May 2004: Bolton Wanderers 4 −1 Leeds United

When it was over, Norman clapped. Sitting, I cupped my tattoo and watched him. When the clapping subsided, and all that was left was song, floating enduringly in the corners of the stands, he crossed his arms and turned to me. There was some part of him that wanted to make a joke of it all. I could tell from the way his eyes were brightening, like little sun dogs in his sockets. He was forcing their brightness, surely. "Don't worry", he grinned. "Worse things happen at sea."

There was a heaviness of finitude in the crowd as we left, a mumbling of the acceptance of inevitable ends. Some folk stopped dead still in the moving rabble to think and made the mass stagnant. Eventually there were so many people stood motionless that reaching the ticket barriers was like weaving through statues. Fields of stone men, unmoving forever. Despite being amongst the last to leave the stands, we were amongst the first to get out of the stadium.

In the car, Norman hummed to himself. Quite cheerfully, he thumbed through the motorway map and fiddled with the radio.

I shut off the radio. "Aren't you sad?" I asked him.

He offered me another grin, broad as hills, twice as assured as the last. "I suppose I'm disappointed", he said, "but not sad. Never sad."

"We're relegated though, Grandad. We can't catch up on points difference now. We're relegated."

"That's right", he said, giving nothing away.

"So why aren't you sad?" I began to feel embarrassed of my tattoo. It was as if his city mattered more to me than him.

Norman sighed. "Well, Fred. Would you rather lead a life like this?" He drew his finger slowly across the air in a perfectly straight horizontal line. He looked at me. "Or a life like this?" He moved the same finger up and down at random, creating towering spikes and gaping ravines that punctuated the memory of the horizontal line, both rising above it and dropping below it. "Well?"

"I'd rather a life like this", I replied, and drew my own line; one that soared endlessly at a forty-degree angle.

Norman laughed. "I'm afraid no one's life is quite like that, lad. They wouldn't be human if it wuh. Of course, the highs are preferable to the lows when yer going through 'em, but the lows are important. The folk that have had the lows are built of stronger stuff. They've experienced life more deeply, more richly. People will know when them folk have gone. By God, I've had ups and downs all me life, but when my time comes, I'll be grateful for the lows. I suppose that's why I'm not sad now." He placed my hand on his soft bicep. "Made of stronger stuff", he chuckled.

I nodded. "Do you believe in God, Grandad?"

"It depends on what you mean. I'm damn sure I don't believe in the absence of God."

"That's the same thing."

He shook his head. "It's not. There's something other than presence and absence. The way I see it, there isn't a something that is God, and at the same time, God cannot be considered to be absent. Neither present nor absent, neither something nor nothing. God, to me, is in-between something and nothing; and I take peace in that."

"That's confusing."

"It is. A lot of things are."

"So you believe in heaven."

"I believe in the belief in heaven. It's very important to believe in things such as heaven sometimes. It helps folk."

I thought for a while. This was the first conversation of this kind we'd had; a conversation between men, equal in height. I spoke slowly and chose my words carefully. "So when you used to tell me the story, when I was younger, about Nana Florrie, and you said she was out at sea — you meant heaven, didn't you?"

Norman didn't answer immediately. His eyes became glassy, as if weighted by memory, as if he had never thought of it before. I had upset him, surely, but then perhaps not, for he grinned again and gave me a knowing look. He was sharing a secret that he refused to speak aloud. "I didn't mean heaven. Every story I've ever told you and yer mam is a true story. You'll realise some day what I mean. By that time, you'll have stories yerself to tell." He started the engine and chuckled buoyantly to himself. "My lad, my lad", he said. "You have an inquisitive mind already. Never stop asking questions."

As we drove slowly out of the car park, Yorkshiremen were just beginning to leave the stadium. They stood apart, quite lost, staring out over the landscape. They looked through us as we passed and went about their lonely searches. There was a silence to be testified to, laying itself down with no indication of how long it intended to stay. It was bright still, and as I closed my eyes, colourful shapes danced in the darkness. I watched them lazily, and the quietening Leeds fans, in their white-and-yellow scarves, fell gently through the clouds in comfort, and became leaves.

Every now and again, without realising it, you do something you are used to doing for the final time. Your mother, at last, places down the iron, and you thank her, as you do daily, as you put on your concluding school shirt and rush out to collect your exam results. You run away from your teachers as if you will soon return to their lessons, almost promising over your shoulder to see them on Monday. You lay down your jackets as goalposts. You play football with your schoolmates, the same ones as *always, having met for a match every week for years. As it gets dark, you ask no questions, before leaving, unbeknownst to you all, forever.*

A fool chooses manhood as his preferable condition. The land of men is an untouched one. It is the companionship of quiet. It is so many darkened boats, heading their own ways, in the night.

July 2017 (V)

Since Norman's funeral, I have not slept a full night. Whilst I *had* been in the habit of waking early, I have found myself recently to be getting up at increasingly inhuman hours. At 4.50am to start with. Then 4.30am. 4am. 3.30am. It has come to a point where I must force my head down whenever tempted to stir, for fear that all this will make me fall asleep by teatime.

The stack of papers I have built in the process of writing this object, whatever it may be — novel, list, monologue, history, confession, dream diary, folklore — is perched uncomfortably on the table opposite my pillow. The heap sits there, under a paperweight, trembling for the window is open and, though warm, the draughts that escape capture still bicker every night. It cannot be at peace, watching me watching it. Though I have composed it, I am not its author. I think, forgivably, it may turn on me.

Clearing out the house. The scent of Scouse stew hung in the hallways till sundown. Mam and I wandered, like rag-and-bone men, with bin liners, with supermarket carrier bags and boxes. It took time to convince Mam to get rid of anything. She sat to look at it all, as if now that she had sat she would never move again. Even the dated contracts for boiler repairs, signed in Norman's familiar script, avoided the bin for hours. There were, of course, many things that could never be discarded. Books. Sports trophies. Squat iron footballers. The palm-sized golden gloves. The dusty harmonica. The Leeds United and the Lads' Club badges. The forty-five-year-old sheepskin coat from when Norman had been the firebrand of Rodney Street. Letters and photos. A couple of self-portraits in charcoal that we had never seen before. The wedding ring he had worn until he met Brenda, kept safe in its box at the bottom of a drawer.

If I were to collect every trinket dotting his bedside table, his vacant desk and his shelves — then form, from them, the shape of a man on the carpet — I might have convinced myself Norman was still there. If a man is the sum of many parts, he is also the sum of many artefacts and can, with patience, be rebuilt again.

I brought down Norman's box of writing; laid it at the foot of the bookshelf in the front room. The weatherman was on, predicting rain. *You can see the blues pushing away the yellows and the oranges*; his hands moving like a magician's. Outside, the moon was breaking.

Norman's papers, putting the volume of my own to shame, were mountainous — a lifetime of work, unanswered speech talking softly to itself. I dipped my hands in and parted it, allowing the type to flow over my fingers, wading through to the bottom. Then I ordered it, for the papers were grouped almost at random, placing in small peaks the pages that seemed to co-ordinate with each other, to construct each of the many stories.

On close inspection, it became clear that not everything was his, at least as far as the handwritten pages were concerned. I knew Norman's hand. Where in capitals, the words were spiked and blockish. Few alterations were made, so there was rarely a scribble. Anything put down had been lain there for a purpose, and so must stay, whether successful or not.

The work in blue pen, then, was Brenda's, of a joined-up hand and awkward in places and marred by alterations. Clearly, she too had tried to write, then abandoned it, for only half a dozen of the pages were hers. She would not let Norman have anything to himself. She had infected his stories with her own. Such is the effort of self-assumed victors to maim and poison history. I moved these gruffly to the other side of the box, then took one up to read:

~~We went to funeral~~
We buried me uncle the
other week
That was 'cos 'ed died
Friends and family all turned
up
~~and~~ everybody cried.
Me aunty Bunny – that was his
wife.
Gave a speech about his life.
~~But how he was an husband~~
~~gentle kind and true~~

They ate the funeral feast and
    supped on tea and sherry.
Aunty face was blooming — I
    swear that she was merry.
Then I heard her giggle as she
    declared with glee
"At last the buggers gone left
    his money all to me"
So let us read the will and
    discover his true worth
She took anoth sip of sherry and
    giggled full of mirth.

Witch. I cast the poem aside and poured myself a large glass from the Grouse bottle stored under the sofa. I turned my eyes to a diary entry — typed. Brenda's again.

11th JANUARY 1994

As I start to type tonight (the time is 1.30am and sensible people are tucked up in bed)my hand is shaking and my stomach is tied in knots. The reason? Well for the past few weeks I have tried to pretend that nothing is wrong and that I am coping in my usual way – not true. I have decided to stop work and spend some time at home. I HATE my job, everybody seems to think that I am good at what I do but I know that I am one big sham. I know that every time I enter a meeting looking confident and sure of myself it is just a sham. I spend half the night when I should be sleeping worrying myself and crying. I have seen the doctor who says that I am having a breakdown and that it is time to give in to it.

She must have been referring to the last job she had, because certainly for twenty years she hadn't lifted a finger. I faintly remembered her working in a nursing home. *How many people had died on her watch?* Another swig of whisky. I turned her papers over on their face, then, finding this not satisfying enough, shoved them violently under the sofa, so I could spend time on what his box was meant to contain: Norman's writing.

What was first? A long short story, set during the 1986 World Cup in Mexico. A group of rowdy English players, tracksuited and booted, mulleted and marauding around the pitch. *Ah. That's better already.* In the first chapter, the final footage of a commercial for the tournament is playing:

```
The closing scene of the film showed a game of one touch football
with the ball zipping from player to player with unerring accuracy and
lightening ppeed.  An ariel shot of the game revealed a telepathic understanding
between players as they executed a bewildering range of positional interchanges.
As the camera moved higher into the sky the snene became larger and the players
smaller to finally becoming lost in a vista vision view of the surrounding
mountains and coutryside.
```

What next? A Bassetlaw boxer tries to make it big and, at the same time, keep his glamorous wife happy. A guerrilla uprising on a fairground in South Shields. A British marine posted in the Falklands interrogates a bound Argentinian, who bewitches him, and is not quite there, and may not be who the Brits believe they have captured. The life and times of Gretchen, the laundrette lady. The epistolary accounts of Günter Müller, the author of secret free-verse poems in 1970s East Berlin. A dozen pages of notes about boats and the sea.

Then, ideas for a foreword he had written for the Hunslet

Lads' Club's seventy-year anniversary booklet. Memories of Hunslet during the Second World War.

I placed it with the rest, telling myself I would find the booklet later. Finally, then, at the bottom of the box, a rough plan for the start of a novel that was seemingly never written.

I held this page for a while, caught off guard. It was without a date so could have been written at any time. It didn't sound like one of his more charming stories. It was one I was glad I would never have to read.

I still hadn't told Mam I'd been sacked by the *Herald*. I quickly jotted down a reminder on my hand, drained the whisky and put Norman's writing away for the night, deciding I was too drunk now to appreciate it. Then I went to check on Mam, who had gone to bed early but was not asleep.

That night, I lay on the sofa, peaty-mouthed, in a half-intoxicated daze. The motorway was thunderous. Cars bolted through the unlit sky. As the weatherman had predicted, it rained heavily, for it could, and the last of the day's revellers stumbled home sodden, each clasping the other's shoulder, shaking rivers from their hair.

The shadows, cast by streetlights, levitated on the wall, making mountain goats and fan plants and forests thick and moon gods. I watched them hovering, waiting patiently, and tried to make some story from them. Perhaps somewhere, in the vague uncharted nebula, Norman was attempting to do the same.

I closed my eyes, but there the figures of shadow were again, not yet leaving. Perhaps I was lonely. In which case, I thought, the room populated by imagination is preferable to the room populated by nothing at all. Imagination, at least, remains perpetually pregnant, a demigoddess on her rock-cloud, empowering her followers to step beyond what is human and what is machine. Such an ability to imagine is critical in a post-truth world, for now that truth is so readily distorted, not only is reality threatened, but the good will, the affectual power and, indeed, the duty of stories is undermined and put at stake.

I wished I had asked Norman more about his tales, or possibly I just wished he had explained what he meant by them, properly, in practical terms — which parts had been true, which parts fabricated, and why. There had been no need to make an enigma of the bloody thing.

Now I knew I would not sleep — I had got myself worked

up again — so I felt around for the Grouse bottle under the sofa and, recalling myself finishing it, decided to pick up one last drink, something to knock myself out with. I would have to take the car down to Balm Road at this hour. Tetchily, I dressed, stuffed my feet in Norman's slippers and padded softly out into the street.

Thankfully, the light in Mam's bedroom was off. There was no need for her to know I had gone.

I drove round to the Oval, and down beyond the supermarkets, south onto Balm Road and past the Mecca Bingo Hall. It was colder suddenly, for no good reason. Glacial in July. An act of rebellion. Behind the rows of uniform council houses, an owl was sounding off. I wondered if owls have a language beyond that of the body. They must do; a language of which we know nothing. If this is the case, I wonder if owls tell stories.

Stories call, without answer, to those who once lived them. In brutal denial, folk burn evidence of their memories, and the impassioned outsider must take up the embers and attempt fruitlessly to piece them together. All these fragments, scattered in the plains where epics once stood.

Before thinking of what I was doing, I had swerved west, away from the shops, veered out the way of an oncoming Corsa, towards Pontefract Road, then onto the M1.

We know nothing of people who did not write — even those who were written about escape in the mist of the author's gaze. Nothing, then, is safe from myth — from aggrandisement or erasure, from idealisation or slander, from false depiction or ideological manipulation. Unintentionally, I too have become a maker of myth. Where I move my hands, all manner of legends grow. I click my fingers, and they snap shut at my command. What ability to commit injustice has been granted to us, we scriveners and criers.

Then again, if the world — the post-truth world — is fast becoming myth, surely it is only possible to write it as myth. Anything else would be unrealistic. But then, if this is the case, and one hopes to make a change through writing, why write? Myth is not beneficial to the progressive transformers of the earth. Surely myth, in all its seduction, is what hinders the betterment of the real. Without the betterment of the real, how can we hope to advance towards our desperate utopia? But what is utopia if not a myth itself, and a well-placed bait to serve a bid for power? Here we are, then, wandering aimlessly between myths — between our interpretations of life, meaning, past and future — pitting them against one another, denouncing one another, purchasing and parading what legitimates our fantasies. Creatures imagine and inhabit their worlds. What a situation we find ourselves in.

In attempting to frame an empirical reality and finding that unintentionally they have written myth — in discovering that such reality has been so long dissipated that it refuses to let itself be imagined anymore — the critical thinker is instantly tempted to destroy their work and accept the world's constant elusive instability. But if such writing is destroyed, what — if anything — dictates? And how do we live without dictation? Without meaning? Such a life is unthinkable. The stark, disorientating nature of the world would swallow us up.

What is the answer? Stories? Those unmanufacturable utopias of the non-place. Those agents — even weapons — of the real, those attempts at a collective sharing, those ventures to communal or universal meaning. The last bastion of the real, surviving the post-truth blast under the clever guise of fictionality. The rift between inhabitation and barrenness, between the something and the nothing. The river that gives way to the sea.

I had been driving for close to an hour when I found myself stopping; stopping at the North York Moors, at the very same gate we had stopped at before. The rain, too, had stopped. Light was already beginning to shatter on the trees, to spill on the road, renewing what it touched. To the south, a small herd of fallow deer noticed the car and galloped off into the brushland. I headed away from them, north, into the humid field, Norman's slippers skidding on the panorama of mud. As I clattered through the branches, a ring ouzel and a skylark took flight to the treetops, in fright of the restless outsider that had come disturb their peace.

Lake Gormire, this, isn't it Dad?

The lake lay, as it always had, flanked by its band of watchful trees. Still, in its muteness, it gave nothing away. It seemed then that even the sound of the birds could not reach it. The water was as still and unchanged as the sky.

I stood waiting, as if it would speak. It did not, so I ran at the water and kicked it. An uninterested stream ran from the slipper. I tore off a branch and threw it at the surface. It floated where I'd thrown it and did not move.

Gormire is a place populated with stories, Fred. Perhaps I'll be able to tell yer all of them one day.

I shook a lean tree, but it made no sound, then turned my feral head to the birdless sky. I lay my ear to the water in attempt to hear it breathing. Desperate, I stomped up and down on the bank, leapt at random from bog rosemary to cornel, snatched erratically at plants, trying to pluck them from their moorings. Eventually, exhausted, I fell on my back, eyes and lips open, in defeat, to the sky.

Then, an owl called. Another, or perhaps the same one as before.

I looked. It could not be seen. The noise of it had sailed from across the lake. It had to be north, hidden in the oaks or cliff. I followed it, frantically, slipping down the bank, until I was waist-deep in water, wading in the unnatural heat of the lake. The sound came again, this time from behind me. I turned quickly to face it. The owl was still nowhere. The bloody thing was invisible — or could it have the face of a tree and wings of foliage? Abruptly catching my foot in the mire, I dropped to my knee and resurfaced, fracturing the water. Mucid and grassy, I spat it back out, raised my arms and found them to be caked with mud. I howled with laughter and splashed intensely. The water churned and erupted and finally took notice. On the far bank, mottled brown snipes made themselves known, shuffling away from the lake. The owl called again, and I thrashed out a response, inventing my own language. The clearing was alive now for the ashes and the birches seemed to sway at my intrusion. Even the disparate clouds took heed and migrated to their vacant territories. I could hear them. The birds in the upper branches squawked in wild rhythm.

I went further out until I could not stand, and shouted boastfully, and whipped my back against the water, and took Herculean strokes up and down the width of the lake. The sun was coming, without warning, as always, and the shrews and the foxes and the voles faded away, for the ceaseless hurry of time had caught up with them. I dunked my whole body under and hovered, looking through the misty film of colour that stretched on into the infinite. Underwater, my lashing was as silent as smoke. Triumphant, I came up for air and lunged back down. Down I went now to seize the belly of this hot, so-called bottomless lake. Let me be the real disturber! Let me put the legend to rest! I swam deeper, searching; searching for the Abbott's white mare, for the remains of Portland stone lions, for a phantom hand, for the underwater town, for the Gytrash, for a capsized rowing boat, for carvings in skin, to recover all lost and the innumerable hiding. All these years, and still all this life! Look. Look how deep I can go. If only you could see me now!

Acknowledgements

Thank you to Amy Jenkinson of Leeds Industrial Museum, Dennis Robbins of the Hunslet Club and Terry Nichols of Holbeck Working Men's Club for supporting my research. Thank you to my family for their stories and memories.

Repeater Books

is dedicated to the creation of a new reality. The landscape of twenty-first-century arts and letters is faded and inert, riven by fashionable cynicism, egotistical self-reference and a nostalgia for the recent past. Repeater intends to add its voice to those movements that wish to enter history and assert control over its currents, gathering together scattered and isolated voices with those who have already called for an escape from Capitalist Realism. Our desire is to publish in every sphere and genre, combining vigorous dissent and a pragmatic willingness to succeed where messianic abstraction and quiescent co-option have stalled: abstention is not an option: we are alive and we don't agree